Soulhunter
GUARDIAN

A Hidden Novel

COLLEEN
VANDERLINDEN

Soulhunter: Guardian
Colleen Vanderlinden

Published in the United States
by Building Block Studios LLC

ISBN 0692447202
ISBN-13 978-0692447208

http://www.colleenvanderlinden.com
http://www.buildingblockstudios.com

CONTENTS

PROLOGUE

Creation of the Guardians
As told to the Fates by Nyx, Darkness be Her name

Nyx created the Universe, the Aether, the
Nether, and watched
As Aether and Nether destroyed one
another,
As they created the heavens and earth, the
moon and stars,
As they gave birth to Anger, Strife,
Jealousy;
But also gave birth to Love, Honor,
Loyalty.
And in the wake of their destruction, she
realized her time was past.

She set in motion the creation of others.
Beings great and terrible, who would create
man.
But she knew, in Her wisdom, that they
would not be enough.
She created the Furies, who would punish

those who'd done wrong,
And the Fates, who would record the
stories of gods and men alike,
And the Guardians, who would collect the
souls of the dead for final judgment.

She created twelve Guardians. Twelve to
shepherd the dead to the afterlife.
And she watched, and the Gods came into
being, and the first Man walked the earth.
The first deaths. The first judgment.
And Nyx saw more. There was something
missing in her Twelve.

So she created the thirteenth. And to her,
She gave empathy, and loyalty, and tenacity.
And with Her indomitable soldier created,
With the souls of the dead in good hands,
She rested.

.

CHAPTER ONE

I stood on the sidewalk outside of the loft in Detroit's Cultural Center. I could have reappeared anywhere, of course. The sensible thing would have been to appear in the living room, or the kitchen. Except, then I would not have had this moment; this ridiculous, nonsensical, blissful moment of looking at the limestone building against the backdrop of a perfect blue-skied Detroit autumn day.

Home. That word is one I never really understood. Homesickness, even less so. It was a concept that made no sense to me. There was never a reason for me to comprehend the idea of it. And what I'd thought of as family, compared to what I have now, compared to the people who lived in the loft, was like comparing the light of a candle to the brilliance of the sun.

There is no comparison.

I took a breath, breathing in the familiar scent of car exhaust and leaf decay, a perfume so quintessentially Detroit that it brings me back here every time. I'd been looking forward to this day almost since the moment I'd flown away nearly two years ago. I'd left. I'd left my best

3

friend, my sister, my queen and god, at a time when she needed me.

I'd left, hoping I could come back stronger and better able to serve her. I still hadn't found what I was looking for. Perhaps I never would. But I did feel somewhat less lost. I traveled. I lived. I thought. I still did not know what this life expected of me. Perhaps I'd figure it out at Mollis's side after all.

I took another deep breath, then walked into the parking garage and hit the button for the rickety elevator that would take me up to my friends. An imp met me as I waited, and gave me an approving nod.

"Welcome back, Guardian," it said, its coarse voice a welcome intrusion into my nervous, excited thoughts.

"Thank you," I answered, giving it a nod in return. "How is our Lady?"

It gave a toothy grin. "Terrifying as always."

I smiled. The elevator came to a stop, and the imp and I stepped in. I hit the button to take us up to the loft. I focused, feeling the power signatures nearby. Several imps, as was always the case when the Goddess of Death was nearby. The shifter. The frenzied, chaotic power signatures of at least two children.

And, roaring over all of it, her power. I practically jumped up and down, giddy over seeing my friend again. The elevator came to a stop, the doors opened, and I heard a crazed cheer from inside the loft. Within seconds, the gleaming wooden door was thrown open, and Mollis Eth-Hades, Queen of the Nether, Goddess of Death, was flinging herself at me, tears rolling down her pale cheeks.

I hugged her just as hard as she was hugging me, and we laughed in each other's arms.

"You're back. You're back," she murmured.

I squeezed her harder, enjoying, more than I would have imagined, this simple embrace. I had not realized how the simple act of hugging could be so satisfying.

One of many, many things I've learned since my world was turned upside down.

I patted her back, squeezed her one more time, and we pulled part. We looked at each other, both of us with tears streaming down our faces, and Mollis laughed.

"Look what you made me do," she chastised, wiping the tears away. I laughed. "Oh my god, E. I'm so happy you're back."

"I am happy to be back, demon girl," I said, and she smiled at the familiar old nickname. She took my hand and pulled me into the loft after thanking the imp for escorting me up.

The loft was the same, and not. The brick walls, the gleaming wood floors, the huge windows looking out over the city, the large empty area in the middle where the team members trained and sparred... all of that was the same.

And yet, it was different. Family photos, framed in matching black frames, covered the brick wall near the living room. Toys were scattered throughout the living room and dining room. And, at that moment a blond-haired boy was chasing a raven-haired toddler across the training floor.

"No running!" an exasperated voice called from the kitchen. I turned in that direction, and the shifter, Brennan, was standing there, looking exactly the same as he had the last time I'd seen him, though his blond hair was longer, and his beard was shorter, as if he'd shaved and then decided to re-grow it. A t-shirt and jeans covered his muscled frame. "Hey, E," he said in greeting, his slate-blue eyes flicking over me, seeming to take in every detail. "Glad you're back," he added.

"I am glad to be back," I said. He smiled, then bent down and listened intently to the little girl, her mass of black curls bouncing as she talked to him, the lisp of her baby voice seeming to charm him. He crouched next to her, listened, said something in a firm voice to his son, Sean. The boy nodded, then took the girl's hand.

"Zoe has grown so much," I said, watching Sean and Zoe as he led her toward a bin of blocks in the living room. I remembered that she'd just had a birthday. How quickly the time had passed.

"She has. And she has every male in this household wrapped around her little finger, apparently," Mollis said, ribbing Brennan.

"And… how are things?" I asked, nodding toward Zoe.

Mollis gave a rueful grin. "Some days are better than others," she said. "We have to spend a lot of time in the Netherwoods. Which I guess works out because this whole God of Death thing kind of never lets up." Mollis had found newborn Zoe beside the infant's deceased mother. The woman had tried to give birth to her daughter alone, in an abandoned home, and it had apparently been too much for her. What Mollis hadn't known when she'd made the decision to raise the baby herself was that she was a half-demon, half-shifter. It was a combination that almost never happened, which was a blessing. The shifter side constantly repressed the demonic side, causing insanity, rages, and violence. Even upon learning that, Mollis had been determined to raise Zoe as her own. In all honesty, it seemed to have made her even more stalwart in her dedication to the baby. "We'll work it all out," she said after a moment, giving me a small smile.

I took her hand in mine. Like all creatures of the Nether, she had cool skin. We were similar in that way, among others.

I could already feel myself relaxing, just being around her and her daughter. Another type of homecoming, and I relished it.

"And where is the new addition?" I asked, glancing around. Mollis and Nain had sent photos of their new baby, a child who should have been an impossibility. Demons and death deities are not known for their ability to create life, and it had been a shock when Mollis had shared the news. I'd been in New Mexico at the time, and an imp, as always, had found me to tell me they'd come through the birth fine, and had given me a small stack of photos.

Mollis smiled. "Sleeping," she said.

"Finally," Brennan added as he settled another toddler dispute in the living room.

"Finally," Mollis agreed. Her hand was still in mine, and she pulled me toward the kitchen. "Hot cocoa?" she asked, and I smiled.

"As long as you have marshmallows," I answered, and she made a face. An old joke between us, and the comfort of it, of being here in the place I'd come to think of as home, soothed me.

"I do," she said. "Just for you."

I laughed, and she let go of me. I took a seat on one of the stools at the granite countertop in the kitchen, the sounds of Mollis's household surrounding me. The oldies station playing on the kitchen radio, the boisterous sounds of children playing, Brennan's deep tones as he talked to Sean.

I watched Mollis set the pan on the stove, add milk. She stirred it, glanced at me and gave a small smile.

"I love your hair like that. You look amazing, E," she said.

I ran a hand over my hair, forgetting how different it looked since I had last seen her. I had always worn my dark hair in a long braid. In New York, I'd had it cut into a sleek bob, with long layers at the front and sweeping across my forehead.

"Thank you. It is much less heavy than it used to be," I answered, and she chuckled. She added cocoa powder and sugar, stirred some more. "Where is the demon?" I asked, noting that her mate, her husband, the demon known as the Nain Rouge, was not around. If Mollis was nearby, Nain usually was as well.

She was still smiling. "He's on patrol. He should be back soon, assuming nothing stupid happens."

"And…how is married life treating you?" I asked.

She blushed a little, and I knew then that things were good between them. Nain was the only one who could put that particular expression on the face of the God of Death.

"Married life is good," she said softly. "Not that I don't want to kick his ass often, but it's good."

I laughed, watched as she poured the cocoa into two white mugs. Milk glass, I remembered. She collected a lot of antique things. Well, *antique* to one who hadn't even been alive for forty years, I amended. Though I did have to admit that the things she collected were often quite pretty. And I benefitted as well.

"Oh, you got it! Good," she said, looking at my t-shirt. It was a black Van Halen t-shirt from the 1980s. I had mentioned in one of my many letters that I was working my way through learning modern music and things like that, so she began sending me vintage concert t-shirts, usually with a letter telling me which songs I should check out by whichever band was on the shirt. It was one of the many ways my best friend and I had stayed connected over the past couple of years.

"Van Halen is not my favorite," I said, raising an eyebrow. "But I love this shirt."

"It's a great shirt," she agreed.

"You are not going to stop giving me these now that I am back, are you? I am starting to understand this obsession you have with collecting weird objects."

"You started buying your own, didn't you?"

I nodded. "They are not easy to find, but I have come across a few."

She grinned. "I'm more than happy to keep your collection going, then," she said. She sat next to me, and we blew on our cocoa. I added several marshmallows to mine.

I took a sip, the explosion of chocolate making my toes curl in my boots. I took a few more sips, and glanced at Mollis to see her watching me.

"What?" I asked.

She shook her head. "You have adapted much better to this world than the rest of them, other than Heph. Do you know that Artemis still wants to carry her bow and arrows with her everywhere?"

I laughed, not at all surprised. "Well, they all had some semblance of life in the Aether." The realm of the immortals, the world I hail from, is divided into two legions. The Aether is the realm of most immortals. These are the ones most humans have heard of: Zeus, Hera, Ares, Aphrodite. There is also the realm of the Nether, home to demons, death deities such as Furies and Guardians. I am, technically, one of the latter. We all served one immortal, the being known as Hades. Now, those of us that remain serve His daughter, Mollis. "And the rest, as well," I continued. "To me, it feels sometimes, as if my life didn't even begin until that night you avenged your husband."

Mollis nodded, a shadow crossing her features. Even now, even after getting him back, after bonding with him again, after creating life with him. Even now, that night, the night he died, haunted her. I wondered what it would be like to love that deeply. In all honesty, it seemed terrifying. To give someone that kind of power... it was, perhaps, another of those things I probably would never completely understand.

"I'm going to take them to the park for a while. They need to get out," Brennan said to Mollis, and she nodded.

"Thanks, Bren." She got up to bundle Zoe into her little red coat, put a hat on her head, which Zoe immediately pulled off with a glare that she must have learned from Mollis herself. After a few moments of negotiation, Mollis got her to keep the hat on, and Brennan left.

We ended up taking our cups into the living room, each of us curling into an end of the huge leather sofa there.

"So. That guy in Texas? What happened with him?" Mollis asked me, and I rolled my eyes.

"It was Oklahoma. And he became clingy."

"E, you were there for like two weeks. How clingy could he really get?"

"Clingy enough to make me happy to bid him farewell," I said, and she laughed.

"And the girl from Wisconsin?"

I shrugged. "She is sweet. We remain friends."

Mollis nodded.

"I know what you are thinking," I said.

"I thought I was the telepath here," she answered, lifting an eyebrow.

"You wear your every thought and feeling on your face, my friend. You always have. You worry that I will never feel like I belong here. You want, so badly, for me to find something here that comforts me."

She was silent for a few moments. Then: "Fine. I don't think I'm quite that obvious, though."

"You are," I answered. "And I love that you care enough for me to worry."

"I feel responsible, somehow," she said.

"Of course you do. You believe you and you alone are responsible for fixing every single thing wrong in this world. If you were not immortal, I would warn you that you are going to worry yourself into an early grave."

She rolled her eyes, set her empty cup down on the end table. "You want it too, though. You want a place in this world, and you don't believe you've really found it yet."

I studied her. "I am beginning to believe my place is at your side," I said softly. "I am content there."

There were a few moments of tense silence between us. I became uncomfortable under her gaze, wondering what she was seeing in me, she who can see everything. There is no hiding from Mollis's sight, the power she inherited upon her father's death. She can see everything a being has ever done. The good, the bad, bravery, cowardice, lies. She sees all.

"This is not all there is for you, E," Mollis finally said, her voice soft. "You are so much more than you realize."

It was like a punch to the gut, hearing her say it. Hearing her address the fear I have had since the day my role in our world became less clear.

It was the worry that I have no purpose at all. That I am a fluke. That my kind should have been wiped out the day my sisters betrayed what we are. Why hadn't I been part of it? Not that I wanted to be, of course, but why? And why was I still here when my skills, my reason for existing at all, were totally unnecessary?

Mollis was about to go on when her phone rang. She held up a finger, gave me an apologetic look. From her end of the conversation, it sounded as if she was needed.

She hung up and sighed. "That was my aunt. There's a soul being uncooperative," she said in irritation. "Do you want to come with me?"

For some reason, I was not interested in feeling or seeing the Nether just yet. I shook my head. "I think I will get settled in here. Is my old room still available?"

"Of course," she said. Then she hugged me, and, within moments she was gone.

I sat in the empty loft, feeling at home and yet even more lost than before.

CHAPTER TWO

A while later, I heard one of the upstairs bedroom doors open. I turned and I glanced up from my spot on the sofa to see Tisiphone carrying a wiggling bundle in her arms. She threw a smile my way.

"I thought I felt you here," she said. I stood up and bowed my head in deference to Mollis's mother.

"Tisiphone," I said softly, and she came up to me and put her fingers under my chin, raised my face to hers.

"It is good to see you again, friend," she said, a small, sad smile on her face.

"It is good to see you as well," I answered. I glanced at the bundle in her arms. Mollis and Nain's son was just over three months old. He lay in his grandmother's arms, bright blue eyes taking in everything around him, and finally, resting on me. I wondered if he could sense another being of the Nether. Ridiculously, I found myself smiling at him.

"So, that is the new member of the family," I said.

Tisiphone smiled again, a more normal smile. I had the feeling that, even now, those were rare from her. Two mortal years since losing her mate, Hades, undoubtedly felt like nothing at all.

"This is he," she said, and she pulled the striped blanket completely away from his face so I could see better. From the nose up, he looked just like his mother, with Mollis's narrow nose and high cheekbones. From the nose down, he reminded me of Nain, right down to the tiny cleft in his chin.

"What did they end up naming him?" I asked.

Tisiphone met my eyes. "Hades," she said softly, and I rested my hand on her arm. "I wasn't sure how I would handle that, the constant reminder. But, as she often does, my daughter seemed to see more clearly than I. It comforts me that in more than one way, he lives on."

"She has some experience in loss."

Tisiphone nodded. "That she does. She asked how I felt about it, and I was unsure. And she said that some days, the smell of her mate's shirts was all that got her through, all that anchored her to sanity." I remembered those days, those first days and weeks after we'd believed Nain to be dead. Mollis had been inconsolable, often clinging to shirts he had worn. She'd cradled his pillow almost nonstop. I knew Tisiphone would still be feeling that. The cost of the demon marriage bond is a high one. Tisiphone gave another small nod. "Besides, I think Hades would have enjoyed having another god named after him."

I laughed. "I think so, yes. He did suggest they name Zoe after him."

She nodded. "Would you like to hold him? I'm going to get a bottle."

I held my arms out awkwardly, feeling as though it would be rude to tell the Fury I had no interest really in holding the tiny being. What if I dropped him? I could just imagine having to explain to the Goddess of Death and her demon husband that I'd hurt their baby.

"You are not going to drop him," Tisiphone said, a wry tone to her voice as she walked to the kitchen.

"You do not know that," I said, frozen in place, afraid to even move rather than risk losing my grip on him. I looked down at his face to see his gaze fixed my face.

"His eyes glow, surely?" I asked.

"They do. White like hers, but only when he's upset. He is a perfect combination of their human forms."

"I wondered if he'd look more like a demon," I said, looking down at him.

"It seems that my daughter's blood cancels out the demon form," Tisiphone said distractedly, as she poured a bottle. "Which really makes no difference, since he'll be plenty strong without it."

I nodded and breathed a sigh of relief when she took him from my arms. She carried baby Hades into the living room, settling into one of the overstuffed armchairs. I took my spot on the sofa again and watched Tisiphone feed the baby for a few minutes.

"It is so quiet," I finally said.

She smiled at me. "Only now. Any minute now the demon and Artemis will be returning from patrol, and my daughter will be back from the Netherwoods, and Brennan will bring the children home. Hephaestus and his family usually end up here as well. It will likely be a full house tonight, once everyone hears that you have returned."

As could be expected, the Fury was right. Within moments, I felt Mollis's presence, as well as the demon's. They walked in, and Nain folded me into a bone-crushing hug before heading into the kitchen with his mate.

"It's Brennan's night to cook," he grumbled.

At that moment, the door opened, Sean and Zoe running through and up the stairs into Sean's room. Brennan followed them in and dumped coats, hats, and toys on the table near the door. "Actually, it's Stone and Ada's night," he said.

"It's not our night," Ada argued as she descended the stairs from the room she shared with her husband, Stone. I could smell the woodsy scent of rosemary, the pungent bite of mint wafting along with her. She often spent her days making teas and medicinal potions for the team and some of the humans that were allied with us. "Don't even try to get out of it, son."

Brennan shook his head. "I watched the two tornadoes all day. If I cook, you're all getting Cocoa Pebbles."

"Which would be fine, except that we're out of milk," Mollis said. "I forgot to stop off at the store. Sorry."

"Dry Cocoa Pebbles then," Brennan said, shaking his head. "I honestly don't even care right now," he said with a laugh.

Mollis started flipping through the drawer in the kitchen that held the many takeout menus we hoarded. "Were they insane?" she asked Brennan.

"Aren't they always?" he asked.

"Pizza," Nain cut in, and Mollis nodded. "I'll call Heph and ask him to pick some up on the way over. Buddy's?" he asked Mollis and she rattled off her order as Nain relayed it to Hephaestus. I sat and observed, amused by the flurry of activity, the noise. I was also well aware that, if I were to live among it every day, it would drive me slowly insane. Mollis had settled into this life, this messy combination of family, friends, duty, and violence, and somehow she was making it work. I reflected on how she'd grown, how she'd matured from the confused, rage-filled vigilante she'd been to the woman she was now. There was still that rage. Violence, always. But her violence had a focus now, and she wielded it with a wisdom even I had not foreseen when we had first met.

Her father would be proud, I thought to myself, still feeling a pang for the loss of the being I'd given my loyalty to for most of my existence.

My morose thoughts were interrupted by the booming roar of a familiar voice, and I stood with a smile.

"Where is she? Where's my frigid little nightmare?" Hephaestus boomed, and I laughed. His wife, the witch

Meaghan, trailed behind him shaking her head and calling a cheerful greeting to me.

"Hello, Meaghan," I called back just as Hephaestus swung me into his arms. It was like being attacked by an excessively snuggly grizzly bear, I thought, laughing as he hugged me to him.

"Ah, she's back. I have missed you, you little terror," he said, rumpling my hair in his usual annoying fashion.

"Must you do that?" I asked him, though I knew I did not sound nearly as stern as I meant to.

"I have two years of annoying you to make up for!" he said, planting a kiss on my cheek before setting me down. I smacked his arm, and he laughed as he headed into the kitchen. As usual, the only thing that could distract the giant immortal, besides his wife, of course, was food. I shook my head and exchanged an amused look with Meaghan, who seemed to be thinking the same thing.

"It is a good thing you are able to grow so much of your own food," I said to her, and she laughed. Meaghan was an Earthwitch. Her power was in working with nature. She made plants grow larger, faster, made crops flourish. The Earth goddess Gaia had taken Meaghan under her wing since returning to the mortal realm after the gateway between the human realm and the realm of the immortals had been destroyed, exiling all of us here together.

Reunions out of the way, we began eating, all of us gathered around the long, gleaming dining room table as we always had before. The main difference being that now Sean and Zoe ran around us, Mollis held baby Hades in her arms and talked to Hephaestus, who was holding his son, Michael. It was as if there had been an explosion of children, the beginning of a new generation of immortals.

Everything was much, much louder.

Soon enough, the loft was filled with old, familiar faces: old friends (very old friends) such as Artemis, Asclepias, and Gaia joined us. After dark the vampires made their appearance. Rayna, Ronan, Zero, and Shanti (who greeted me with an ear-splitting squeal and a hug that practically knocked the air from me) all welcomed me back home. I listened to the stories of the team's exploits over the past couple of years. They'd discovered another cell of vampires in the city who'd been causing trouble and seemed to be ready to move against Rayna, and there was, it seemed, never any shortage of supernaturals who believed that their power granted them the right to endanger the humans. I laughed, and listened, and felt full. After a while, children started drifting off on the sofas, or, in Sean's case, on the living room carpet, snuggled with a blanket, and talk turned as usual, to strategy. I took this opportunity now that they weren't so focused on entertaining me, to slip out. I knew Mollis would fill me in later on anything important.

I made my way up to the roof, breathing a sigh of relief. I'd gotten used to quiet once again. I loved being back, but it was a bit of a shock to my system.

I pushed open the door to the roof deck, and when I stepped out, I saw that Brennan was already there. He had turned when the door opened.

"Oh, I am sorry. I did not know someone was up here already," I said, preparing to turn around.

"It's okay," he said. "You don't have to go. Unless you want to, I mean. Or if you want to be alone, I can take off."

"It is fine," I said, walking the rest of the way across the roof. He was sitting on the wall surrounding the roof, feet dangling over the side of the building. I sat a short distance away from him. "It is much quieter up here."

He nodded. "Thank god,"

I laughed, and, after a moment, he joined me. "They are talking work down there, if you are interested."

He shook his head. "I know it all already."

I smiled a little, looked out over the city. "How I've missed this view," I said softly.

"It never changes," he said after a few moments of silence.

I glanced at him. "You make that sound like a bad thing."

"It's not," he said, shrugging. "Never mind."

I studied him, and he seemed to be doing the same with me.

"You're taller," he said finally.

I laughed. "I am."

"Why?"

"Being very short is almost the equivalent of being very tall. It makes people notice you. I didn't especially want to be noticed anymore. Hence, I'm taller, and I take the lead from our Lady and wear an enchantment to hide my wings when necessary when I am out among the humans."

"Yeah, but your wings are totally badass. Hey, can you fly in front of the moon? It would be like a real-life bat signal."

I gave him a disbelieving look, and he grinned. "I…what? You are strange, shifter," I said with a laugh.

"So have you done that before?"

"Make a bat signal?" I asked.

"No! Change yourself like that," he asked with a laugh, watching me.

"My sisters and I were always able to evolve as necessary. We started out looking similar to what you'd think of as harpies… you've seen art with them in it before?" I asked, and he nodded. "That was similar to our original form. Over time, we evolved to look more like the others, like Hades. It made sense. We all presented a more uniform front. The only thing we kept of ourselves was our wings." Indeed. My bat-like wings were nothing like the humongous feathered wings that the Furies, Hades, and Mollis shared. "And our diminutive size. It made sense at this point, that I could be what I wanted. So I grew taller and get fewer curious looks."

I sat with him, and we both looked out over the city. I felt myself decompressing. I'd been feeling overstimulated. Loved and happy, yes, but overstimulated nonetheless.

"It sounds like your life has been exciting the last couple years," he said after a while. "An entire vampire cell? Really?" he asked with a raised eyebrow.

"It wasn't a very well-organized one. And they were feeding on children," I added. "It felt right."

"Where was that?"

"Portugal."

He looked out over the city again. "Is Portugal nice?"

"It's beautiful. It's a lovely country, the food is outstanding, and the people are generally warm and friendly yet they know when to leave a person alone. I liked it there."

"How long were you there?"

I shrugged. "Maybe a week or two? Not very long."

"I'm not gonna lie. I'm envious. Before, I'd just kind of take off when I wanted to. Nain usually wasn't happy about it, but he got it."

"Wanderlust," I said, understanding the feeling.

"Yeah."

"Well. There is a trade-off, yes?" I asked, and he turned to look at me. "You are a father. You have friends and family here. You're an important man. Director of a federal agency, leader of the shifter coalition, valued member of Nain's team. You have a lot of wonderful things in your life."

"I do. And I'm grateful."

I watched him. "But you are also a shifter, my friend. When was the last time you ran, just to run?"

He went still. His eyes met mine, and he gave a small shrug. "I don't know."

"Don't you think maybe that is part of what is bothering you? You are ignoring an essential part of what you are."

"There's no time—" he began, and I stood up and held my hand out.

"Come," I said.

"What?"

"We are going for a bit. And you are going to run."

"Huh?"

I laughed, waved my hand, urging him to take it.

"What if they need me? They don't know we're leaving."

I glanced to the shadows. There was an imp there, as always. "Can you please inform our Lady that we have gone to get some fresh air?" It nodded and disappeared. I turned back to the shifter. "All right?"

"Why are you doing this?" he asked.

"Because you are this close to snapping, I think," I said, holding my finger and thumb up, demonstrating how close he was. "Or falling into depression. And you have not been taking care of yourself, as usual."

"Look who's talking," he huffed.

I smiled. "Yet I had the sense to listen to myself. When I needed to leave, I left."

"I can't just leave," he argued.

"For a couple of hours, you can. Come."

This time, he took my hand, and I focused.

Moments later, we reappeared, and I heard his sharp intake of breath. I looked around. It was night, as it had been in Detroit. The air was perfumed with the scent of clean forest floor, orchids. A river roared in front of us, and jungle spread for miles and miles all around. I watched as Brennan turned in a circle, staring in wonder.

"Where are we?"

"The Amazon," I said. "It seems to me that a panther should, at least occasionally, be able to run in a place like this."

He stopped looking around and stared at me. "This is amazing."

I smiled at the child-like wonder on his face. "Do you know what would be even more amazing?"

"What?"

"If you let your panther run free for a while."

He grinned, and I turned toward the river as he started removing his clothing. I could feel the prickle of power that came with a shapeshifter changing, could hear the sound of bones popping. A few moments later, the panther was gently butting my leg with its head.

"You are a beautiful panther," I said to him. "Go on. I will be here when you're done." I sat on the ground, and after a moment, the panther bounded away.

I sat there for some time, enjoying the scents around me, the quiet, occasionally catching sight of Brennan's panther, like a shadow streaking through the trees. I could tell he was enjoying himself. Every once in a while, he roared. That was one of the things, in addition to his ridiculous size, that set him apart. I'd heard panthers in this jungle. They tended to make a high-pitched, almost screaming sound when they called out. Brennan, and Artemis, his grandmother, did not sound like that. I suppose that when a god becomes a giant cat, they may as well be able to roar. And they did. Artemis's roars, the times I'd seen her run in the Aether, had been so loud the ground shook with them. But of course, Artemis did everything full force. Brennan's were loud but more controlled, somehow. And, like Artemis, he could turn into any animal he chose, but this, the enormous panther, was his favorite.

I smiled to myself as I caught the sight of black streaking through the trees again, and sat and enjoyed the quiet.

After a while, the panther loped up to me, butted his head to my shoulder in such a way that I ended up swaying under the impact, and then he dropped next to me on the ground. He lay on his side, back pressed to the side of my thigh, legs stretched out as he gave a luxurious stretch. He closed his eyes, and a deep purr emanated from him.

"Better now?" I asked. He just gave a long, lazy swish of his tail in response, and I laughed. I rested my hand on his shoulder, then gave him a scratch behind the ear and he purred more loudly.

"Is it offensive to pet you this way?" I asked, and in response, he moved his head closer to me, urging me to scratch some more. "Oh, you magical, beautiful beast. Artemis never would let me do this." I gave him a few more scratches, then rested my hand on the sleek fur of his side, feeling the rise and fall of his body with each breath he took.

We sat that way in companionable silence for a while. Eventually, he got up with a sigh and walked behind me. I felt the prickle again, a sign that he was turning back. He came back to me, jeans on, pulling his t-shirt over his head, and I looked away. Brennan sat down next to me and pulled on his socks and shoes.

"Thank you for that," he said, and I looked at him. He gave me a smile and I smiled back. "How did you know?"

"I am very, very old and smart. And I pay attention. It wasn't all that difficult to tell something was wrong."

He laughed, bumped my arm with his.

"And I know you," I continued. "When we all believed Nain was dead, we were the only ones Molly would allow near her for a while, remember?"

"I remember. We'd sit with her in shifts, even when she didn't want us to."

"She usually did not want us," I said.

"True," he agreed.

"How many times did I force you to finally take a break to get some sleep, because you were practically asleep on your feet? And you argued with me every single time, claiming you were fine."

"And how many times did I have to do the same to you, those first few days?" he asked in return, and I shook my head. "It was weird, wasn't it? As terrible as it was, as broken as she was, it felt like we all became more of a team after that than we had been before."

"You all had something to rally around," I said. "And I knew that my place was by her side."

"I'm glad you're back, Eunomia," he said.

I looked at him in surprise, noting the use of my whole name instead of simply E, as they usually addressed me. He seemed to know what I was thinking, and met my eyes. "I like your name. I think you deserve a hell of a lot more than one letter." I shook my head, unreasonably pleased by his observation. He continued, "we should go back. Sean probably has them tied up by now." I nodded and took his hand.

"Hey," he said before I could focus on rematerializing us.

"Yes?"

"Thanks again. I haven't felt that way in years."

"We will have to do it again sometime. I bet you would love running in the desert. Or on the grasslands in Africa."

"You've been to those places?"

"I have been everywhere, shifter," I said. "Wherever there are people who die, I've been there." Then I focused, and, within moments, we were standing on the roof at the loft again. He gave my hand a gentle squeeze before letting go.

He glanced at me, then went to the door and opened it. He held it for me, and we went down the stairs that led into the loft. Brennan went to retrieve Sean, and I went and sat next to Mollis in the living room. The evening passed as so many had in my days with the team. I listened to Rayna explaining the latest issue she'd had with attempts by her enemies to pry control of the city from her. By the time everyone finally left, I was more than ready to sleep. I dragged myself up to my old room, changed into pajama pants and an oversized t-shirt, and slipped into bed. As I listened to the sounds of the household settling in for the night, of Stone and the vampires leaving for the night patrol, Mollis murmuring softly to one of her children in the room below mine, I began to doze. I smiled. I was home.

The next morning, I woke to a pounding at my bedroom door.

"Wake up, sleeping beauty. I need a patrol partner," Hephaestus's booming voice called from the hallway. I pulled my pillow over my head, glancing at the alarm clock beside the bed with a grimace.

"Don't you already have one?" I said back, my voice muffled by my pillow.

"Yeah, but Brennan bugged off on me. Some work thing he absolutely *had* to attend to."

I didn't answer.

"Come on. You know the main reason you came back was to hear my stories, E," he said, and I could hear the smile in his voice.

I threw back my covers. "All right. Keep your trousers on."

"Pants, E. They call them pants around here," he said.

"What difference does it make?" I asked as I pulled on a pair of jeans, knowing he would just stay out there talking, because that is how Hephaestus is.

"You sound like a ninety year old woman saying it like that," he said.

"Then I would be sounding young, considering," I replied.

"Except that you look like you're in your twenties, so it's weird. Didn't we teach you anything about how to blend in?"

I rolled my eyes and tugged a brush through my hair, then pulled on my leather jacket.

"Do you mean like shouting like a fool so everyone within five miles can hear what you are saying?" I asked sweetly as I opened the door.

Hephaestus grinned at me. "You know you missed me, you chipper little thing."

I tried to hide the smile that was sneaking its way onto my lips, and failed. I smacked his arm and he laughed. "Idiot," I muttered, and he slung his arm over my shoulders.

"Just think. You have the next five hours in a sixty-seven Chevy with me."

"You know, there is this work thing I have to do…" I said, and he laughed again.

We made our way down to the garage and he showed off his current project, a 1967 Chevrolet Impala that he'd lovingly restored over the past several months. For the first hour of our patrol, he filled me in, in absolute detail, about how he'd found all of the parts, made what he couldn't find. I enjoyed the familiar landscape out the window as he drove and talked.

"Ah, damn. I'm sorry. I'm goin' on and on. Sorry," he said again after going through how he rebuilt the engine. I shook my head.

"You are not. I like hearing about your projects, even if I have no clue what you are talking about most of the time," I said, and he laughed. "Tell me about your son," I said, and off he went.

Three hours into patrol, after settling a dispute between two rival shifter packs on the west side, we were back in the car again and he was pressing me for details about my life.

"So no one special? Not one lucky guy or girl who's won your prickly little heart?" he pressed, and I ignored him. The "prickly" thing was a joke between us, since most of the immortals believed I was a little on the aloof side, apparently. In reality, I am choosy about who I give my attention to, and most of the immortals are annoying.

Hephaestus, being among my actual friends, knows better, I suppose.

"No."

"But there have been romances. You told me so."

"There have been companions," I corrected.

"Ah, Eunomia girl. We need to find you a nice person to settle down with."

"No we do not."

"We do. Don't you want someone to come home to at night?"

"I have approximately twenty people to come home to at night, now that I am back. I am not lonely."

"Yeah, but most of us can't do any of the really fun stuff for you," he said, wiggling his eyebrows at me.

"That is what companions are for."

"Most people would call those flings, you know."

"Can we stop talking about me now?"

"But nobody? Not a single person who makes your heart pound?"

I ignored him.

"Oh, wait…" he said, and I looked at him.

"What?"

"You're not hung up on Nain or anything like that?"

"Oh for the love of Hades, honored be His name. No, I am not hung up on Mollis's mate."

"I mean, I'd understand if you had been."

"I'm not. And I am really regretting telling you about that now." There was a time when we had believed Mollis lost to us. She had been trapped in the Nether, away from the mortal realm, for years. Her bond to her mate, Nain, had broken in the process, and along with the revelation that she had bonded another (Brennan) during the time we'd believed Nain dead, things were a mess. The demon went through sexual partners the way most people went through tissues. I had been one of them.

In fact, he had been my first. And I had asked him to do it, because I was curious. We both knew it for what it was: one night, and I have never felt anything deeper for him. "Absolutely not," I reiterated to Hephaestus.

"Nobody?"

"I am going to leave if you keep asking. The answer is no, and I do not need anyone."

"But why not?"

I looked at him incredulously. "Shouldn't you be focusing on patrolling?"

"I can multitask. Why not?" he asked. "And know I'm only being a pain in the ass because I love you. Right?"

"Or because you are nosy."

"That too, sure."

I looked out the window.

"I have no idea why I am here. Why am I the only of my sisters who didn't betray what we stand for? What is my purpose? Do you see?" I asked, turning to look at him. "I do not even know what my role in this world is. I have nothing to offer anyone else."

"Oh, E. You know that's bullshit, right there, yeah?" he asked, his voice softer, a tone of sadness in it.

"Until I figure out what I am doing, it would be selfish of me to let someone else get lost along with me. All right?"

He shook his head, a look of consternation on his face, but he let it go.

After driving in silence for a few minutes, he looked over at me with a wolfish grin. "So, if you're not doing anything else then, do you feel like babysitting for my beautiful wife and me?"

I gave him the kind of glare I've only used against the most annoying souls I've ever had to deal with, and he drove on with a laugh. I shook my head and looked out the window. We pulled up to a red light, and, out of nowhere, an imp appeared in the backseat, tapping each of us on the shoulder.

Hephaestus let out a rather unmanly shout, and I had to suppress my own gasp of surprise.

"Will you stop doing that shit?" Hephaestus boomed, and the imp bowed as if in apology but didn't look at all sorry, giving me a mischievous wink.

"Our Lady sent me. Needs you in Netherwoods when you're able," it said to me, scratchy voice comforting in its way. These, like Mollis, were creatures of the Nether, and I felt most comfortable around them.

"I will go now," I said, and the imp bowed and disappeared with a "crack." I glanced at Hephaestus. "Unless you need me?"

"Ah, no. I'll just drive around talking to myself. It's fine. Really," he said, squaring his shoulders.

"Very well then," I said, patting him on the shoulder. And then I focused, appearing just outside of the Netherwoods. I wondered what she could possibly need from me, that it couldn't wait until we all got home later.

I looked at the woods before me, took a deep breath, and walked into the trees. I supposed I would find out soon enough.

CHAPTER THREE

I made my way through the Netherwoods. Even now, years after its appearance, the fact that it existed at all was a wonder. After the gateway between worlds had been destroyed, Mollis and her family believed their duties, those deeds they'd always done, of judging and punishing the dead, were no longer possible. Without Tartarus to hold the souls of the dead, there was no way to collect and control them. It looked as though all of us, Guardians, Furies, and Hades alike, were adrift here in a new world. It wasn't until Gaia had appeared in the city that things had changed. She'd tried to heal the Earth, furious over the pollution caused by the humans. Instead of creating a virgin forest as she'd meant to, she'd ended up creating an Earthside version of the Nether. The best guess any of us had for why it happened was that there were so many creatures of the Nether gathered in the city, including Hades himself. At any rate, the Nether immortals had moved in and taken up their work once again.

As I walked, I observed this new Nether, which we'd dubbed the Netherwoods. It was similar in some ways to the Nether I'd always known, yet not. The trees were the same; ebony trunks and branches dripping with nearly luminescent black leaves, like black pearls strung on a necklace. The sky, which had been overcast in Detroit, was the normal violet, the way a Nether sky was supposed to be.

And yet, things were different. Mixed in with the usual forms of the trees were trees native, not to the Nether, but to Michigan. I could recognize maples, pine, and elm. Not in their usual colors, but in the muted tones of the Nether. I wondered how much of that had to do with the fact that the current Lady of the Nether had spent most of her existence in the mortal realm, and how much of it had to do with the fact that the Netherwoods mirrored a bit of Michigan itself, thanks to Gaia's attempts to heal the environment there.

Likely, it was a combination of both.

Hades, before his death, had created a large black stone castle for himself and his mate to live in. A place where he would judge the dead and the Furies would exact his punishments. An enormous, never-ending walled field receded into the distance, full of the souls of the dead. In his day, Hades had changed the appearance of his home at will, according to his whims. It appeared that Mollis had not yet learned how to do that, because the castle was very much not her style. Or, perhaps she could do it and chose not to, preferring to leave it as her father had created it.

Just inside the iron front gates that led into the palace's courtyard, there was a garden that had not been there the last time I'd visited. An enormous black metal statue of Hades towered over the world there, taller than even the highest tower of the castle, a mass of black and silver blooms at the base. I looked up at it, recognizing Hephaestus's handiwork. It was uncanny, almost chilling, how much this inanimate object looked like the former God of Death. Hades, the fallen king. Hephaestus had captured his firm, cruel mouth, his narrow nose, even the haughty gaze we had all seen so often. He stood tall, straight, threatening, his enormous wings billowing behind him, his muscular arm holding a sword as if he was ready to strike.

It was breathtaking.

At the base, tiny in comparison to the gargantuan sculpture, a figure knelt. A curtain of straight coppery-red hair cascaded down her back and over her shoulders, covering her face. Her head was bowed, and she was dressed in long black robes.

Persephone. Hades' former wife apparently still mourned him, despite everything that had happened in the last several years. Not only had she discovered the daughter he'd created, against all odds, with another, but she had insisted on breaking their marriage bond. Hades had bonded afterward with Mollis's mother, the Fury Tisiphone.

And then we had lost him.

I considered going to her, saying a word, but it looked like a private moment, and she did not seem as if she wanted to be disturbed. I studied the sculpture, then glanced at Persephone once more and continued on my way.

I walked the stone path to the castle, and was admitted immediately by two demon guards. I asked where Mollis was, and one of them answered "office," pointing me in the general direction.

As I approached, I slowed. I could hear voices behind the door, and I'd learned, in my time with the mortals, that walking into a room unexpected could yield embarrassing consequences. I could hear Mollis and Nain.

That was definitely not something I wanted to walk in on. But then I heard words, and realized it was all right.

"I don't want to send her away already," Mollis was saying.

"I know you don't," the demon responded. "But this shit can't go on and she's the only one who can help you. You know this."

Mollis didn't answer, and I knocked, ashamed to have listened in on any part of a conversation that wasn't my business. Well. That had probably been my business, but I supposed I would find out soon enough.

Mollis called for me to come in, and I did, walking into the large office. This had definitely taken on Mollis's personality. Gone were the severe stone tables and black furniture. An antique wooden desk sat at one end, near a window that looked out into the Netherwoods. In true Mollis fashion, it was piled with an assortment of papers, magazines, books, and the occasional baby toy. A pair of long red sofas flanked the enormous stone fireplace, and Mollis sat on one of them. The demon stood behind the sofa, his fingers pressing small circles over her temples, as if soothing a headache.

"What is wrong?" I asked.

Mollis smiled at me. "You never beat around the bush, do you?"

"Not really," I answered.

"It's a headache," Mollis said. "Nether has been acting up today, and I'm tired." The Goddess of Death was, aside from our strongest immortal, also the prison for a violent, confused primordial god. It was a constant effort to keep Nether contained, and it seemed that some days were better (or worse) than others.

"That's not all," Nain said, still rubbing his wife's temples. This was why they worked so well together, I realized. They were both brutal, demonic beings. Both of them took a certain amount of joy in pain and violence. But they were both so completely protective and devoted to one another, it was clear in every movement, every glance. And when Mollis behaved as she usually did, taking on too much and refusing to ask for help, he had no problem telling her what she needed to hear, whether she actually wanted to hear it or not.

"That's not all," Mollis ceded after a moment.

"What do you need?" I asked, and she smiled at me. She patted the sofa beside her, and I went and sat. She waved Nain's hands away, and he stopped with an irritated sound, then went and sat on the other sofa.

"I want to talk to E alone," she told him.

He narrowed his eyes at her. "Why?"

"Because," she answered in a deep, gruff voice, imitating the tone he'd had. "My mom is probably ready for a break."

"It doesn't matter. I'll get any secrets out of you later," he said, getting up and heading for the door.

"You can have fun trying, anyway," she said to him, and I caught the barest of grins on his face as he closed the door.

"You two are as ridiculously enamored as ever, I see," I said, and Mollis laughed.

"Sometimes," she agreed. Then she sobered. "It's good having you back, E. I missed you so much."

"But my stay will be short-lived, will it not?" I asked with a small smile.

"I didn't want to ask you yet. I wanted you to settle in and relax for a while," she said, and I could tell how much it bothered her. Mollis never has been good at keeping her feelings to herself.

I took her hand in mine. "What do you need, demon girl?"

"Did my father ever tell you how he knew someone had died?" she asked me, still holding my hand.

I shook my head. "That was something only the Lord of the Dead knew."

She took a breath. "When someone dies, I feel it. Doesn't matter where they are, how far away. It's like part of my brain lights up, as if there's this pinprick of awareness." She paused, thinking. "And until they're brought to me, it's like a niggling irritation, that something that belongs to me is out there somewhere. It only calms when the crows have brought the souls here and they are contained and waiting for my judgment." After my sisters had betrayed Hades and his family, there were not enough of us left to collect souls of the dead. Nyx, our Creator, had assigned that task to special crows of Her own creation.

I listened. "That must be rather overwhelming. Considering how often my sisters and I had to go collect souls… I have a good idea of how often people die."

She nodded. "It is. It took some time to get used to."

I waited, watching her.

"We're having some problems with lost souls," she finally said, and her clenched jaw, the set of her shoulders let me know everything I needed to know about how she felt about that.

"Lost?" I asked.

"The crows can't find them. I've had the imps look, once the crows failed. Nothing."

"How many?" I asked. "Going back how long? Because I am sure we never lost one."

She smiled at me. "You're right. You and your sisters never lost one. I'd know. There have been other issues, however. When the gateway between the original Nether and this world began to fail… when Tartarus itself began to fail—"

"Some escaped," I said quietly, picking up the direction she was heading in, and she nodded. "How many?" I asked again, more quietly.

"Twenty-seven," she said, and I let my head fall back, looked up at the ceiling. "I know," she said, an apologetic tone to her voice.

"And how long have you been dealing with this?" I asked her.

She shrugged. "Pretty much since I inherited my dad's power and role. I didn't recognize what it meant until after I'd experienced a few deaths, and then I realized some were missing and it was wearing on me."

"Do we know which ones?"

"I hope you weren't expecting sweet, kind, gentle types."

"I know better than to hope for that," I answered. She nodded, stood up and walked over to the desk. She rifled through the stacks there, and picked up a sheet of yellow paper on which she'd written a list of names and dates.

"These are our lost souls," Mollis said, sitting down beside me again. "I added their locations and dates of death. I don't know if that will make it easier for you or not."

I looked down the list. I'd escorted the souls of some of these beings myself. "Some of these were hundreds of years ago," I murmured. "This information will help. Souls are somewhat tethered to the area of the world where they died, where they lived. They tend not to wander, which is why it is generally so easy for us to collect them in the first place." Usually, I thought to myself.

"I was wondering about that, if souls tended to return to their old stomping grounds. Does this happen often?" she asked me.

"No. It definitely does not. Only once did we have souls escape, and that was during a period of time when Zeus and Hades were in one of their spats."

"What happened?"

I kept my eyes on the slightly messy writing on the page in front of me, though my mind was thousands of years away. "Zeus was being a reckless imbecile, and threw lightning at Tartarus, killing several of the demon guards. A few souls got out. All returned to where they'd last been in the mortal realm."

She was watching me. "Will it be difficult?" she asked. "I mean, I know the crows can't do it. But is this dangerous at all?"

My mind flashed back. Memory. I threw her a smile. "They can be tricky when they want to. And some of these…" I shook my head as I looked at the list. "What are the odds that these particular souls would escape?" It was, essentially, a list of notorious serial killers. "There is something behind this."

"Damn," she muttered. "I was hoping I was just being paranoid again. Isn't it possible these are just the worst, so of course when they had a chance at escaping judgment, they ran fastest?"

I shook my head. "It's possible…"

"But you don't think so," she said.

"No, I do not." I looked over the list again. "Why were they still there?"

"What do you mean?"

"Some of these died a very, very long time ago. How is it that they were still waiting for their judgment?"

"I asked my mother the same thing. Apparently, for some, the wait for judgment is part of the punishment. They get to stand there, waiting, for hundreds or even thousands of years. Plenty of time to think and be afraid."

I nodded.

"E," she said, and I looked up.

"Yes?"

"Can they do things in the mortal realm? Can they hurt anyone?"

"Spirits can't actually, physically hurt someone by laying hands on them," I began slowly. "In fact, the only beings they can manage any physical contact with at all is my kind, and I suppose the crows, because we have to be able to physically escort them to you." I paused. "What they can do, is cause disruptions. They can manipulate physical objects. When you hear stories of 'hauntings' sometimes, though it's very rare they are actually real, it can be blamed on errant souls, opening and closing doors, lifting and throwing objects. Sometimes we took too long in getting to a soul, and it wandered off and caused problems."

"Can people hear them?"

"Some can," I said. "Those that are more sensitive to the line between this world and the next. Those are few and far between, though," I added.

Mollis nodded.

"So a bunch of dead serial killers, and they're free, and they can mess with people. I asked the imps to start looking for stories about any weirdness that sounded like it could be caused by something like this, but of course that's useless because how many quacks believe they have a ghost living in their house?"

I laughed. The presence of the spirits of the dead in the mortal world was extremely rare. Most things can be explained by other things. Usually, it has something to do with imps or demons, the occasional vampire. It didn't stop the mortals from believing places were haunted.

"I think we need to work on figuring out why. Why these spirits, specifically? Because there is no way this is a coincidence, my friend," I said.

"I know. And we will, but I need you to start tracking them down, E. Find them, and bring them back to me. And we'll figure out who or what is behind it all."

"I will," I promised her.

"Do you need help? Should I send anyone with you?"

I patted her hand. "Are you forgetting who you are talking to, demon girl? I hunted many of these souls in the first place."

"But this seems…bad," she said.

"It does. But I am hardly new to that, either." I stood up.

"When will you leave?" she asked, standing up with me.

"Now?" I asked.

"Oh, don't do that. Wait until morning! Spend one more night home with us." She shook her head. "I feel like such an asshole for sending you out again already."

I shook my head. "It is my duty to serve the Lord, now, the Lady, of the Dead. It is my duty and my honor to do this for you. And I am the only one who can do it."

"Can Aunt Meg help?" she asked me.

I gave her a gentle smile. "Mollis, you are a Fury. Are you capable of physically detaining a spirit?"

"No," she grumbled.

"No. You can punish them, but that is only after they are contained, which only happens after a Guardian has apprehended and shackled them. Yes?"

"Yes," she said. "Okay. You're right."

"Of course," I said, and she rolled her eyes.

"Stay with us for tonight," she said again.

"I will," I promised. I gestured toward the window. "I saw the sculpture of your father. Hephaestus?"

Mollis nodded. "He did an amazing job, didn't he?"

"He did. As always. I saw Persephone out there."

"She is there almost every day since Hephaestus finished it. She comes in the morning, and she kneels there. Sometimes she's still there when I'm heading home for the night."

"She mourns."

Mollis nodded. "It has been hard on her. For the first couple of weeks or so after my dad died, she stuck around. She was with my mom a lot. And then she just kind of started drifting away. She seems to want to be left alone... and I can't even blame her. No matter what my mother and Hades had, no matter how much passion they had, she lived by his side for thousands of years. She loved him. And from what I know, he was a shitty husband, but he loved her, too. I can't imagine what she's dealing with," she said, shaking her head.

"We all grieve differently. The only way out is through, right?" I asked, and she nodded. "All right. I will let you finish up here. I will see you at the loft."

She hugged me, and I left, promising again that I wouldn't go off yet.

As I walked through the Netherwoods, it was difficult not to be annoyed. Of course, I was pleased to help her with this. I was more annoyed that no one had anything sooner. If they had told me about this immediately, I could have most likely easily tracked the souls to where they'd died. Souls always returned there.

Morbid things. But it had been years since these souls had escaped. I had acted more confident than I was that they would actually remain in the place they'd died. Would they eventually venture away? And while I understood that for Mollis's own mental state, these souls needed to be captured, it bothered me that they didn't seem to be looking more closely at why. The fact that we were looking at some of the most degenerate beings humanity had ever produced was enough to make my stomach turn over.

I took a deep breath. I would figure it out. Souls had to be captured. That had to be my first order of business, because the longer they were out, the longer they could cause harm. The longer they were in the mortal realm, the more ability souls gained to manipulate things. Some, though it had only happened once before, figured out how to gain a corporeal form once again.

That would be bad.

I glanced down at the list again.

This would keep me busy for quite a while.

That evening at the loft, it quickly became apparent that my departure was not being discussed. Mollis didn't say anything about it, and neither did Nain, who undoubtedly knew what was going on already. I understood why. If it was revealed that she was having difficulties due to these lost souls, that she was weakening, it would make things even more difficult. There was no shortage of enemies for my Queen, and the first sign of weakness would be like blood in the water, beckoning the sharks. She also played the role of unshakeable leader to most of our team, and it would do no good for our allies to have to worry about her. I was fine with keeping my departure to myself. It would only draw additional attention to me, and they were just beginning to not focus on trying to amuse and entertain me, now that I had been back for a few days.

We ate, and we sat and talked, and, slowly but surely, people started drifting off toward their homes or their rooms in the loft. Mollis, the demon, and their children prepared to retire, and Mollis hugged me. I murmured that I would likely be leaving early, and she thanked me and hugged me once more. We parted ways, and I headed up to my room.

I tossed and turned in my bed. I wondered if it would be rude to just leave in the night so I could get on with it. But, they were expecting that I would stay until morning, and I'd hate for them to need me for something during the night and find me gone. After glancing at the clock for about the thousandth time and seeing that it was just a little after one a.m., I got out of bed with a sigh.

I walked down the stairs, still wearing my pajama pants and a t-shirt. The loft was mostly dark, other than a light in the kitchen area and a lamp in the living room. It took a moment to realize Brennan was sitting in there, laptop open, hunched over it. He glanced up when I reached the bottom step.

"You are up late," I said.

"So are you."

I went into the kitchen, considered hot chocolate, but that would only make me want more hot chocolate. I put some water on for tea instead, and measured some of the chamomile Ada stocked the kitchen with into a tea infuser. I stood and waited for the water to boil, glancing at the refrigerator, which was covered with a hodgepodge of takeout menus and children's drawings. Once the water was nearly boiling, I poured it and brought the cup into the living room.

"Did you want any?" I asked Brennan, and he shook his head. He set his laptop on the coffee table as I settled myself onto the sofa, tucking my legs beneath me. I set the cup on the end table. "You don't need to stop on account of me," I told him, nodding toward the laptop.

"No, I know," he said.

"Work?"

"Work," he answered. "The amount of paperwork we have to file is ridiculous."

"Doesn't Jamie help you with that?" I asked, referring to one of our shifter friends who Brennan had brought on board once he'd become director of the supernatural division for the federal government.

"She does, but," he shrugged. "You know. I'm choosy about what actually goes into the official reports."

I gave him a small smile, nodded. It was the entire reason he had the job to begin with. He knew, because he'd been approached, that the federal government had a department focused solely on keeping track of and learning about supernaturals. He'd joined so he could know exactly how much they knew about his friends and teammates. Over time, he could "clean up" their files so that, officially, the government knew only a minimal amount about those he cared for. As an added benefit, when something was happening at the federal level that affected supernaturals, our team was usually the first to know about it.

"And now they're opening offices in eight other cities, so mine, being the first one in the U.S., is serving as kind of a model for how to handle things," he continued. The existence of supernaturals had been a shock to the human population. Things were still tense, and fear ran rampant. In all honesty, I had expected the humans to figure it out a long time ago.

"So lots of time answering questions then, is what you are saying," I said, and he nodded.

"Did you know European and Asian countries have had supernatural affairs departments for decades? Sometimes even longer than that?" he asked me.

"It does not surprise me. Having so many older cities, places in Europe and Asia have even more supernatural activity than we do here," I said. "But we have a concentrated population of exiled gods. I am pretty sure we are unique in that."

"I hope so. Can you imagine if there were others running around?" he said, and I laughed. He was watching me. "You're leaving again," he finally said.

I took the infuser out of my tea, set it on the saucer. "How did you know? Did Mollis tell you that?"

He shook his head. "She was specifically not answering questions about your patrol schedule when we were trying to figure it out for next week. That tells me you're not going to be on it, and I know you, so I know that if you were going to be here, you'd insist on being out patrolling."

I didn't answer, just sipped my tea. It was still too hot.

"So where are you going, and why the big secret?" he asked, leaning forward and resting his forearms on his knees.

"My Lady has a task for me," I said.

"You're not a servant, Eunomia," he said.

I smiled. "Do you go where the demon tells you to go?"

"That's different."

"It isn't. You recognize Nain as your leader, you do as he says. This is the same. She is my leader and my friend, and if she asks something of me that makes sense, I will do it."

"You just got back, though," he said after a few moments.

I smiled at him. "And I plan to be back again soon." I studied him for a moment, made a decision. "I do not think she wants word to spread about what I am doing for her. But I think you can help me, if that is something you want to do."

"If I can, I will. What's going on?"

I filled him in on the lost souls, and who they'd been, and how the crows had been unable to find them. He sat and listened intently. "So, with that in mind, if you hear anything about something that could have anything to do with this, unexplainable violent activity, people being hurt by things they weren't able to see… if you could tell me about it, it would be a help."

He nodded, lost in thought. "I'll do some digging, too. Now that we're more out in the open with the rest of the law-enforcement community worldwide, I actually have contacts. I'll ask around. I won't say what happened," he said, stalling my reminder to keep it quiet. "But I'll poke around and see if anyone has heard anything."

I smiled. "Thank you. I honestly do not know if there will be much. I rather hope there isn't, because that will mean our lost souls are still unable to cause any actual harm. But it has been a while, and I am not sure if they've been free long enough to start being able to manipulate their environment or not."

"You shouldn't be doing this alone," he said after a few moments.

I laughed. "Shifter, I am thousands of years old and have dealt with the dead since the moment I came into being. This does not worry me."

"They're serial murderers," he said, exasperated.

"And I cannot die," I said, shrugging. Of course there were dangers, but he did not need to know that. "Unless Mollis decides to end me, but I find that rather unlikely." My best friend was the only being capable of killing an immortal.

"But you're saying someone's behind it. What if it's another immortal? They can't kill you and keep you dead, but they can kill you enough to have you end up trapped on the other side, like Zeus."

"You worry too much," I said in irritation.

"And you don't worry enough," he answered.

"Will you be helping me find information, or not?" I asked, meeting his eyes. He looked away, still annoyed.

"I'll help. You know I will."

"Without being moody and over-protective," I added.

He gave me an incredulous look. "I'm never like that."

I didn't dignify that with a response.

"All right. Sometimes I am. I will try not to be. Okay?"

I smiled. "Thank you." I have known his grandmother, Artemis, long enough to know that, like her, Brennan did not mean to be annoying when he went into protective mode. It was the way they were, the way, essentially, all shifters were. It had something to do with instincts and pack alliance and things I did not really understand. Artemis had tried to explain it to me once by asking if I had ever seen a mother wolf when her pups were threatened somehow. I'd nodded, and she had explained that that was what it was, except it was not just their own family they cared for. It was anyone they cared about, anyone they had, in one way or another, started thinking of as "theirs." It meant that, to have a shifter, or even more, one of Artemis's line, as an ally, meant knowing that someone was looking out for you.

Which was nice, but ultimately unnecessary for someone like me.

"If you need more help than that, you'll ask though, right?"

I finished my tea, stood up and patted his shoulder. "If I need anything else, you will be the first one I ask."

"Really?"

"Really. I am going to get some sleep now. I'll see you when I see you."

"Be careful."

I patted his shoulder again. "I promise I will be."

I washed my cup and saucer and headed up the stairs, giving him a wave as I did. He just shook his head.

I smiled to myself. I had just saved myself weeks of trying to find out who knew what. If anyone knew anything, he was the man who would be able to ascertain how much information we really had.

After a few hours of fitful sleep, I woke, packed the small black duffel bag with the few things I'd need, and focused. My first target had died just outside of Paris. And that was where I would begin my search.

CHAPTER FOUR

For all its modernity — the newer-model cars that filled it streets, the modern style of clothing — I still saw Paris as it had been long ago. The clomping of horse hooves on cobblestone streets, the flurry of women in their flowing empire-waist dresses, the sounds of haggling surrounding me in its many small marketplaces.

I sat at a bistro table at a cafe near one such market, *cafe au lait* warming my hands as I took in the scenery around me. Cars rumbled by intermittently on the narrow street, and men and women bustled past, on their way to one of the many shops and bistros nearby. In the distance, I could hear the bells ringing at Notre Dame cathedral, and they sounded just as they had the last time I had visited Paris, nearly one hundred years ago.

So much the same, and yet, so very different.

Old cities had that in common, I'd found. I could see the way they had been, beneath all the layers of modern life. Still the same, but different. And I mourned for what was lost, perhaps more than I'd ever mourned a death, I mourned the beauty the world had lost, even as it gained beauty in other ways.

Hephaestus would laugh at me, I realized as I took a sip of my coffee. He, who was so completely enamored with every new thing humanity came up with, while I longed for the days of horses and carriages. Plays instead of television, letters instead of email. The fashion was so much better then, I thought, glancing at a young woman wearing neon orange sneakers.

"Good Hades, you really are a cranky old woman," a wry voice said to my left.

"Megaera," I said, greeting the Fury as she sat down in the chair opposite me. She was one of the very few people in existence who could pick up my thoughts when I wasn't specifically trying to shield them. "Did she send you to check on me?"

She smiled. Megaera, like her sister Tisiphone and her niece, Mollis, had flowing waves of nearly-black hair, skin so pale she could have been one of the marble sculptures in the Louvre, and eyes that usually glowed white. Today, she'd enchanted herself to at least have normal looking eyes. She was improving in that regard. Sometimes, we forgot to make concessions to the mortals. I was relieved she had remembered this time.

"She did not. I needed to get out of the Netherwoods for a while, and she mentioned you'd be around here, most likely. Any luck?"

I shook my head, frustrated. I'd spent the last two days looking for any sign whatsoever of my current lost soul, with not even a trace.

"Which one is this? There were a few from France, from what I remember," Megaera said as she waved down a waiter and pointed to my coffee, ordering one for herself. Of course, I would end up being the one to actually pay for it, I thought with some amusement. She still hadn't really grasped the whole concept of paying for things that the mortals held so dear.

"Do you remember 'the Vampire of Paris'?" I asked. We stopped talking as the waiter brought Megaera her drink, as well as another for me. I watched him as he walked away, out of earshot.

"Oh, yes. That was a mess," Megaera said with a grimace. "It was around fifty, right?"

"Fifty-seven victims," I said, nodding.

"Not an actual vampire, though," Megaera said, sipping her coffee.

"No. Honestly, calling that one a vampire is an insult to some vampires we know."

Megaera nodded. "He was a monster."

The infamous 'Vampire of Paris' had been nothing more than a middle-aged human male who, after catching his wife with her lover one evening, killed her and her lover, and then went on a rampage in the late 1800s, killing nearly sixty women over the course of five years. One per month, on the same day each month, until he was caught and executed.

"The vampire name was catchy, though," Megaera said, and I shook my head. "Though no actual vampire would even bother biting the ear. So many better body parts to feed from. That's just stupid."

"It was the draining in addition to the bites, of course," I said.

"Well yes there is that. Creepy bastard," Megaera replied. "Where will you check next?"

I'd checked the usual places for souls to return to: the place he'd died (via hanging, messy business), the place he'd committed his crimes, which was the same home he'd shared with his wife. Still there, still occupied, but very much only by the living. I visited his grave, which was marked with a very small granite stone, as if he'd been given the barest amount of recognition in death. Even that was more than he deserved. He hadn't been in any of those places, and, part of what I, as a Guardian, can do, is pick up the energy signature left behind by a soul, even after it's left a place. I can track the energy signature, follow it, until I'm able to capture it and take it to the Nether.

Unfortunately, the energy signatures fade over time. If he had been in any of those places, it was quite a while ago.

I pushed the irritation away, that if someone had told me this sooner, maybe his energy signature still would have been fresh enough to track. What was done was done, though, and I would just have to search harder.

"He was employed at a slaughterhouse not too far from here."

Megaera made a face. "You think he would return there, of all places?"

I shrugged. "It is as possible as any other place. Reports from the time indicate that he murdered the women with knives he'd pilfered from his workplace. I read an article that said that, after his capture, he joked that the only thing his knives had ever been used for were slaughtering cows, of both the human and bovine variety."

"If only we could kill him all over again," Megaera said with a snarl. I shook my head. Furies. That blood lust, that streak of violence was always there, just below the surface. How often had I seen it in Mollis, just waiting, barely constrained, ready to explode at any moment? Tisiphone was no less violent, but a bit better at concealing it than her daughter and sister seemed to be.

I stood up, and she followed. I paid for our coffees, left a tip for the waiter. Megaera watched the entire process as if it was some grand performance.

"Did you plan on coming with me?" I asked as we walked, the shadows from the buildings shading the sidewalk on our side of the busy street.

"Would you mind if I did?"

"Not at all," I said, stuffing my hands in the pockets of my leather jacket, all the while wishing she would return home.

Megaera laughed. "You Guardians. You do know there is no point in your subservience now, don't you? You're not under anyone's thumb anymore. Not Hermes', not Hades'. Mollis wouldn't even consider treating you as a servant."

"I have never considered myself subservient," I said quietly.

Megaera was quiet, and I was aware of her watching me. "But you were. All of you. You did every single thing Hermes asked of you, and, even after he transferred command of the Guardians to Hades, you all continued on the same way."

"We were not all apparently working in Hades' best interests," I said, reminding her of my sisters' betrayal. They'd turned on Hades and his family, choosing to follow our old commander, Hermes, when he'd decided to go after Hades' daughter. They had not told me about any of it. I still failed to understand why, but I was grateful to have been left out of it all.

"But always more than willing to be ordered around," Megaera pointed out. I rolled my head a little, stretching my neck, a very human action that I found made me feel better, especially when I became irritated. "They stopped listening to Hades, but they listened to Hermes. And you just kept listening to Hades, and, now, Molly."

"I don't listen to anyone," I said, looking ahead. "I do things that must be done. If it soothes the occasional ego to believe they have me under their boot, it matters not at all to me. If I am underestimated because I am seen as nothing more than someone's errand girl, all the better." I turned my head, studied Megaera. "I don't care what anyone thinks of me. The only opinion that matters is my own, and I am at peace with how I handle my life."

"Right. That's why you went away for two years," Megaera murmured.

I didn't answer at first. "You are just as old as I am. Those years are nothing."

"They are to those who have lived their lives as human. To Molly, it seemed to be a very long time. And you knew that. And you're missing the point."

"Here is a question," I said. "Of the two of us, which is still doing the same thing she's done every single day since coming into existence, and which has found herself in a whole new reality?" I watched her, and she gave me an irritated look. "You speak of things like subservience and never changing, yet you are the one who has had an easy transition."

"My sister betrayed us as well," she reminded me. The third Fury, Alecto. Her name was no longer spoken.

"I know. But you are not the last of your kind. You have your sister, your niece. You have whatever Mollis' son will become. You are in a different place, but your life is largely the same, no?"

After a moment, she nodded.

"And you are grateful."

She nodded again.

"Right. Now imagine if you were here, with none of your family with you. With your very reason for coming into existence at all, stripped from you. Think about that, and then you can lecture me about how I should have handled myself."

"I am sorry I have angered you, Eunomia," Megaera said.

"I do not get angry."

"Maybe you should."

We were nearing the abandoned slaughterhouse. We could have rematerialized there, but I wanted to walk. It was much easier to pick up the energy signature left by a soul that way.

Unfortunately, it also meant I had Megaera's company.

"Why? So I can be like the rest of you?" I asked, glancing at Megaera again. "Running on rage all the time, ready to cause pain at the drop of a hat?"

"No one could doubt that we are alive. That we feel, that we have emotions. You... I wonder sometimes if Nyx left something out when she created you."

"Yes. Stupidity. Go back to Mollis now," I said, focusing, then rematerializing inside the slaughterhouse.

Ah. There. My irritation with Megaera (who had always been the most annoying of the Furies) faded away as I picked up the faint, barely-there sensation of an energy signature. It felt like prickles along my skin, like a chill up my spine. I closed my eyes and let myself feel it, let myself decipher this particular signature.

I have watched enough late night television now to know how often actors in crime dramas search for fingerprints. Energy signatures are my version of fingerprints. No two souls' energy signatures are alike, and, much as I know exactly where to collect a soul of a person who has just died, I can identify which person's energy signature I am feeling.

I kept myself open, focusing on not losing the faint energy trail. This was my lost soul. This was Edouard Biset, "the Vampire of Paris."

He had been difficult to apprehend in the first place, and that had been with two of my sisters at my side. I was not particularly looking forward to facing him again. I followed the trail anyway.

The old slaughterhouse was essentially one huge, cavernous room. The brick walls were slick with algae. Holes in the failing roof let in an almost useless amount of daylight. Not that light was necessary. I would see a soul even if I could see nothing else.

Large iron hooks hung from heavy chains. Not many; there had likely been more once upon a time, but over the years, scrappers had taken what they could. Usually, all that was left in these old abandoned buildings were things that couldn't be easily removed. There were several old wooden worktables around, and I hit my knee on one of them, not focusing on where I was stepping.

The scent of death hung over the place like a veil. Old death, but death nonetheless. And Biset's energy signature was getting stronger the deeper I followed it into the building.

I went around a brick wall, into another area of the facility; this looked to be an area where the butchering had been done. Tattered, yellowed posters showing the various cuts of meat hung on the walls.

He wasn't there. I looked around in irritation. I'd almost missed it, but there was a door to the left. I slipped across the room and pulled it open.

Hooks hung from the ceiling. A cooler. There was another doorway on the next wall, leading I guessed, to another cooler, and I opened it, stalked through.

"You again, eh?" a high, reedy voice said, and I spun. He'd somehow circled behind me, and now stood in the doorway I'd just stepped through. "It is convenient, being able to walk through walls," he said in French.

I slid the tiny dagger I had concealed in my sleeve down into my palm and sprung at the soul. He dodged, cackling wildly, and circled around me again, swinging out and punching. He caught me just under the jaw, and my teeth clicked painfully together.

I forced myself to focus, trying to get in close, trying to angle in with my dagger.

A dagger seems like a useless thing to use against a soul. The goal, of course, isn't to make them bleed. The daggers I use, the daggers every one of the Guardians used, are honed from almost glass-like black stone from Tartarus itself. They were honed and fashioned by Hephaestus, blessed by Hades. The moment a soul gets stabbed or cut by one of the blades, they weaken. They slow. They lose their ability to walk through walls or slip away easily.

The crows that have since taken over our jobs, those created by Nyx Herself, are a special strain. Their beaks have the same properties as our blades. Of course, most souls are ready to go and don't fight back. I wondered what one of the crows would have done in my place as I received another bone-rattling punch to the side of my face.

He was talking the entire time, raging. Mostly about how he was forced to do it, how if the women hadn't been evil, he never would have killed them.

I didn't answer. Arguing with deranged souls is about as useful as arguing with someone after they have had a few too many drinks. They're unlikely to make any sense, and you just end up looking foolish. I focused, instead, on trying to get my dagger into him. Unfortunately, this was not his first confrontation with a Guardian, and he knew what to watch out for. He continued dancing away from the blade. He tried to head toward one of the walls to escape, and I ran at him, crashed into him, knocked him down and back onto the floor to prevent him from escaping. He called me many vile things as we scrambled around on the floor, though they sounded much nicer in French. I focused on trying to get my dagger into him.

He surprised me by grabbing my dagger hand and suddenly shoving it toward my face. I turned my head away, and the dagger narrowly missed my eye, but I felt the razor-sharp blade draw down the side of my face, down to my neck.

He cackled. "It bleeds just as any bitch would," he said.

While he was distracted, I wrenched his wrist around, hard, and stabbed toward his neck.

The dagger hit home, and he howled. I pulled it out, grabbed the back of his neck, and whipped him face-down onto the floor. I plunged it between his shoulder blades and left it there as he screamed in agony.

"Burns, doesn't it?" I asked, my voice calm. "It always does, for those who have much to answer for in the afterlife." He continued screaming, weak enough now with my blade leeching his strength that his thrashing had no effect at all. I pulled the threadlike chain from the pocket of my jacket and wrapped it around both of his wrists, behind his back, shackling him to bring to the Furies. I shook my hair out of my eyes, watched drops of blood from the cut on my face splatter onto the floor.

It would heal. Mostly. It was a good thing I have never been vain.

I stood up, hauled him up with me. It felt like nothing, like lifting a hollow shell. He'd lost any strength he had gained in the mortal world.

I grimaced. He'd had much more strength than he should have had, given what I knew of the way souls regained strength and eventually, solid forms. They retained some strength right after death, so some of them, like this one, fought back when the Guardians came to claim them. That strength, that energy, usually faded fairly quickly. Time in this realm, if a soul was free for quite a long time, would result in them being better able to manipulate objects. This was different. He should not have been as strong as he was. He should not have been able to fight me so easily.

"How did you get strong?" I asked him, and he cackled. I knew how it happened, of course, no matter how badly I wanted to believe otherwise. It just didn't make sense — how had this particular soul come so far, so fast? He continued screaming. "Who helped you? Tell me and I will remove the dagger."

He shook his head wildly, his screams echoing off of the walls of the cooler. I was the only one who could hear them, of course. And I was more than ready to be rid of him.

I focused, and we rematerialized moments later in the Netherwoods. I handed him off to Megaera, who looked me over but said nothing. "Please try to find out how he gained so much strength. This one was much stronger than he should have been," I said to her.

"I will. I am sorry about earlier," she said.

"It is fine. You can make it up to me by making sure that one doesn't get out again."

Megaera took his arm and laughed. "I promise." She pulled him into the large building the Furies used as a holding facility for souls awaiting punishment and I was more than happy to see both of them go.

Moments later, I was standing in the parking garage below the loft. An imp stood near the elevator, silently guarding is post.

"What time is it here?" I asked him.

"Nearly dawn," he answered. "Looking worse for wear, Guardian," he said, nodding to my face.

"Are they awake up there?"

"One of the small ones was awake a while ago. Sleeps now, I think."

I nodded my thanks, headed onto the elevator, and went up. I was exhausted. My injury was healing, which took energy. My own blade had been used against me, and it seemed it had nearly the same effect on me that it did on souls; I felt much more tired than I should have. The thought of pulling it together to rematerialize again just made me feel even more tired. So I took the elevator up and let myself into the loft.

When I walked in, I felt the shifter nearby, as well as his son. Both were in the living room. The only light was the television. Brennan got up, wrapped a blanket around his son, then came toward me.

"Do you never sleep, shifter?" I asked, turning away from him before he could fuss over my appearance.

"Not really," he said, a light tone to his voice. He followed me into the kitchen. I grabbed some paper towel and wetted it under the faucet. I could at least wipe the worst of the blood away.

"Well, you should. What is the little tornado doing up?" I asked, washing the side of my face. I glanced at the paper towel, grimaced when I saw that it was fully red. I wet another paper towel, went back to work.

"He had a nightmare. What are you doing?"

"Cleaning up. Which I meant to do in private, but there are always people awake."

"You could have rematerialized," he said.

"Too tired. This soul was not a fun one to bring in," I said, wiping down my neck.

Brennan took my arm gently in his hand, turned me around to face him.

"Do not overreact. It is fine," I said immediately. I watched as he forced himself to suppress whatever it was he was going to say. He was looking at the side of my face.

"Pretty bruised and cut up. It looks like Tinkerbell got into a brawl or something."

"Tinkerbell is blond, you idiot," I said though I couldn't keep the laugh from bubbling up. "And I am not a fairy. Are you trying to insult me?"

"You'd be like a nightmare fairy, maybe, with the bat wings and all that. Dark Tinkerbell."

"Can you stop now?" I said rolling my eyes.

He ran his fingertips down the side of my face. "It's not bleeding anymore, anyway. Why is it still there at all? When Molly and Tisiphone heal, it just kind of disappears as soon as it's closed up."

It was like a fog settled itself over my mind, and all I could feel were his fingertips first at the side of my face, then down over my jaw, then onto the side of my neck, tracing the path my blade had taken.

"I…" I shook my head a little, pushed his hand away. "We are different from the Furies in many ways," I said. "Is there still a lot of blood on me?"

He shook his head. "It'll heal all the way eventually though?"

"I will have a scar. It is not my first."

"Why?"

"Why, what?"

"Why won't it heal the way Molly's injuries heal? She doesn't scar."

I shrugged. "For whatever reason, Nyx decided that we do not have the same level of healing as the rest of the immortals. Maybe so we would have some sense of what the mortals go through. Maybe to keep us humble. Maybe she just didn't care about much beyond ensuring we could survive an attack. Our appearance hardly matters."

He was watching me. "But you're the one out there actually collecting souls. Apparently it's dangerous work. The rest of them aren't exactly doing work like that."

"Who can guess Nyx's mind? As I said, how we look doesn't matter, which was why, I guess, she gave us and only us the ability to change things about our appearance permanently. Growing taller, changing our features, things like that."

"If you change again, will the scar be gone?"

I smiled and shook my head. "I will have it forever. And I will wear it as a mark of pride. I faced an adversary and prevailed. There is no shame in it."

"There isn't. It just seems unfair," he said.

"The immortals can be cruel," I said with a shrug. "Surely you have noticed."

He didn't answer. It bothered him. Injustices bothered him, great and small. He practically internalized them, wanted to find ways to fix every single one. This one was beneath worrying about, and I wanted him to see that.

I pulled off my jacket, set it on the island in the kitchen. "Look at this, shifter." I pointed to a long pink scar on the backside of my left arm, from my elbow to the base of my hand. "This, I received apprehending the soul of Jack the Ripper."

"Bastard."

"Bitch, actually. She was horrible."

He stared at me, and I smiled.

"And this one," I said, pushing my hair back and pointing to a puckered scar just under my left ear. "This one, your American gangster called Al Capone gave me. He was very much not ready to go when his time came."

He gaped at it.

"This," I said, pulling the neck of my t-shirt down so I could show him my right shoulder. There was a round wound there, with a matching one at the back of my shoulder. "This was from Genghis Khan."

"Oh yeah?" he asked, a mischievous glint in his eyes. "Well I got this from a wolf shifter in Alaska." He pointed to a jagged mark on his forearm.

"Very impressive, shifter," I said, laughing.

"Genghis Khan? Really?"

"Really."

"How are you even real?"

I laughed. "You have not even seen my best ones yet."

He crossed his arms. His face became serious again. "How many of you were there?"

I sat on one of the stools. "There were thirteen Guardians."

"And you're the last."

I nodded. "From what Tisiphone and Megaera have said, most were killed that day in the Nether." I did not need to tell him which day. He knew as well as I did. "And the rest perished during Mollis' time trapped in the Nether."

"Did Molly kill them?"

"That is what I hear."

"Do you miss them?" he asked, taking the stool beside mine.

"They were traitors."

"Do you miss them?" he repeated.

I smiled. "You assume I have the same ability to feel that you do. I do not."

"Bullshit. You love Molly. You care about Shanti. You and Hephaestus clearly have a warm relationship. You can feel."

"Those are exceptions to the rule, and I do not understand them. Perhaps it is a defect on my part. None of my sisters ever developed emotional attachments to anyone."

"Why did they betray Hades?"

I shrugged. "My guess is that, like Hermes and the rest of them, they believed Mollis would destroy our world, and they joined the side that aligned with their interests. It wasn't out of loyalty for Hermes, or spite toward Hades."

"Cold logic then?"

I nodded.

"Maybe I should call you Spock instead of Tinkerbell," he said.

"You assume I know what that means. I do not."

The trace of a smile turned the corner of his mouth up, just a bit. "Yet you knew Tinkerbell. Ask Heph about Spock."

"The Furies enjoy Disney movies," I said with a shrug. "Is this 'Spock' thing something Hephaestus enjoys?"

Brennan nodded. "It is."

"Are you setting me up to have him yammering on for hours on end at me?"

He laughed, and I shook my head. He stood up, went to the refrigerator, and brought back a pie. "Nain ate most of this already. Freaking bottomless pit."

"I have seen you eat, shifter. What's the phrase? 'Those who live in glass houses shouldn't throw stones?'"

He handed me a fork, took one for himself, and we both dug into the remaining slice of pie left in the pan.

"Ada's pumpkin pie is maybe the best thing I have ever tasted," I said, taking another bite and sighing in contentment. It was flavorful, rich, the perfect blend of flaky crust and silky filling.

"That's the truth," he agreed. We ate in silence, and when we were finished, he pushed the pan aside. "Which one was this?" he asked, glancing at my new scar.

"The Frenchman. Edouard Biset."

He grimaced. "I read up on him. He was something else."

"He was."

I looked down at my hands, folded on the dark granite countertop. He was studying me again, and I found it unnerving.

"Wouldn't it be better to have someone with you? I know, no one else can actually do anything to help you catch the souls," he rushed to say before I interrupted. "But just to be there, in case you need to be protected or taken care of or… I don't know," he finished. "It just seems stupid that you're doing this alone."

"There is not a single thing any of you can do that would help me. None of you can touch a soul. None of you can fight one. And if one went after me, it would walk right through you as if you weren't even there, shifter." I rubbed my arms, remembering the feel of Biset's icy grip. "Anyone who came with me would only distract me. Megaera showed up today, and I was grateful she left before I actually came upon Biset."

"What was she doing there?"

"Checking up on me. And she is growing restless, I think."

We sat in silence a while longer. "Even if no one can help you… aren't you lonely?"

"I don't have much need of others."

"Yet you sit here and talk to me as if it's the most natural thing in the world."

I traced the squiggly pattern in the granite of the countertop with my fingertip. "Only because you never stop asking questions, and it's easier for me to simply answer them than try to distract you."

He laughed. "Just admit you like me."

"You are growing on me, maybe."

"Who are you hunting next?"

"I think I am heading to Ireland. Boyd O'Connor," I added. "I think there is another there as well. I need to check the list again."

He was thinking. "He was the doctor who killed a bunch of his patients, right?"

I nodded.

"Dublin?"

"He died near Cork. I will head there first."

"His file said he spent a lot of time in Kilkenny, too. He had a girlfriend there or something."

"That may end up being helpful. Thank you," I said, genuinely meaning it.

"I hope so. I hope this one is easier on you," he said, his gaze going to the cut along the side of my face again.

"One can hope. One of my sisters led the operation to bring him in, and I don't remember him being much trouble."

Brennan nodded. "When are you taking off?"

"Early tomorrow, most likely," I answered, glancing toward the large windows that looked out over Detroit's Cultural Center. The sky was dark, the air crisp… I needed to get out for a while.

"Shanti has been bugging me about going out with the vampires. When you get back, maybe you can come with me and do that?" He looked hopeful.

"Why?"

And then he looked uncomfortable.

"What?"

"Rayna is going to be there."

"And?"

"She was pretty forward last time about being interested in…uh…" He threw his hands up in the air in irritation. "You know."

I raised my eyebrow at him. "I think the vampire queen enjoys seeing you flustered, maybe."

"Maybe."

"She's a beautiful woman. You should take her up on that," I said, sitting back down, finding myself more than happy to be amused at the shifter's discomfort.

"I'm not intersted."

"Why not?"

"Vampire," he said, deliberately pronouncing each syllable of the word, as if it was obvious. "Immortal blood in my veins. Biting...ugh."

"Biting is not always such a bad thing," I said, trying not to laugh at his discomfiture.

"Have you had a vampire bite you?" he challenged.

"No. But I hear that if it is done correctly, it can be quite pleasurable."

He stared at me in disbelief, and I shook my head.

"Ronan would kill me."

I crossed my arms. "He would not."

"Oh, he would. He told me so."

I nodded. I did not know the brawny vampire well, but what I knew was that he was utterly devoted to Rayna. "He is quite protective of his sister."

"That's putting it mildly," Brennan agreed.

"If it was not for that..." I asked, urging him on.

He shook his head.

"You are not the least bit curious?"

He sighed. "No. I'm really not. I went through the being with a badass leader type before. Let's see what else. Spelled by a witch to get her pregnant so my own son could be used against this team. A bunch of meaningless crap before Molly. My track record isn't exactly impressive, you know?"

We sat in silence for a few moments. Then he continued. "So I guess what I'm saying is, I either want to be alone, or I want a nice, normal, sweet, warm woman to come home to at night. I'm done with superheroes and other badasses."

"Shifter..."

"What?"

"Are you honestly telling me you would be happy going home to some sweet little thing who will 'yes, Brennan' and 'no, Brennan' you all the time? Someone who can't protect herself? Seriously?"

"You say that like it's a bad thing," he said.

"Do you like me?" I asked him. He looked up at me in surprise.

"Uh, yeah."

"Why?"

"You're loyal and you have that kind of awesome dry humor thing going. And you're scary and… ugh. Shut up, Tinkerbell."

I laughed. "I am merely suggesting that you have maybe begun to fantasize about something that, if you had it, would likely drive you up the wall. So why not give Rayna a chance?"

He studied me, then a slow smile spread across his lips. "Not interested."

"Well, you should maybe find someone? Right? You are a male. A shifter male, for gods' sake. I know Artemis, and knew Apollo, well enough to know what that means."

A teasing glint came to his eyes. "Are you volunteering, Eunomia?"

My jaw dropped, and I felt a ridiculous flush creep to my face. "N-no! I am not volunteering."

"Why not?"

"I— you— because!" I finally managed, and stood up again, as I should have several minutes ago. He was openly grinning now, his arms crossed over his chest. "I meant someone else. Rayna, or one of the shifter females, or Athena or Hestia…"

"Athena would behead me before she'd even let me touch her," he said, laughing. "Why not you?"

"Why are you fixating on me?"

"Because I just realized you're my type."

"And what type is that?" I demanded, though I was not entirely sure I wanted to know.

"Feisty, cute as hell, and unwilling to let bullshit pass."

I scrunched my face, and he laughed. "Yes, I am all those things. Thank you for noticing. I am also the aforementioned deadly badass type. And I am *much* too old for you, cub."

"Experienced," he countered, and I found myself blushing again. Stupidly.

"I am leaving now," I muttered, and he laughed. "Is this payback for bringing Rayna up? Because if it is, I am really sorry I did so."

He grinned, and stood up, much too close to me for my own comfort. I could smell him, and he reminded me of cool forests and warm fire. "Partially," he answered, and I forced myself to look up at him. "But more because I realized the other night how completely amazing you are. I want to know more."

"More," I murmured, forcing myself to look away from his eyes.

"So much more," he said, his voice low, a little rough, and the sound of it made something curl deep inside me, made my entire body warm.

"I think that is a terrible idea," I whispered.

He leaned in, even closer, and I felt utterly dwarfed by him. "I excel at terrible ideas, Eunomia," he said softly.

I could not look at him, yet my legs seemed unable to move, when I knew I should have been backing away. What in the Nether was he doing to me? Did shifters release some type of pheromone that made their prey completely stupid? I would have to ask Artemis.

"I need to go. I have work," I said, managing, barely, to find my voice. My throat was so dry, and my voice, usually so strong, so steady, was shaking just a little. I could hear it, and hoped he did not.

"Running, Tink?" he asked, and I could hear the humor in his voice.

"Not running. Just doing the sensible thing."

"Which is?"

"Walking away," I said, forcing myself to meet his eyes. There was still a hint of a smile on his lips, and his gaze was warm.

"I believe I've managed to spook Death's hunter," he said.

"I am not spooked, you ridiculous male."

He laughed, and turned toward the side of the loft where his rooms were located. "If you say so, Tink. We'll talk more when you get back." He turned back to me. "Be careful, okay?"

I nodded. And once he was in his own rooms, I felt as if I could breathe again.

Oh, I would most definitely be asking Artemis about this! I have never in my existence behaved so stupidly with anyone, male or female. I added it to my mental list, and focused, irritation with myself gnawing at me as I rematerialized at street level, just outside the loft. I needed to clear my head.

CHAPTER FIVE

I walked past the library, around the corner and back toward the Detroit Institute of Arts. I'd often admired the building from the outside. Its limestone facade was lit with bright floodlights, making the building appear to glow in the night. The reproduction of Rodin's "Thinker" sat, ponderous as always, near the entrance.

I reminded myself that I still intended to check it out. I enjoy museums. They are interesting, though I often end up feeling depressed about how little humanity has actually managed to save.

The conversation with the shifter had unnerved me more than I cared to admit. Obviously, he was toying with me. That entire thing had come out of nowhere, and I mentally kicked myself for starting our conversation on that path at all. That was a complication I definitely did not need in my life.

Once I was around the museum, I glanced around, then quickly shed my jacket, hiding it beneath shrubbery. Looking around one more time, I spread my wings, gave them a few strong flaps, and rose into the air.

A few powerful movements had me high above the city, perfect, empty darkness all around me. This. This was the single best thing about being me. It was not long life, because, really, at times I honestly wondered what the point was of living forever. It was not strength, the ability to heal, or the ability to touch and communicate with the dead. Flight. If I could spend eternity soaring through the air, I would.

I smiled to myself and kicked off, flying faster into the emptiness, feeling the biting autumn air on my face, my arms as my wings propelled me faster, farther, and I dove, then swooped up again, flying circles in midair. This was what made eternity bearable, because even after thousands of years, nothing felt the same when I flew. It was always exhilarating, always freeing, always just a little frightening. Hephaestus believed it was the thrill of setting myself apart from the world. Perhaps it was. I have no desire to be human. There is no shame in celebrating the things that make us unique.

The Detroit River came into sight before long, and I gently dove toward it. As I did, I felt several beings nearby. Immortals.

Most immortals who chose to live in the city were known to Mollis and the rest of the team. These, I could feel already, were not immortals that were part of our usual group. For one, they were not strong enough.

Lesser gods, then, I thought, grimacing at the derisive name Zeus, Hades, and the others had given to those who were beneath them in the immortal hierarchy. Technically, I am one of them. A lesser god.

Less of a pompous ass, perhaps.

Still, any immortal, lesser or not, was dangerous. And a group of them here, in our city, was probably not the best sign.

I brought myself in for a landing, my feet settling gently on the wet sand of the beach on Belle Isle, which was an island park located just off the coast of Detroit. I could hear the water splashing as gentle waves crested onto the beach. Downtown Detroit sparkled in the distance.

I studied the immortals, who were standing there as if they'd been waiting. I knew every one of them, of course. Triton, son of the sea god Poseidon and a sea nymph. Cithaeron, a mountain god who was a former lover of Mollis' mother. Iris, one of the many earthly gods, and her close friend Aeolus. Nature gods, followers of Gaia. Eiar and Thelos, the goddesses of spring and summer, respectively. Rounding out the group was Ares' and Aphrodite's son, Eros. I was not exactly pleased with his presence. There had been a very unpleasant incident a few years back, in which Eros had schemed with his brothers to punish Hephaestus for the death of their parents at Mollis' hands, as well as his loyalty to Mollis. While Eros had eventually overcome his anger toward Hephaestus and done the right thing by not harming Hephaestus' mate, Meaghan, I still did not trust him entirely. His parents were cruel beyond any beings I have ever known. I have no reason to believe he is different.

I lowered and folded my wings, taking my time as I nonchalantly inspected the group. They were tense, that much was clear. Not a friendly face among them, for the most part. Though, to be fair, my kind are not known for making friends.

"This is an odd place for sightseeing," I said, keeping my hands at my sides, ready to pull the daggers from my holster if it became necessary.

"We are not here for pleasure, believe me," Aeolus said, looking around in disdain. "The things the humans have done to this world."

"Yes. Well. More help from their gods may have helped, maybe?" Most of the nature gods fled the areas where they were actually needed, choosing to live in places that were pristine, untouched. A waste of their power.

"As if it would matter. They destroy everything they touch," Iris added, glaring at me. She was definitely not among my favorite immortals. Despite her cheerful, bright appearance, her rainbow-streaked hair that flowed to her ankles, the way her skin seemed to shimmer, she was among the most unpleasant beings I have ever encountered.

Eros looked as perfect as always, as if he'd stepped out of a magazine. Aeolus, with his flowing white hair and gray eyes, looked every bit the god of the winds. The goddesses of spring and summer would have been mistaken for fairies. Shimmering wings. Like Tinkerbell.

I groaned inwardly, annoyed with myself for remembering the shifter's new nickname for me.

"They do not care. Why waste our time?" Iris pressed.

"Time is something you have in abundance, no?" I shot back, crossing my arms.

"Maybe not," Triton said, and I finally forced myself to look at him. It brought back a flood of memories I would rather not think about. The god standing before me, with his long red hair, full beard, and sparkling green eyes symbolized everything that was wrong with me. He symbolized the moment I realized I was damaged, that even among my sisters who looked, sounded, and acted like me, I was alone.

Defective.

We'd become friends almost immediately. He was the first friend I'd ever had, and that alone made him strange enough, considering that my kind do not develop bonds like that. My friendship with Hephaestus and Artemis came much later, after I learned to accept whatever it was that was wrong with me, that made it so that I felt things my sisters did not. We are, by nature, meant to be aloof. Separate. Above entangling alliances and petty disagreements. My friendship with him made me suspect there was something wrong with me.

And, more so, the moment I realized I had deeper feelings for him, feelings he never suspected or returned. Everything I'd felt for him, for thousands of years, made me feel confused and wrong, somehow. It played into every insecurity I'd had about myself, magnified every way in which I was different from my sisters. It bothered me less now, especially now that I had seen what my sisters were capable of, but the memory of my shame and confusion still haunted me, not to mention my embarrassment over the ridiculous unrequited longing I had once had for him.

I looked away from him. "Surely you have not just now decided to start panicking about my Queen?" I asked him, keeping my voice flat, devoid of emotion. I was quite good at pretending, even if inside I was nothing but turmoil.

He threw a small smile my way, and I steeled myself against it.

"No. Not for my part, anyway, Eunomia. If you trust her, that is enough for me."

I nodded, his warm tone, that small smile, relieving me more than I would have expected.

"I am glad to hear that, Triton. You should meet her some time," I added.

"I would like that very much. My father respects her."

"Let me know, and I will set something up for you."

"Thank you," he said with a small bow, and Iris cleared her throat in irritation.

"If we could get on with the reason you thought it would be such a great idea to come to this hellhole, Triton?" she said, looking around in disgust.

"We have a problem, Eunomia," Eros put in before the immortals could start debating one another.

"And that is?"

I watched as the gods exchanged several uncomfortable glances, as if they were waiting for someone to speak up.

"Well?" I pushed, and Triton smiled, his eyes crinkling at the corners the same as they always had.

"Still not one for niceties, hm?" he asked.

"Too old and cranky for nonsense, perhaps." I crossed my arms, though remained at the ready in case an attack came.

"You were born old and cranky," he said with a laugh.

"I was not born at all."

"That was a... never mind," he said with a smile. "I convinced the others to come here because we need your help and there are few I trust other than you."

I kept my face blank. "All right. What can I do for you?"

"Typical Guardian," I heard Iris whisper derisively to Aeolus. I chose to pretend I had not heard it.

Triton met my eyes. He'd heard it as well, of course. I gave an almost imperceptible shrug, and he nodded in response. "A few among our number have gone missing."

I raised my eyebrow. "Perhaps they wanted to be alone. We all do that from time to time."

He shook his head. "That is not the case this time, unfortunately. These are immortals who rarely left those places they were most comfortable."

"Our sisters would have told us," Thelos said, the waver in her voice signaling her distress.

"Autumn and Winter are missing?" I asked, using the common names for them. Thelos nodded. "For how long?"

"They went missing four days ago. I cannot find them."

I studied Thelos, shifted my gaze to her sister, Eiar. That was unsettling, at the very least. The four Seasons could feel one another. They rarely left one another's sides. Inseparable.

"Who else?" I asked. I looked down at my boot. My Queen would have to hear about this. One more thing.

"Pthinoppen. Cheimon. Nemesis—" Thelos began.

"Nemesis is unlikely to actually be in danger," Triton interrupted.

"Says you. She would not just take off like that," Eros said.

I shook my head. "Zeus's children do as they like. You know that, Eros," I said.

"She would not," he insisted. "And you well know she is not like most of her siblings."

"I know," I said, meeting his eyes. Ever-protective of his closest friend. He was not wrong. While Zeus's other children, including Athena, had more than a fair share of their father's warlike temperament, the spirit daemon of retribution was among one of the most level-headed, fair-minded immortals I'd ever known. "Besides those three?" I asked Triton.

"Angelia and Penthus, as far as we know. We are still trying to get in touch with the others."

I stood still, considering. Lesser gods. Spirit daemons. Most of them had kept to themselves during Mollis' battles with the gods. The spirit daemons, other than those who chose to antagonize Mollis on purpose, simply had continued doing what they'd always done; living among the mortals, whispering, maneuvering the actions of humanity as if it was all nothing more than one grand game.

"So what do you want me to do about this?" I finally asked, meeting Triton's gaze once more before looking away.

"We want you to do what you do best. Track them. Find them."

"I track the dead," I reminded him.

"We all know you do much more than that. You tracked Hades' daughter, after all, when no one else even realized she existed."

"How exactly did you manage that, Guardian?" Iris asked, more curious than disdainful, for once.

"Lucky guess," I muttered. "I am currently working on something for Mollis. I will work on this as well, as long as I have her blessing to do so. I will need to tell her about this. It concerns her world, after all."

The lesser gods nodded.

"None of you have presented yourselves to her. Why not?" I asked.

"She is not my Queen," Iris said. "I follow the rules and laws of one, and one only. Mother Gaia."

"And Mother Gaia has allied herself with Mollis," I pointed out. "This is an ally you want. Believe me."

"I need no allies," Iris said, flipping her multi-colored hair over her shoulder.

"I intended to go," Eros said, looking uncomfortable. "But I did not know where I stood after that unpleasantness I was part of regarding Hephaestus and his mate."

I thought of several things to say to him, and none of them were kind or reassuring. In the end, the best I could come up with was, "if she wanted you dead, you would be."

"I've been in hiding," he admitted.

"She would have found you. Or she would have sent me to find you," I said, and he nodded.

"I will pay her a visit."

I glanced to Triton, and he gave me a small smile.

"Why don't you come with me tomorrow? We can tell her of this issue together then, and you can fill her in on any details that may come to you between now and then."

He nodded his agreement. "Can I meet you here in the morning, then?"

"Sure. Eros?"

He grinned. "I'm not ready to risk my life just yet."

"Hephaestus is more likely to try to kill you than Mollis. I think he is mostly over it."

"All right," he sighed. "I'll meet the two of you here then."

I told them what time to meet me the following morning, watched as, one by one, they disappeared, each of the lesser gods leaving to rematerialize elsewhere. Eventually, it was just Triton standing there with me. He smiled.

"It's been too long, Eunomia," he said.

"It has," I agreed with a nod.

"You've been keeping busy."

"Of course. I am me, after all."

He laughed. "Still the same."

I shrugged. "Only in some ways."

He was standing close enough to me to reach one long arm out, and before I realized it, he was tugging my hair as he always had, a brotherly gesture thousands of years old. I laughed, and swatted his hand away.

"You are ridiculous," I muttered, and he laughed again.

"I will see you in the morning, little ghost," he said, a nickname very few others could get away with.

"I hate it when you call me that."

"I know you do." And in the next instant, he was gone. I was alone, and I shook my head. After a few moments of blessed quiet, I rose into the air again, and headed toward the museum to gather my coat, and from there, I rematerialized into my room at the loft. I did not think I would sleep, but once I was settled, I was grateful for the heaviness in my eyelids, the grogginess of my thoughts, and I soon felt myself drifting off to sleep, hoping all would go well the following morning with Mollis.

I was not completely sure she would not try to kill Eros, after all.

CHAPTER SIX

"Why the hell didn't you just come here? I would have healed you," I heard Mollis's voice berating someone as soon as I opened my bedroom door. I trotted down the stairs to see Nain and Mollis standing side by side, glaring at Brennan, who was sitting on one of the stools at the kitchen island, his shirt off, a large gauze pad over his left shoulder.

"Because stitches work just fine. I'll heal fast enough anyway," Brennan was saying. Mollis and the demon both started arguing with him.

"Rough night, shifter?" I asked over them as I headed for the stove, turning on the burner under the tea kettle.

"A scratch," he said, winking at me.

"From what?"

"Werewolf. We've been having more problems with them lately. They used to be so good at making sure they were contained around the full moon," he said, shrugging his uninjured shoulder.

"He went to the stupid hospital instead of letting me heal him," Mollis said to me. I measured tea leaves into the little green tea cup I liked. "Tell him how stupid that was."

I shrugged. "Does it really matter?"

"Thank you," Brennan said. My gaze darted to him, and I saw way too much muscled flesh before I looked away, my face heating after the odd conversation we'd had the night before.

"You would let me heal you if you were hurt, right?" Mollis pressed me.

"It would depend on how bad it was. It is not as if most of us are in any danger of dying from a cut," I pointed out.

Mollis rolled her eyes. "Fine."

"It's stupid. She heals me all the time," Nain said.

"Well you get your ass kicked a lot. You need all the help you can get, old man," Brennan said, standing and pulling his shirt on with a wince. Nain made a rude gesture in his direction, and Brennan grinned.

I stirred my tea around. "Mollis."

"Yeah, E?"

"Several lesser gods approached me last night. They report that there are some of them that have gone missing. They are asking for my help, and I told them I wanted to inform you of what was happening before I began."

"How many are missing?"

"Five that we know of. They are still trying to track down others. You know how they are. They all generally do their own thing and we won't see them for hundreds of years at a time."

She nodded slowly. "Do you want to help them?"

I met her eyes. "Of course. Tracking… I can do that much. Perhaps I can even see what I can turn up while I look for your lost souls."

Brennan and the demon were standing, listening to us.

"As long as you want to, it's fine with me. But I want to be in the loop. I need to know what's going on."

I nodded. "Two of them were hoping to meet with us this morning to go over the situation if that would be amenable to you."

"Sure. I'm about to head to the Netherwoods with Zoe but bring them by and we'll talk."

"Perfect. We will see you there shortly, then." I watched as she scooped Zoe up, and the next instant the two of them were gone. I could feel Tisiphone in the loft, which likely meant that she was caring for Mollis's son. Artemis was there as well, to take care of Brennan's son for the day.

"Did your grandmother see you like that?" I asked him, nodding toward his injured shoulder.

"Yes. And she told me I'm too slow," he said.

I let out a short laugh as the demon walked out, heading out to patrol with other members of the team.

We watched them leave, and after a moment, Brennan continued. "This meeting you're having with Molly and these lesser gods. I'd like to be there, too. What's going on might affect my job as well," he said.

"Very well. I can take you to the Netherwoods when you are ready, and then I will retrieve them."

He nodded. "I'm going to go get cleaned up a little, and then we can go, if that's okay?"

"Of course. Take your time," I said, waving him off. I started hunting through the refrigerator and settled on a cold piece of fried takeout chicken. Really, I was lucky to have gotten to it before Nain, Stone, or Brennan had.

By the time I'd finished my not-precisely-filling breakfast and tea, Brennan was coming out of his room, dressed in the dark suit and tie he usually wore for work, his long hair pulled back, which for some reason made his eyes seem even more vibrant.

Or perhaps that was just me being ridiculous.

He walked over to me, a small smile on his lips. "Have I told you how much I like that coat?"

I glanced down at myself. I had picked up the jacket in Greece during my travels. Black leather, form fitting, and long enough to cover my wings. It had a hood, and a cowl that I was able to pull across the lower half of my face.

Thin metal chainmail was imbedded in the stomach area, though it was hidden between the layers of leather, making the jacket both attractive and functional. It was, other than my dagger, my most treasured possession. "No, you have not," I said.

"I do."

"Lovely. I do as well," I said, and he laughed.

"Prickly, Tinkerbell," he murmured.

I suppressed a sigh and held my hand out. He took it, tangling his fingers with mine, and I tried to ignore the way my skin prickled in awareness at his touch, the way my heart beat just a tiny bit faster.

He did not, though. "Just admit you like me, Eunomia," he said, smiling.

"You are a completely ridiculous male," I said, and he squeezed my hand.

"Someday, Tink."

"Do not hold your breath, cub."

I shook my head, and focused, and we rematerialized just outside of Mollis' office in her home in the Netherwoods. Without a word, I pulled my hand from his and focused again, this time on the beach on Belle Isle where I had agreed to meet Eros and Triton. They were there, Eros shifting nervously from foot to foot, hands clasped behind his back. Triton wore a pair of well-worn jeans and a gray t-shirt. He looked like a beach bum, with his flowing red hair and casual clothing. Beside Eros, he looked completely unkempt.

"Can you sense the Nether?" I asked them. I knew most Aether immortals had a hard time sensing it. Once they were able to, they could usually get themselves there without much trouble. Both Eros and Triton shook their heads. I nodded, took Triton's hand, then Eros's. "Off we go, then."

I took them to just outside the Netherwoods and dropped their hands. "You can sense it now, I assume."

"Oh, sure. Now I can," Triton said, smiling, and Eros let out a small laugh.

"Come," I said, and they followed me into the woods. The second we were inside, the sky changed from blue to violet, the trees from green to black, shades of steel gray. We walked silently along the pathway that led to a larger walkway flanked by rows of tall trees that resembled the weeping willows of the human realm. This path led to the entryway of Mollis' palace. I greeted the large gray demon guarding the door and he bowed slightly, his eyes narrowing as he inspected Eros and Triton.

"She is expecting them," I told him quietly. He nodded, opened the large door, and let us through. I led the way through the corridors to Mollis' office. The door was open, and Mollis was in the process of judging a soul. The other gods and I entered the room silently, standing near the door. Tisiphone and Megaera flanked the Goddess of Death, who, like her father before her, chose to stand as she judged the dead, looming above them. On the other side of the throne room/office, Brennan read quietly to Zoe on one of the sofas. I shook my head a little. Mollis had certainly put her mark on what it looked like to be a death deity. So much life surrounded her, even here in the realm of death itself. Eros and Triton watched, listened intently as Mollis judged the soul before her, an older woman who stood with her head bowed before her judge and jury.

"Your name?" Mollis asked. Of course she knew it already. The way Mollis' powers worked, she could see everything about a person, good and bad, the instant she looked at them. Such was the curse of her powers.

"Theresa Angelino," the woman said, head still bowed.

"You have been brought before me to be judged. Your time in the mortal realm has come to an end, and the question now is, how much pain did you cause during your life? What things, Mrs. Angelino, do you need to answer for? Be aware that I know them all."

The woman began speaking in a wavering voice. Arguments she'd had, lies she'd told. All in all, not a terribly harmful life. A life well-lived. She'd loved her family, worshipped her god as best as she could have. She kept her head bowed the entire time, spoke respectfully to the being before her, who, here, in her own realm, did nothing to hide what she was. Mollis's eyes shone with an almost painfully bright white light, and her enormous wings were no longer enchanted, the tips of them touching the floor. Her waist-length black hair was braided in a thick rope over her shoulder, and the black uniform, the same one her mother and sister wore, fit her like a second skin. Her only adornments were her wedding band, another ring that made it possible for her to become invisible, and a delicate black chain around her neck, with a pair of tiny black wings that hung at the hollow at the base of her throat. She looked every bit the goddess she was, especially there, her Furies and imps lined up to do her bidding, the soul of the dead bowing before her.

It was the fist time I had seen Mollis in the role she had inherited from her father. He had been chilling. Cold. Mollis was not that way yet, and I hoped with everything I was that she would not become so.

"You have lived a good life, Theresa," Mollis said softly when the woman finished speaking, and tears rolled down the soul's face. "You have minor sins to atone for, which you will do at the hands of the Fury Tisiphone." She transferred her gaze to her mother. "Ensure she relives any pain she caused by her deeds, and then she can go to the Fields."

"Yes, my Lady," Tisiphone said. She stepped toward the soul, who clasped her hands as if in prayer.

"Thank you, my Lady," the soul said.

"Go and be cleansed of your sins," Mollis said, and everyone in the room watched as Tisiphone led the soul of Theresa Angelino away. Mollis saw me, nodded, then turned to her aunt.

"I have something I need to do here. I will call when I am ready for the next one."

"Yes, Mollis," Megaera said. She left, closing the double doors that led into the corridors behind her. I watched Mollis take a deep breath. I knew she hated things like this. Meeting other immortals. Her experience, though not nearly as long as ours, told her that an immortal was usually nothing but trouble. And, in that, she was absolutely correct.

"Mollis Eth-Hades, may I present Triton, son of Poseidon, and Eros, son of Ares and Aphrodite," I said, falling into the formality of life in the Nether as easily as breathing.

Mollis stood, studying both gods. I knew she was sizing them up, that she was seeing them the way only she could. Their sins. Their good moments and bad. Their lies, the harm they'd caused. I could only imagine how overwhelming that might be, upon seeing someone who had thousands of years worth of actions to sort through. As she did, I felt Brennan come up behind me, Tisiphone having come to claim Zoe and take her from the room for the meeting. I stepped back, next to Brennan, more than happy to let the other gods talk to Mollis as I observed.

"Isn't he the one who kidnapped Meaghan?" Brennan asked me softly, leaning toward me, nodding toward Eros.

"Yes."

"Is he suicidal?" he asked, and I bit back a smile.

The initial barrage of information seemingly over, Mollis took a deep breath and nodded first to Triton, then Eros.

"Triton, it is nice to meet you. Your father is an honorable god," Mollis said, and Triton bowed deeply.

"Thank you, my Lady. He speaks highly of you as well. I meant to come before. Please accept my apologies for not doing so."

Mollis smiled a little. "Apology accepted. How is your father?"

"He is well, thank you. Last I heard, he was spending some time in the Arctic. He is amused by walruses," he said with a shrug, and it seemed as if Mollis was hiding a laugh.

"I will have to ask him about that some time," she said.

"I think it's the way they move on land," Triton said, imitating their waddle. "You should see the way he laughs at them sometimes," he finished, and Mollis did laugh then, shaking her head.

"All right, then. It is nice to meet you." She turned to Eros. "Eros," she said, the warmth gone from her voice.

"My Lady," Eros answered, head bowed.

"I believe Hephaestus owes you a few punches to your stupid perfect nose. You should let him do that."

I saw Eros gulp. Hephaestus has a mean swing when he is angry. "Yes, my Lady."

"Good. Now, Eunomia tells me we have a few immortals missing. This," she said, gesturing toward Brennan, "is Artemis's grandson, Brennan. Also the head of supernatural affairs here in the city. This affects his work as well." Triton nodded, seeming to take Brennan's measure. Mollis continued. "What can you tell me?"

She gestured toward the sofas near the fireplace, and she sat in a chair nearby. Triton and Eros settled onto one sofa, and Brennan and I sat on the one across from them. I listened and watched as Triton did most of the talking, filling Mollis and Brennan in on what was going on. I was amused. His gestures hadn't changed at all. He still rubbed his hand across his beard when he was thinking. He still sat the same, elbows resting on his knees, leaning forward as he talked.

"So how did you find out they were missing? Who told you?" I asked him after he had given Mollis and Brennan the basics of what he'd already told me.

"Eros came to me," he said, meeting my eyes.

"And Iris came to me," Eros said, picking up the rest of the answer. "After the two Seasons went missing."

"She is still close to the Seasons, then?" I asked, and both Eros and Triton nodded.

"All right. So that explains how you all knew about Eiar and Thelos," I said. "What about the rest? Nemesis?"

"Iris told us about those, too. She knew I'd be worried about Nemesis, especially," Eros said.

"Nemesis?" Brennan asked quietly, leaning in toward me.

"Zeus's daughter. Goddess of vengeance."

"Oh."

"She is quite nice, actually. Not at all what you are likely picturing."

"Well, that's a relief," he said, and I hid a smile.

"All those who have gone missing are immortals I consider friends. I think Eunomia would as well," Triton said.

"Well. I would not go that far. I would be unhappy if they were harmed," I said, and Triton smiled at me.

"Still a loner then?" he asked with a smile.

"I keep very exhilarating company. My own," I told him, and he laughed, his eyes warming, crinkling at the corners.

I could sense Brennan's eyes on me. Mollis was watching me, and I wonder what she saw. I chose not to dwell on it. Wishing she could not see everything I was ashamed of was pointless, at the very least.

"Mollis has given her blessing, and I intend to track the missing immortals as you asked," I said, looking at Eros, then Triton. "I am currently working on a few other projects, but I can fit this in with the other roles I have. I need to know where they were last seen and who was with them at the time. I need to know if they were angry with anyone, involved with anyone—"

"Romantically, you mean?" Triton asked.

"Of course."

"Why?"

"Because it may be important."

"Why?" he pressed.

"Because very often when someone goes missing, the person they were fucking, or someone who wishes they were that person, was the one who made it happen," Mollis put in, studying Triton.

"She has some experience in this matter," I said.

"I was involved with Thelos for a while. We grew bored of one another, though," he admitted, looking uncomfortable. "I had nothing to do with her disappearance."

I looked at Mollis, met her eyes, and she gave a nearly imperceptible nod. I released a breath I wasn't aware I had been holding, relieved that I would not have to see Triton as some kind of psycho. Brennan seemed tenser than usual beside me on the sofa, and when I glanced at him, he was watching Triton, an unreadable look in his eyes.

"Nemesis," I said, bringing the conversation back around. "Was she involved with anyone?"

Eros shook his head. "You know her. She could have been a Guardian, as little interest as she has in stuff like that. No offense," he said to me, and I kept my face blank.

"Was she in any type of disagreement or anything like that with anyone?"

He shook his head. "Not that I know of. She always kept pretty much to herself, except for me. But she went off for a while. She wanted to visit some of the old temples. I think she was feeling lost, considering how much things have changed," he said with a glance toward Mollis. "It has been unsettling."

"For everyone. I know," Mollis said. "All right. Eunomia is going to help you. My only demand is that I be kept informed of the status of the search, and she has agreed to do so. Know that anything Eunomia finds out, I will know as well. If there is any kind of fuckery that I see as a threat to my realm or my friends or family, there will be pain." She paused. "So know that. If she finds something… if one of you had anything to do with any of this, and she doesn't mess you up first, I most definitely will." Then she smiled, that smile that has, rightfully so, been rumored to have made demons and other monsters lose control of their bodily functions. "But knowing E, there won't be much left for me to do."

"Oh, I think I can save some for you, if it becomes necessary," I said, and she nodded.

"I hope you find them. I hope you deal with whoever did it. None of them were the types who had grudges against them. None of them were causing trouble. They were all peaceful, quiet beings. I don't understand what's happening. What could anyone hope to gain by taking one of us?" Eros asked.

"Why are we assuming they've been taken?" Brennan asked. "Maybe they just took off."

"Nemesis would have told me," Eros said, shaking his head. "I can't contact her. That's never happened."

"And Thelos and Eiar would not have gone off without their sisters," Triton said, looking to me for confirmation.

"The Seasons are very close. Inseparable," I said to Brennan. "If they are missing, it is not of their own choosing. The two of them disappearing this way is all the proof I need that something is wrong here."

Brennan nodded.

"Where were they last seen?" I asked. At this point, it was clear this was my meeting to run. Mollis was sitting back, watching. I knew after working with her so closely that she would fill me in later, in private, if anything had struck her as odd, or if she'd seen anything that might help me.

"The Seasons were last seen by their sisters. They were all in Hawaii at the time. Pthinoporon and Cheimon were last seen when the sisters all settled in to sleep under the moonlight on one of the beaches. When Eiar and Thelos woke the next morning, their sisters were gone. They told me they did not hear a sound during the night and slept soundly," Triton said. "Angelia and Penthus were together, from what we understand," Triton finished.

Brennan nudged me gently, and when I looked at him, he raised his eyebrows questioningly.

"Angelia is the spirit of tidings. Messages," I explained. "Penthus is the spirit of mourning."

"That's kind of an interesting combination," he said.

"Opposites attract," Eros said. "They have been inseparable for eons."

Brennan glanced at me again, and I nodded my agreement. "They have been together for as long as I can remember. Where there is one, you will find the other."

"Romantically, or friends, or?" he asked.

"Mates," I answered, and he nodded.

"So who saw them last?"

"Iris said that Lethe, who is close friends with them, is the one who told her they were missing," Eros said.

"Spirit of forgetfulness," I said quietly to Brennan before he had to ask.

"Are we sure she didn't just forget where she'd last seen them?" he joked, and I hid a smile.

"We should ask her. Where did Iris see Lethe?"

"Somewhere in Ireland, I believe," Triton said, and Eros nodded.

I looked toward Mollis then, who was looking at me. "Well that is convenient. I am leaving for Ireland soon to check on something. I will see if I can speak with Lethe while I am there."

Mollis nodded.

"Be careful, Eunomia," Triton said. "I don't know what's going on, but it feels wrong. It doesn't make any sense. I don't like the idea of you going off alone tracking them."

"You asked me to do so," I pointed out.

"That was before I thought about it. If there's something dangerous going on—"

"I am the best one to handle it," I finished for him.

He gave me a stern look. "Do not be over-confident."

"I really am not in need of your advice about how to handle myself, Triton," I said softly.

"Eunomia can handle herself," Mollis said. "And she is not going alone. Brennan, you're going too."

"I was just going to suggest that," he said, as I stared, open-mouthed at Mollis. I remembered myself, and clamped my mouth shut again.

"I was not," I said, looking coolly at first Mollis and then Brennan. "I do not need a babysitter."

"I know. But he can actually help with this. And I would feel better if you were not alone. Especially with people knowing where you're going."

"Are you saying you don't trust us, my Lady?" Triton asked irritably. "You must mean us, right? We're the only ones here."

"Obviously," Mollis said drily.

"I would never hurt her. I want the same thing you want. To find them and figure out what happened," he said.

She was watching him, and I wondered what she saw. "Then surely you have no issues with her having backup, right?"

"Of course not. I just think that if you're looking for someone to mistrust, it is not anyone in this room."

Mollis stood, which was a clear indication that she was finished with the meeting. "Ask him about trust," she said gesturing toward Eros. "He's already proven that he has it in him to lie and a whole lot more. And my experience with immortals tells me there's not a fucking thing most of you won't stoop to. You're clean right now. Your conscience is weighed by nothing. Which is really good for you, because if you'd come in here guilty of something, your throat would have met my blade instantly. Don't give me a reason to rid the world of two more immortals," Mollis finished.

Triton and Eros stood. "We are on your side, my Lady," Triton said.

"Fuck my side," Mollis said. "I don't care about me. Just don't be a lying asshole and we'll be fine. Thanks for stopping by."

With that obvious dismissal, Eros disappeared. Triton turned to me.

"Be careful," he said, stepping toward me. He hugged me gently, gave Brennan a nod, and stepped back. Then he, too, disappeared.

"They weren't hiding anything." Mollis said, answering my first question. "I still don't like this. I know you like to work alone, but please just take Bren with you. Okay? For me?"

I tamped down my irritation. I did not need help. And spending time traveling with Brennan was not exactly what I needed at the moment. But arguing with Mollis over it, especially in front of the shifter, would not help my case.

"Very well," I said.

"I'll do some searching. I'll see if anything weird has been reported that we could possibly tie to this," Brennan said, and Mollis nodded.

"Artemis will watch Sean, right?" she asked.

"Sure."

"Tell her if she needs any help, to just ask. Between Nain and me and Ada and my mom, we'll work it out."

"It'll be fine," Brennan said.

"Okay. I need to get back to work," Mollis said. "Be careful, E."

"I will, demon girl. Go hurt somebody."

She grinned, gave us a wave, and then was gone.

"Ready?" I asked Brennan, and he nodded. He was watching me closely, and there was that ridiculous tingle when he touched me, when he clasped his hand with mine. I forced myself to ignore it, focused on rematerializing. We appeared in the main living area of the loft. It was empty. Even the younger ones were gone. I knew they often went to the park with Tisiphone and Artemis. Everyone else was likely out on patrol.

I let go of Brennan's hand and started walking toward the stairs that led up to my room. I wanted to double-check my bags before I left for Ireland.

Before *we* left for Ireland, I reminded myself.

"Tink," Brennan said, and I turned back to him, my hand resting on the railing of the stairway the led up to my room.

"Yes?"

"What's the deal with you and Triton?"

I froze. Damn perceptive shifter male.

"What do you mean?"

He walked toward me, slowly, reminding me of the way he moved in panther form. Graceful. Deadly.

Why did I want to flee?

"You know what I mean. I've never seen you that uncomfortable around anyone."

I did not answer.

"Did he do something to you?" he asked, and his voice had that growl to it. "Because you don't act like someone who's in love. Or even just hot for someone, which is what I thought at first when I saw you two together. You act like you're ashamed of something."

I simply stared at him. How in the Nether did he see so much?

"I think you have an over-active imagination," I said, and he looked down at me. There was no smiling now. There was an intensity to his eyes that practically took my breath away.

"Eunomia."

"Brennan," I said, trying to sound more irritated and less stupidly breathy. I am not sure I was successful.

"Did he do something to you? Did he hurt you?"

I shook my head. "It is nothing like that. We have known one another a very, very long time. He would never hurt me. He has not. Any so-called 'weirdness' you saw was all my own. I have a fair share of that. Or had you not noticed?"

He was still watching me. "I like your weirdness."

"I should finish packing," I said, taking a step back from him, still gripping the stair rail. "I would like to leave soon."

"I'll pack up, and I want to say bye to Sean before I leave. Then we can go. Okay?"

I nodded, turned, and climbed the stairs, more than happy to be away from him.

Once I was in my room, I closed the door and leaned back against it, closing my eyes.

I rubbed my hands over my face in irritation, my fingers rubbing along the raised scar at the side of my face from where Biset had managed to cut me. In truth, it still hurt.

I have only been struck by a Guardian's blade on one occasion before, and it was the day I realized my life would never be the same.

I stood, and tried to center myself, and remembered the first time I had ever been afraid. Mollis had gone to meet with Hades, and Brennan, who had been her mate at the time, had been kidnapped and held hostage by my sisters. Tortured. We realized what was happening when one of the imps alerted us that the shifter had been taken, and I had been in charge of getting Brennan out of the Nether.

The blood.

The blood was something it would take me a long time to forget. I was starting to believe I never would. I have taken part in my share of battles. I have been wounded more times than I care to remember. Seeing the way my sisters sliced and broke the shifter's body at Hermes' command was one of those things I just could not quite unsee. I saw it every time I looked at him. Perhaps that was why he was working his way into my life. Guilt on my part? Because my sisters did that to him? Maybe. Maybe I admire that, despite the fact that they were in the act of torturing him when I arrived, he'd refused, stubbornly, to give them what they wanted. He'd refused to scream, and, more, he'd refused to break.

We'd fought, my sisters and I. One plunged a dagger into my thigh as I ran past her. I'd grabbed the shifter and lifted him into the air, preparing to fly away. Another of my sisters had barreled into me in midair, stabbing her dagger into my wing, slicing it all the way through.

My wings flexed beneath my coat, a response to the memory of the excruciating pain. We barely made it out, and two of my sisters fell at my hand. From what I understand, they resurrected only to later be cut down by Mollis herself, permanently.

I had flown Brennan out of the Nether and into the deserted Packard Plant in Detroit, where the gateway between this world and the world of the immortals had once stood, both of us bleeding, barely hanging on to consciousness. And even though I knew I must have been hurting him as we fell through the gateway, he never made a sound.

Everything after that was chaos and panic, and it is only thanks to Ada's quick skill that I can fly at all.

I shook my head and walked over to the small dresser in my room. I tossed a few t-shirts, jeans, underthings into my duffel bag, along with the small laptop Hephaestus had given to me. I went through a box of different currencies I kept on hand, grabbing a few Euros for the trip, and I tucked them into my jacket pocket.

I tried to keep my mind from reliving that day in an endless loop. These were things I did not particularly want to think about. I did not want to think about what it felt like to really fear something. Yet I had a feeling, like an irritating gnat that just would not go away, that I had a reason to fear something now. I just did not know exactly what that was.

I tried to shove the thoughts aside and zipped up my bag. Hopefully this would be a quick trip. Hopefully she would send someone else with me next time. Hephaestus, maybe. Yes. Hephaestus would be better. Less likely to make me feel like some kind of awkward adolescent.

All I had to do was make it through a few days in Ireland. How hard could it be?

CHAPTER SEVEN

Less than an hour later, Brennan and I rematerialized in an alley behind a row of storefronts in Cork. I'd already tried it once myself to ensure it was a good place for two people to suddenly appear out of nowhere. We were between two large trash receptacles, and while the smell was horrid, it did ensure that no humans saw us.

"Ugh. Welcome to Ireland," Brennan muttered. He did not release my hand, instead, he pulled me out from between the dumpsters and toward the opening at the end of the alley.

"It generally smells much nicer than this," I told him.

"Good to know." We walked in silence, turning onto a main thoroughfare, surrounded by cars, people about their business. He glanced at the duffel bag I carried. "Only one bag? I expected more."

"I do not need much. A change of clothing. Laptop. Local currency, because if you have money, you can buy anything else you may need." I had that in abundance. One doesn't live for thousands of years without amassing a sizable fortune, especially if one plans on trying to pass for human.

Brennan was smiling, and he shook his head.

"What?"

"I've heard that before. Nain taught you how to pack, didn't he?"

I let out a short laugh. "I did not need him to teach me to pack, but he shared his advice nonetheless."

Brennan laughed. "He tends to do that."

"He was not wrong," I admitted, and he shook his head. We walked, and I took in the tall, narrow buildings on each side of the cramped street, some in muted, natural tones, and others in bright pastels. The air smelled of bakery bread, and I breathed it in. We passed a cheese shop, and the scent of sharp, fragrant cheese wafted out when a customer opened the door.

"Did you know my grandparents were from here?" Brennan asked, reading the name on the cheese shop's sign.

"I did not," I said. I considered pulling my hand out of his, but did not. The man made me do nonsensical things. I am perfectly capable, more so than he is, of walking on my own. Yet I understood. I knew, from the time I had spent in the shifters' company, as well as with Artemis, that their kind thrive on physical contact. I blushed at that, stupidly.

I made the mistake of glancing over at Brennan to see him watching me, a small smile on his lips.

"Your mother's parents, or your father's?" I asked.

"My mother's. My great grandfather owned a small cheese shop here in Cork. A long time ago. My mom's parents emigrated to the U.S. after they were married."

I nodded. "And you would like to see the location of the shop. Even if it is not your family's any longer."

He did not answer, and I smiled. "We can do that."

"It's stupid, I know."

"It is not. It is part of your history. Your past. It is good to honor our history. It makes us who we are."

He squeezed my hand. "If we have time. Did you have a place you preferred to stay while we're here?"

I shook my head. "I was not thinking ahead. I just planned on finding a place once we arrived."

"I reserved two rooms at this small inn near the center of town. If that's okay," he said. "We can change it if you want."

"That is fine," I said. "Thank you."

"So, look. We can get checked in, and then I'm meeting with one of the supernatural affairs guys here at four o'clock," he said, pulling his phone out of his pocket. "It's one thirty now, local time."

"Perfect. You can find out what you can from him while I look for the lost soul," I told him. "And then I will see you when I am finished, and you can tell me what you've learned. And then we will go look for Lethe."

He sighed. "I still don't like you dealing with these dead assholes by yourself."

I let out a short laugh. "I have been doing it for thousands of years, cub."

"I know. And you're scarier than they are," he said with a small smile.

"Of course."

We walked through the streets, ending up at a large stone building just off the main thoroughfare. We went in, and Brennan did the talking as a woman who identified herself as the owner of the inn, an older human with snow-white hair and too much perfume, openly studied us. We definitely looked like an odd pair, Brennan in his very official-looking suit and tie, hair neatly pulled back, ready, friendly smile. And then there was me, with my leather coat, faded Nirvana t-shirt, and knee-high black leather boots. At least she did not know about the daggers strapped to my body.

One did not need to be a telepath to see that she very clearly thought Brennan could do better. I hid a smirk as she gave Brennan the keys and looked disapprovingly at me, as though I was an irritant to her somehow.

Humans are strange beyond all reckoning.

She told us which rooms were ours, and Brennan and I headed there, hands still clasped.

"She thinks I have seduced you and I am not nearly good enough for you," I said when we got to our rooms. He was unlocking the door, and he fumbled, dropped the keys, swore under his breath.

"What made you think that?" he asked after he recovered and picked the keys up.

"She thinks you are a nice boy and I have corrupted you. She hopes you grow out of it."

"You are not a telepath," he reminded me as he pushed the door open and waved me in.

"No. Just very, very old. And humans are easy to read if you pay attention," I said, walking into the room.

"This room connects to our other one," he said pointing toward a door on the opposite wall. "Corrupting me, huh?" he asked, dropping his bag on the bed.

"Mhmm," I said, walking over to the door, opening it. The other room was identical to this one, and I tossed my black duffel bag onto the bed with its bedspread of gaudy mauve roses.

"Only if I was really lucky. Feel free to corrupt me, Tink," he said, shrugging his suit jacket off.

"You wish," I said.

"That's exactly what I'm saying. Glad you get it," he said, grinning at me, and I felt my entire body heat. I looked away, and he let out a short, entirely too intimate sounding chuckle. "You blush an awful lot for a badass immortal who claims she has no emotions whatsoever, you know that?"

"I am not blushing," I said, crossing my arms over my chest.

"Sure you are. It's cute."

I did not dignify that with a response, and he chuckled again. He unbuttoned the top button of his white shirt, started tugging at his tie.

It was much too warm in our rooms. Much too warm.

"I should get to work," I said, well aware that I was mumbling. Though part of me was very interested to stay and see how many more items of clothing the shifter planned to shed.

Damn it.

I headed for the door. "I will see you later," I said.

"Be careful, Eunomia," he said.

"I always am," I answered, closing the door behind me and realizing after the fact that I could have simply rematerialized from our room. Now I had to walk through the inn and risk the glares of perfume-woman, since two other visitors were currently standing in the hall with me and chatting near the stairwell.

I blamed Brennan and his pheromone power for my lapse in planning. I really did need to ask Artemis about how to counter that.

I made my way out of the inn, out onto the street, and then around a corner where I ducked between delivery trucks outside a small grocery store. Now, I was able to get to work.

I reappeared in a large pasture, relieved that this part of Cork hadn't changed much since the last time I'd been there. It would not have done at all to have reappeared in the middle of a cafe or, worse, someone's bathroom. I had that unfortunate experience once, and it left both me and the poor human emotionally scarred for sometime afterward, I am sure. I got my bearings, and started walking east. I felt calm settle over me as I eased into my work, and I was grateful for it. I focused on my reason for being in Ireland: Boyd O'Connor. The kindly doctor, or so he'd once been considered, had murdered eleven children in his care over the course of seven years. At least, that was what the public knew about him. Those tasked with judging and punishing souls know better. In addition to the eleven deaths he'd been accused of and successfully tried for, he'd also murdered at least six other people, always people who had turned to him for help. One had been an unmarried woman who had found herself pregnant after a tryst with a man who worked for her father. She sought the doctor out to help end the pregnancy, and he'd given her a concoction, telling her it would do that very thing. Instead, it caused a slow, painful death, and he sat and avidly watched every single moment, the woman tied to a chair in the root cellar of his home in the country. That was where I would head first. Even if the home itself was gone, souls were usually drawn to places they'd had a strong emotional attachment to in life. Good emotions or bad didn't really matter. All that mattered was the strength of the emotions. And the doctor had definitely had a strong affinity for the things he'd done in that house. Torture.

That had been his particular little kick, I thought as I neared the home he'd lived in. Watching death happen. He'd done it with every one of his victims, prolonging it for as long as possible, as if it was a show he never wanted to end.

The old stone house was still there, to my surprise. Long since abandoned, dilapidated. It was likely that no one had wanted to live there, knowing a murderer had lived there. The details had all come to light during his trial. I could hardly blame the humans. Even now, even knowing what I know of the dead and spirits, I disliked walking through the gaping front door. The windows were all broken out, the inside of the home littered with leaves and other debris. The roof had long since collapsed, as well as part of the second floor, and daylight flooded into the main floor. I walked through, stepping over beams, making my way to the back of the house. The cellar door was outside, set a bit away from the house. It had been a root cellar, I remembered, tucked into the gentle slope around the house. I checked the house just the same, able to feel the remnants of his energy signature there. It was fairly recent, and I was hopeful that he was not too far.

I stepped out of the house and made my way to the root cellar. Its doors seemed to be gone completely, nothing more than a dark hole in the side of a mound of earth. It was likely that thrill seekers had done that, coming to see, in person, the place where he'd caused death. While he'd killed the children, slowly, so that they wasted away, in hospitals, there had always been rumors that his other victims had been taken here to die. As it was, the rumors were completely true. More so than many realized at the time.

I stood in the doorway of the cellar, and he was there, sitting on the floor.

"Ah, you. I was hoping you'd show up soon. Nice hair," he said, his voice somewhat scratchy, as if he needed a lozenge. Hanging did that, sometimes.

I did not answer. This was not the reaction I was expecting.

"So, let's get on with it, eh? You've brought someone for me?"

I stared at him, shook my head a little and eased my black dagger out of its sheath.

"Why so quiet?" he asked, looking a little more alarmed now.

I leapt forward before he could react, and plunged the dagger into his side. He struggled for a moment, and he was nearly completely solid, much, much stronger than he should have been. He screamed, and struggled, and cursed me as the strength slowly leeched out of him, thanks to my dagger. I turned him over and wrapped the thin black chain around his wrists, leaving my dagger right where it was.

"What in the hell is your problem? Worthless bitch!" he screamed, enraged.

I didn't answer. I numbly took his arm in my hand and closed my eyes, focusing on rematerializing in the Netherwoods.

Tisiphone was on duty in the holding area, and she greeted me with a hug as Boyd O'Connor's soul raged impotently beside me.

I met Tisiphone's eyes. "We have a problem." I debated sharing what he'd said. I wasn't ready. I needed time to figure it out, to process it all. "This one, like the last, was much stronger than he should have been, given the amount of time he was free. We need to find out how that is possible."

"They must have had help," Tisiphone said, catching on. I nodded.

"Have you made any progress with the Biset?" I asked, wondering about the Frenchman I'd captured in Paris, and she shook her head in irritation.

"It is as if there's a blank spot there in his memories, and I'm assuming whoever helped him is there. We will keep working at him, and this one as well."

I nodded my thanks and turned the soul over to Tisiphone, pulling my dagger from his side as I did. He continued to rage at Tisiphone, and one thing became very clear: I'd caught this one by surprise.

When he's been waiting for someone else.

I observed for the next couple hours as Tisiphone did her thing. It was not something it was possible to watch without feeling disturbed. Furies are feared for a reason. Watching the things she did to the soul of Boyd O'Connor reminded me of that, very clearly. I did not merely stand by and watch. I helped. I used my dagger on him, and usually the pain of that alone is enough to get a soul to break. Whatever secret he was keeping, most notably who had helped him escape, and who he'd been waiting for, he was determined to keep it. Or unable to tell us, which was even more disturbing.

There are no secrets from the Furies.

We made him scream. It was not enough. Tisiphone came as close as I have ever seen to losing her temper, and, after a while longer, after she used more mental manipulation on him with no success, she gave me an irritated shake of her head. I retrieved my dagger from his chest. Tisiphone punched him in the face, hard, and I knew that was for her, because she was frustrated and worried about Mollis, more than anything else.

We walked out of the cell together and Tisiphone slammed the heavy door behind us, locked it. She was covered in blood. Which was another bad sign. Souls don't bleed. He was on his way to a corporeal form, just as Biset had been.

"I will have Mollis take a crack at him," she snarled, still angry. So much rage in the Furies. "He will talk."

"Perhaps he cannot."

"We'll make him talk," she growled, her eyes glowing. "My daughter cannot continue like this. Nether attempted to take control today."

I had been about to argue with her, but that news brought me up short. I clamped my mouth shut. "Is Mollis all right?"

"She kept her under control," Tisiphone said with obvious pride. "My daughter is strong. She should not have to deal with this. We have one more. Hopefully that will help her condition," she said, eyes still blazing.

"I will not stop until they are all back."

"I know you won't. There is no one more capable of this than you, Eunomia. Thank you for handling this," she said, beginning to calm down.

"We will get to the bottom of it. I promise you." She nodded. "I must return to Ireland now. I have one more soul to find there, and then the shifter and I will return here until we make our next move."

"Excellent. Make them pay," Tisiphone said, a phrase the Furies often said to one another.

I gave her a small smile. "I always do."

I took a deep breath and focused on rematerializing back in Cork.

Moments later, I was standing in my dark room at the inn the shifter and I were staying in. I could hear the television in Brennan's room, the volume low. It sounded like a sporting event, maybe. I made my way to the lamp beside the bed and clicked it on, kicked my boots off, then made my way into the small bathroom. I washed my hands thoroughly, as if Dr. O'Connor's filth still lingered there.

He'd acted as if he'd expected me, or, at the very least, someone. I closed my eyes and leaned forward on the vanity countertop. The possibility that tiny hint had opened up was one I did not even want to contemplate. I would have to, of course. I would have to tell the Furies, the Goddess of Death.

I needed to see it for myself first. If he'd meant what I thought he meant... I shook my head. If he meant what I thought he did, it meant things were not only messier, but much more dangerous for me. I am a good fighter. Just like all of the Guardians. Warriors. Death's own hunters. If things went wrong when I faced one of them, I could very well see my time in the mortal realm come to an end.

I walked out of the bathroom, eyed the door between my room and the shifter's. It also meant I should not allow company when I was out on a mission. Endangering myself was one thing; endangering another was something I would not abide.

I would tell Mollis so when we returned to Detroit. I was not sure if Brennan was asleep or not. I did not see lamplight beneath his door, so he may very well have dozed off. Rematerializing, for those who are not used to it, can be quite exhausting, especially when traveling great distances, as we had. In addition, the time change would have confused his system.

Why was I disappointed?

I pushed the thought aside and stretched out on my bed and pulled my small laptop out of my bag, booted it up and picked up with the next show in my Netflix queue.

The modern human world certainly had its advantages. Hephaestus was right about that much. I settled the laptop on my stomach and leaned back on the pillows, every once in a while stifling a giggle as I watched.

There was a knock, and then the door opened. I jumped up, making sure the laptop was facing away from the doorway.

"Hey. I saw the light and thought I'd check in and make sure you were okay."

"Yes. I am. I am fine," I said, standing awkwardly next to the bed.

"So I see," he said, leaning against the door jamb. "How did it go?"

"Fine. I was able to apprehend him easily and turn him over to Tisiphone. Tomorrow I will go after the next soul from Ireland. And we will try to track down Lethe."

He nodded. "What's wrong?"

"Nothing," I said.

He was watching me, and I knew he wanted to ask more. He glanced at the laptop. "What are you watching?"

"Nothing." I felt heat rise to my face, and he noticed as well (damn his preternatural shifter senses.)

He grinned. "Why are you blushing? Are you watching porn or something?"

I sputtered. "No. I am not watching porn!"

"I don't judge," he said, still grinning.

"Well, I am not."

"Then what else could it be? What can possibly be embarrassing enough to make an immortal badass blush?"

"Nothing," I said again, edging closer to the bed.

He crossed his arms. "I'm watching soccer."

"Good for you."

"But I'm bored."

"Such hardships," I said in mock pity.

He laughed. "So prickly, Tink." And then he became a little more serious. "Are you hungry?"

I shrugged. I was, but I hadn't realized it until just then, my mind still spinning over what the soul had said to me.

He went into his room, and came back with a grocery bag. I watched him as he carried it over to the dresser. He caught me watching him and he shrugged. "I didn't want to stop for dinner in a restaurant. And I didn't want to eat with the other guests here, so I just stopped at the grocery store after my meeting."

I let out a short laugh. "What do you have?" I asked, giving up, knowing there really was no getting rid of him and that my stomach was now growling.

"Bread, peanut butter, some cheese that I haven't tried yet, grapes, apples, cookies…"

"I will try the cheese. And an apple would be perfect."

He handed a small wheel of cheese to me, along with a green apple.

"Do you want tea?"

I shook my head. "How did your meeting go?" I asked him.

He shrugged, still rifling through the bags. He'd changed into sweatpants and a white t-shirt, and I did like the way the pants hung from his hips.

I forced my eyes away.

"It was good to meet the guy, I guess. Have a face to go with the name. He didn't have a lot to say. Things are pretty quiet here. No reports of unexplained activity. They mostly have shifters and witches here, I guess," he finished. "Sorry I didn't find out more."

"I did not expect much. But it is better to ask around than not, yes?" I settled onto my bed, sitting cross-legged, and used my dagger to cut a thin wedge of cheese. I popped it into my mouth. It was pungent, with a bit of a bite to it, and an underlying creaminess. I cut another wedge and handed it to Brennan, who had settled himself at the foot of my bed, lying on his stomach. He took it, bit into it, and made a face.

"Ugh."

"Very well. More for me, then," I said. I cut a slice of apple, layered a thin piece of the cheese onto it, and took a bite, sighed happily.

When I looked up, he was looking at the laptop.

He was grinning. "You were watching 'The Golden Girls'?"

I glared at him. "Not a word."

"There's nothing to be embarrassed about."

"If you even breathe a word of it, I will acquaint you with my dagger," I warned him.

"What's the big deal?"

"I am death's hunter. This," I said, gesturing toward the laptop, "does not fit the rest of what I am. I do not even understand why I find four older mortal ladies living in Florida as amusing as I do. It is nonsense."

"It's funny, Eunomia. That's why you like it. It doesn't make you less of a badass hunter."

I took another bite of the apple and cheese, well aware that I was scowling.

"It's called 'having a personality,' and it isn't a bad thing, you know," he continued.

"My sisters did not have such frivolous interests," I said, taking another bite.

"Yes, and your sisters were monsters," he said, and the mild tone of his voice made my gaze shoot up to his. "From personal experience," he added.

"I am sorry," I said, chastened. "I should not have brought them up."

"I'm a big boy, Eunomia. I don't need to be protected from the memory of that day, though I notice that you seem uncomfortable about it."

"I am," I said quietly.

"You shouldn't be. You saved my ass. I wouldn't be here if it wasn't for you."

I took another bite of the apple, though I did not feel hungry anymore. The stupidest things came out of my mouth when I was with him, I thought in annoyance.

"I just keep thinking about what it must have been like for you, to have these beings who looked exactly like me, who sounded exactly like me, doing those things to you." I could not look at him. "How can you stand the sight of me now?"

He didn't answer, and long awkward moments of silence stretched between us. My stomach turned, and I regretted eating.

"Eunomia," he said. "Look at me."

I forced my gaze up to his. There was no anger there, no hatred. Instead, I found kindness and empathy.

"You are not your sisters. I know that better than anyone else. Maybe I even know it better than you do."

"And what makes you so sure?"

He smiled, just the tiniest lift of the corner of his mouth. "Because you were the only one saving me. I don't look at you and see them. I look at you and see the one who fought to free me, the one who ended up bloody and torn bringing me out alive."

I hated the way my heart pounded, stupidly. There was no reason for it, and I knew that if I could feel it, he could hear it. "Well. I don't find you all that annoying. I could not just leave you there."

He laughed and shook his head. "You are this close to corrupting me now, smooth talker," he said, winking at me, and I shook my head. "So," he said, still smiling.

"So," I mimicked him, taking another bite of cheese and apple.

"What's the story with Big Red?"

"Who?" I asked with a laugh.

"Triton."

I shook my head and waved it off.

"Come on. If you don't tell me, I'm gonna think the worst of him. And the worst I can think is pretty bad, Tink."

"Leave it alone," I said, meeting his eyes.

"It's just you and me here. And I'm curious. And I want to feel a little less like you're all speaking another language."

"What do you mean?" I asked him, and he shrugged. He lay down on his back, folded his arms, resting his head on his hands. I could have stared at the way his t-shirt stretched across his chest for quite a long time, but I remembered myself and looked down at my ugly bedspread.

"You all have all this history together, right? Literally, thousands of years. You all know each other and there's nothing weird about being immortal or having seen empires rise and fall. And then a couple of years ago, I find out that's in my blood, that I'm going to live a very long time. Not immortal, but still—"

"You may as well be," I said.

"Huh?"

"You have Artemis' blood. You've had Mollis' blood. You have been healed by Asclepias. At this point, I do not think you will age."

"They made me immortal?" he asked, his eyes widening as he looked at me.

"Close enough that there is not much difference, I believe," I said.

He furrowed his brow. "I'm not sure how I feel about that."

I nodded. "Back to what you were saying before? About everything the immortals have seen?"

"Right," he said, picking up his train of thought. "So I'm part of that world, the immortals, but I don't understand a damn thing about it, you know? I don't know who any of these people are, or what their relationships are, or... anything."

"It is a whole new world for you, isn't it?" I asked gently, and he nodded.

I smiled. "We are quite the pair, you and I," I said with a small laugh.

"What do you mean?"

"You have no idea how to be an immortal. And I have no idea how to live among humans. We are lost, cub."

He gave a short laugh. "We are, Tink." His eyes met mine, and the warmth in his gaze made something inside me twist. "We can stumble along together, maybe."

"Maybe," I said, barely able to find my voice.

He rolled over, onto his stomach, and I lay down on my stomach beside him, pulled the laptop over so we could both see it. I hit play with a sigh, and the four human women on screen continued the argument they were having.

"Fine. But tomorrow night, we're watching something else," he murmured beside me.

"We will see."

We watched a few episodes, and I looked over at him when I heard him start snoring. I closed the laptop, rested my head on my arms, and watched him sleep until I drifted off as well.

CHAPTER EIGHT

When I woke the next morning, Brennan was gone. There was a note beside me on the bed, that he was having coffee with another of his contacts in Ireland about some information that had come to light overnight and that he would see me later. Of course, he reminded me to be careful. He added a postscript to his note: "Tonight, we're watching *The Avengers*. Or *Iron Man*. I'll even let you pick. —B"

I shook my head and got up, still holding his note. Really, I should take him back to Detroit immediately. I had the distinct feeling that the moment I set eyes on him, that resolution would go out the window. Unless I found my next two souls before then. Once they were found, we had to return to Detroit. He had work to do, and so did I.

I showered, dressed, and checked my daggers. That done, I focused on rematerializing.

I knew my next target was in the small tourist town of Kenmare, in the southern part of Ireland, so I rematerialized just outside of town. It was one of the most beautiful places I could imagine. Mountains rose in the distance, and the town itself was a mix of tall, narrow buildings, cobblestone streets, and an almost endless parade of tour buses. That part was new, I thought as I walked into town. The last time I'd been there, horses and carriages had traveled the streets. Aside from that, it felt the same. It looked the same, a church spire rising into the sky against a backdrop of verdant hills.

It was mid-morning, and the main road through town bustled with activity. People walked to and from shops, and, while there was not an abundance of car traffic, there were plenty of people on bikes zipping along the narrow avenue. I snaked off of the main street, onto some of the nearby, less-traveled streets. Inns, pubs, shops, and the occasional inn filled both sides of the street. I kept walking, hoping to pick up an energy signature. My next target, Mary Shanahan, had died in this part of Kenmare, burned by her own husband and four neighbors under suspicion of having been possessed by a demon. There had been a trial and a whole lot of speculation at the time, and the husband had been found guilty of manslaughter. He'd deserved much worse.

She did not belong on my list. Every other of the twenty-seven had been murderers, rapists, degenerates of the worst sort. Mary was nothing more than a woman who'd been killed after falling ill. It seemed to me that her only mistake had been marrying a superstitious fool.

As I walked, my phone started vibrating in my pocket. I pulled it out and saw Mollis's number on the screen. I hit the talk button with a grimace. The telephone was among my least favorite modern inventions.

"Hey E. Thanks for finding that soul. My mother is punishing him now and I feel dirty just from looking into his mind."

"I do not doubt it. He was a vile one. And you are welcome. I am on the trail of my next Irish target. We should be back in Detroit tomorrow or the day after, hopefully."

"Perfect. I swear these missing souls are making me nuts. Every one of them is like having my fingernails pulled out repeatedly. And it's making Nether nuts…" she trailed off, and I did not know what to say. I felt badly for her. Her situation was much more difficult than her father's had been. She was trying to work with ancient systems in a new world, a new reality, and she had been thrown into her role without even knowing it was coming.

"I will find them as quickly as I can. I promise you," I said.

"My mother and aunt have been at those two you've brought in already. I even went to work on the butcher, trying to get them to tell us how they got out. Nothing yet, but I swear I'm going to break them."

A sense of foreboding filled me at the tone of her voice. "Mollis, you do realize it's entirely possible they can't tell you, yes? Your mother mentioned a blank spot in their psyches."

"I can break through whatever anyone else did to them. It's amazing how quickly unbreakable things break once the pain starts," she said, and the words sent a chill down my spine.

"Just keep it in mind, or you are going to get even more frustrated."

"Right," she said, and I knew Mollis's "whatever" tone well enough to know she wasn't going to change her stance on this.

"Violence only excites Nether," I reminded her gently.

"Maybe. But it also makes me feel a hell of a lot better. Just find the souls, E. I'll talk to you when you get back." And with that, she hung up and I was left staring at my phone.

I hoped the demon was watching her carefully. Nether's influence wasn't something to take lightly.

And if it wasn't Nether's influence, then it was possible my friend was beginning to some of the humanity that had set her above all other immortals. The powers that had come with her new role as Lady of the Dead were ones I would not wish on my worst enemy. The ability to see every bad thing, every questionable thought anyone had ever had would be a waking nightmare. I remembered Hades's coolness well, the way he held himself away from others. It was, I now knew, for his own sanity. But that separation had made him generally unable to empathize with others, unwilling to justify himself or his actions to anyone else. He'd been a brutal, cold god because he'd had to be, and I hoped Mollis had it in her to hold on to what she had once been.

I knew, however, that she practically craves violence and always has. I just hoped she would keep it under control, lest Nether gain a foothold.

I walked along a quiet road on the outskirts of town. I could feel an energy signature. My lost soul had come this way recently. I pulled my Netherblade from my sheath and kept walking, listening, sensing. All of a sudden, I stopped dead in my tracks. A second energy signature had joined Mary's. I closed my eyes, focused, taking a moment to analyze and identify it.

Quinn Connolly. Dead nearly forty years, and most certainly *not* on my list.

Which meant Mollis didn't know he was dead. Which was absolutely something I'd never heard of before. How could the God of Death not know someone had died?

I took a steadying breath. This was bad, to put it mildly. The way it was supposed to work, a mortal died, and the god or Goddess of Death immediately knew everything there was to know about the soul: who it was, where it had lived, and every single deed it had done in its life. What it loved, and, more importantly, what it feared. At the moment of death, a soul belonged, completely, to Mollis. And because Mollis (and, before, Hades) knew everything there was to know about a soul, the Guardians knew things as well, our mental knowledge of the dead tied to theirs.

But there was nothing here but a name and a general sense of how long it had been since he'd been among the living, and I only knew that from analyzing his energy trail.

I kept walking, and on a field outside of town, I found the two souls. The female sat on a log, looking at the hills in the distance. The male paced several yards away. All at once, he stopped, turned, and his eyes rested on me.

"She can see us," he said in a deep voice, a warm Irish brogue. The woman, Mary, turned and studied me.

"I suppose you've come to bring me back, then," she said quietly, recognizing me for what I am. I took a few steps closer. Unlike the last two, Mary was still very much nothing more than a wisp of spirit. She would feel solid to me, of course, but she wasn't in any condition to affect the living. The doctor and the butcher had both been almost inexplicably strong, well on their way to developing fully corporeal forms.

It was another sign that Mary was different.

"How did you get out?" I asked her quietly. I was aware of the brawny Irishman, Quinn, studying me closely. I would deal with him eventually. I needed to understand how he was possible.

"Please believe me when I say it was never my intention," Mary said, still sitting on the log. That is another thing the living don't quite understand about the dead. They say, "well, they can't pick things up and they can walk through walls, so why don't they just fall down through floors and the earth and how can they even sit?" Hades once explained it best, when he said that the Earth is the creation of the gods, and as such has some of our power in it. Everything attached to the Earth itself gains a little bit of that, meaning that it spans both the living and spiritual realms. So the floor of a building holds some of that energy, as does anything sitting upon it, like a chair or a bed. However, should the spirit try to pick those things up, they would find themselves unable to as soon as the item broke its contact with the floor, and, therefore, with the Earth.

It is also why, in their most desperate moments, mortals find contact with the earth so comforting.

"It was not your intention," I repeated, nodding. "I can believe that. You are unlike the rest of those that escaped."

She smiled a little. "You mean I am not a bloodthirsty raving lunatic? Yes, I would agree with that." Her voice had a pleasant lilt to it. She had been in her late thirties when she'd died, back in the year 1803. She still wore a plain gray dress which went down to her ankles, and her dark hair was held back in a tight bun at the back of her head.

I walked over to the log, watching Quinn out of the side of my eye as I did. He stood in the same spot, watching me, a confused look on his face. I sat on the log beside Mary. "Can you tell me what happened?"

Mary folded her hands in her lap. "One of them... one of the monsters who got out, had claimed me as his own. As a plaything," she said, meeting my eyes briefly, making sure I understood what she meant.

"I am sorry," I said automatically.

She shrugged. "It did not hurt as much as burning, I suppose. Though you may want to mention to whoever is in charge that separate facilities for men and women may help. Not all of us need quite that much punishment while we wait for our final judgment." I nodded, and she continued. "At any rate, when they were freed, he dragged me with him. I broke away from him as soon as I possibly could, and returned home. I met this fellow on the way. He doesn't say much, but it is nice to have someone who can hear me when I talk."

"Do you know who freed them? How?"

She was studying me. "I wish I did. All I knew was that it looked as if several of them were being pulled by an invisible force, and I was grateful to see him going as well.

It is just my luck that at the last moment, he decided to pull me with him."

"Who was he?"

"His name was Bates Downing."

"American," I said, and she nodded. "Serial murderer and rapist."

"Indeed."

"I will capture him again," I promised her. "I know it does not undo the things he did to you."

"I hope he gets a little more punishment for it," she said.

"Oh, he will. His final judgment will take all of it into account."

She nodded, and we sat in silence for several moments.

"What have you been doing since you have been free?" I asked her.

She shrugged. "At first, just trying to get back here. I just wanted to go home. And, since, I have mostly been avoiding the crows when they come to claim the dead. In some cases, I have tried to make sure the crows find the one who just died. There are some that surely need the punishment they have coming to them."

I looked up to see Quinn still watching me wordlessly.

"He's the reason I got into doing that. That is his thing. The crows don't seem to bother with him at all, so he's been leading the crows right to the new souls," Mary said.

"What are you?" I asked Quinn, shaken by the revelation.

He shrugged. "Far as I know, I'm just a man. Ghost, more to the case," he added, still watching me. "What are you?"

"I am a Guardian. It is my duty to collect the souls of the dead and bring them for their final judgment and punishment."

"Then why the crows?" he asked.

"Because there aren't enough of my kind anymore. The crows have taken over the duties that were once ours." I studied him, as he studied me. He was tall, broad, barrel-chested. He was built much like Hephaestus, huge and solid. Reddish-brown hair fell in unruly waves over his forehead and down his neck. His eyes were a shade of bluish-green that I often associated with people from the Emerald Isle, fringed with long dark lashes. He was fair of complexion, and he'd apparently had a bit of a five-o'clock shadow at the moment he'd died. He wore a plain white t-shirt and chinos, cut in a way that would have been typical of the 1960s or so. "Explain yourself, please," I said to him.

A slow smile spread over his lips. "I was just about to ask you the same thing, lass."

I shook my head. "This is very serious. Why is it my Lady of Death doesn't know about you? If she did, I would be here for you as well, not just for her," I said, gesturing to Mary.

He shrugged. "You know as much as I do, then. I expected you to be less clueless."

I let out a short laugh. "Oh, if you only knew," I said, and he laughed as well. I sobered. "Can you tell me your story?"

He nodded, and sat on the ground where he'd been, a few feet away from where Mary and I sat.

"I lived here," he gestured to the deserted cottage across the field, "with my sister and her children. She was widowed, and I was in no hurry to start a family of my own. I was the family's bachelor uncle, I suppose," he said, and I nodded. I could only imagine how frustrating that must have been for any eligible women who knew him. He looked to have been possibly in his early thirties when he'd died. "At any rate, we had all settled in one night, and I woke to the sound of glass breaking somewhere downstairs. I slept in the attic," he added in explanation, and I nodded. "I stumbled down the stairs, and there was a man there, a man my sister had refused after the death of her husband." I felt my stomach tighten. I clenched my fists in my lap. He caught the motion, met my eyes for a moment. "He'd killed my nephews before I'd even heard him down there. I went after him. We fought, and I screamed for my sister to run, but she was of course hysterical over her sons. She charged him in a rage, and he stopped slashing at me with his knife. I bled, and tried to catch my breath, and watched as he stabbed my sister in the stomach."

His tone was flat, as was normal when someone was trying to relate an emotional story without losing their composure. As he talked, it was as if I could read his past, the way I usually could with souls of the dead. It came a little at a time, instead of all at once the way it usually did, as if, by sharing part of himself with me, I was allowed to see more.

"She fell," he continued, eyes still on mine, "and I watched her fall as he stabbed me one more time. I wrestled him for his knife as I bled out, and finally hit home. He and I fell at the same time."

Mary was silent beside me, apparently hearing this story for the first time as well. Tears glistened in her eyes, and she sniffed a little, shaking her head.

"Women who looked like you came. Were you one of them?"

I shook my head. I had not been there.

"They took the souls of my sister and her children, and, in the meantime, her murderer tried to run. I held on to his soul and refused to let go. They claimed him, took him away. It was as if they never saw me at all, and soon I was left alone here."

"I can see you. I wonder why they could not," I said softly. "You are a mystery."

"As are you," he said with a nod.

We sat in silence for several long moments. A plan was beginning to develop in my mind. Mollis needed these souls found as quickly as possible. And this new development was something I most definitely needed to figure out.

"Now that I have found you, it will be easy for me to trace you again," I said. "I offer you a choice," I said to Mary. "Would you prefer to take your place in the Nether, and face your final judgment now?"

"Or?" she asked.

"Or," I said, not fully believing that I was doing it, "would you like to stay here and help me track down the soul of the one who hurt you?"

She'd been fiddling with the ends of her sleeves, and she stilled. "You would allow me to do that?" she asked.

I nodded. "If it is something you want to do, yes," I said. It felt wrong to send her back now. Wrong to lock her away when she had been here, in the mortal realm, helping my Lady in her own way. I would have to try to find a way to explain it to Mollis. "He has likely fled to the U.S. I can take you there if that is what you want."

Her gaze hardened. "I find him, and you take him to be punished?"

"Yes."

"And what about me? What happens to me then?"

I took a breath. This was the part I would have to explain to my Queen. I had a feeling she would not be entirely happy with me. And I could not, for the life of me, understand why I was doing it, only that it felt right. There was just an overwhelming sense of knowing. I have learned several things in my lifetime, and listening to that feeling is one of the reasons I am alive and able to look at myself in the mirror. I had the same feeling the day I met Mollis, when I came to collect the soul of one of her friends. I had it the night I stayed with her after her mate died. And I had it the day I battled my sisters saving the shifter. I would not stop listening to it now.

"That will be up to you. If you feel ready to go, I can take you for your final judgment as well, ensuring that you are judged quickly. Or, if you decide you want to continue helping me, you can do that, as long as we have my Queen's blessing for you to do so." I paused. "There were twenty-seven souls that escaped with you all together. I've now found three. We have twenty-four more to find and return to the Nether, including the monster who tortured you."

"I would very much appreciate the opportunity to avenge myself," she said quietly, her eyes glinting.

"Then you shall have it," I said.

"Thank you, Guardian," she said softly, her gaze still holding mine. "I am yours."

I nodded. "You should not have any trouble contacting me when you find him. We will discuss it more when we are ready to leave."

"Very good. I am looking forward to this."

I smiled a little. "I am sure you are." I turned my gaze to Quinn, who was still watching me. "And what am I supposed to do with you, Connolly?"

He smiled again. "Put me to work, lass. We'll try to figure one another out along the way."

I looked away. I met Mary's eyes.

"My name is Eunomia," I finally said. "If you betray me, your punishment will be never-ending and terrible. I have friends in high places, and I am adept at causing pain myself."

"I do not doubt it. And when I said I am yours, I meant it," Mary said.

"I believe you. I am not sure about you, however," I said, turning back to Quinn.

"That makes two of us," he said.

"I think you should stay where I can easily find you."

"Can I fight and capture souls?"

"Of course," I answered.

"Then that sounds just fine to me."

I sat with the two souls for a while, and eventually Mary wandered off and settled further away, her eyes still on the mountains in the distance. Quinn sat, mostly silent, and mostly watching me.

"She does that often. Stares at those mountains," he explained. "Her memories haunt her. Nightmares plague her. She spends a lot of time closed in on herself."

I nodded, and we sat in silence for a few moments longer. "You are not like any other soul I have come across," I finally said.

"How so?"

"Besides the fact that my Lady knows nothing of your existence, and the fact that I knew almost nothing about you until you told me about yourself… you feel different. Aberration."

"You really have a way with people," he said, a wry grin on his lips.

I found myself smiling a bit as well. "It was not an insult, necessarily. Your energy is odd. You feel both alive and dead. If that makes any sense," I added.

"None at all," he answered, and I laughed. He joined me. We were silent for a few moments. "If we're sharing aberrations, I should tell you that I do not usually flaunt my presence to your kind. I do not know why they don't see me, but I have been waiting for my luck to run out in that regard. I do not know why I sit here, knowing you can see me, and knowing what you are supposed to be doing with me." He paused again. "There are others," he said finally.

"Others? Of me?"

He shook his head. "Others your kind cannot see. I wonder if you will be able to see them."

I clasped my hands around my knees, rested my chin on them. "Where?"

"I know of some here in Ireland, though a few claim to have come from Britain and that they saw more there. I'm not sure if that was true or not," he said with a shrug.

"If you exist here, it is entirely probable there are others like you in other places," I said.

He took a breath he likely did not need. Old habits die hard. "They will be drawn to you, as I was. Do not be surprised if they begin seeking you out."

I studied him, and he bore it patiently.

"I am going to take a wild guess and say you arrived in Ireland the day before yesterday," he said.

I nodded.

"That is when I started feeling the need to find… something. And when you arrived looking for Mary, I realized the compulsion was gone. Your arrival was what I was waiting for."

He must have detected some disbelief in my countenance, because he shook his head and smiled. "You are as confused by it as I am, lass."

"Why now? I have existed a long time, and you have been dead for decades. So why now?"

He shrugged. "You are here now. Have you been on this land in the last forty years?"

I shook my head. "The last time I was here was a little over three hundred years ago."

"And England?"

"Nearly as long," I said quietly. "I worked mostly on mainland Europe and Asia. Occasionally in North America." I looked up into the sky, clouds passing across a deep blue sky. "Why now? Why here?"

"I do not know… What should I call you?" he asked.

"Eunomia is fine. Lass, as you have been, is fine," I said.

"It feels like I should be bowing to you."

I laughed then and shook my head. "While that is not an unheard of response for men to have to me, it is not necessary."

He let out a loud guffaw. "That is not what I meant, though I do indeed see it. I'm saying: I am the one following you. I am telling you now I want to fight for you. This feels like the entire reason I am still here. I can't walk around calling you 'lass.'"

"Then call me by my name. It is enough."

He shook his head. "I hope I'm not making a mistake."

"That makes two of us."

"I am not afraid of facing my final judgment, understand," he said, eyes meeting mine. "I just am not ready to stop doing this. I'm not ready to stop making sure those who are trying to escape judgment are forced to face it."

"By escaping your own judgment," I said with a smile.

"There must be a reason the crows and your kind haven't been able to see me. There must be a reason I am drawn to follow you now."

"That remains to be seen," I said. "But you claim you will help me and for now that is enough. I fear this task my Lady has set for me is more dangerous than I at first believed."

"The Lord works in mysterious ways," he said slowly. "Maybe this is one of them."

Pointing out that we likely did not believe in the same god seemed pointless, so I merely smiled. "Gods do love their mystery," I finally said.

He seemed to catch the general direction of my thoughts and smiled. "It's no surprise to me that the god I've worshipped my whole life is not exactly what I believed He was. And, who knows? Maybe He was. Maybe the gods you know are not the only ones after all."

I shook my head. "I have been here for thousands of years. There has never been an inkling of any others. And be grateful for that, because the ones I know for the most part care nothing for human suffering."

He smiled. "We will agree to disagree. Though I don't doubt your gods are dangerous. You don't exactly seem the peaceful type yourself."

"No?" I asked, raising my eyebrow.

"No. Shall I try to guess how many weapons you currently have on your person?"

I smiled. "Go ahead."

He studied me.

"I am guessing four. Two strapped to your chest or back maybe. Two more in your boots," he said, glancing at my legs.

"So close," I said.

"How off was I?"

"Very close."

"Care to share details?"

"Not a chance."

He laughed, shaking his head. I glanced toward where Mary sat. "I will have to take her to the U.S. Her target will likely be in Florida. And then I have a friend I have to transport back to his home." A friend who I was looking forward to seeing more of, which was stupid and ridiculous. "Can I trust you to stay where I tell you to until I return?"

"You can. I have no idea why, but I know I have no desire to wander now. I would suspect witchcraft on your part, except that I don't believe that works on the dead."

"Well, there are necromancers," I said. "But they use the actual body."

He gave a mock quiver, and I rolled my eyes.

"I will be where you tell me to be."

"So obedient," I murmured.

"Let's not push it, shall we?" he said in a mild tone, and I smiled. "Let's keep that between us, eh? I do have my manhood to think of."

"Is that even a thing ghosts are concerned with?"

"This one is. Yes."

The sky was beginning to darken just a bit, the mountains like a row of uneven teeth at the edge of the earth. I met his gaze. "Be careful. I can see you... who knows? Maybe something has changed. Maybe now others can see you as well."

"I will be. I always am," he said, standing up. I moved to get up, and he held out a hand to help me. I set my hand in his, my hand almost ridiculously small in comparison. He pulled a little, and I unfolded my legs, standing up in one smooth motion.

"I will see you soon," I said.

"Looking forward to it," he said with a nod.

I grimaced. "You'll likely see me do this often, so you may as well see it now. I'm going to leave."

He watched, and I met his eyes, then focused on rematerializing back at my room in the inn. And I was relieved to leave him and all of the questions he raised behind.

CHAPTER NINE

I had intended to go back to the inn, but I did not feel ready to deal with Brennan just yet. I was not entirely happy to have him with me, not because I disliked him of course, but because he confused me. And that is not a feeling I am overly fond of.

I decided that looking for Lethe was a better use of my time and energy than waiting around for Brennan to be ready to go with me to find her. And if I sat alone too long, it would give me far too much time to sit and worry about the appearance of Quinn Connolly and the mystery of his existence in my world. It would give me too much time to second-guess the decision I'd made. I still believed it was the right one. I just wished I understood why I was so sure about that.

I rematerialized myself to a rocky bluff overlooking the coast. This was an area Lethe had always loved, and I could see why. The choppy waters below, the ceaseless wind, the passage of wispy clouds overhead. It was the perfect place for a goddess who dealt in impermanence. The goddess of forgetfulness. She was not responsible for general forgetfulness, such as forgetting where one had left their car keys. The forgetfulness she caused was a gift to those she bestowed it upon. Traumatic incidents, heartbreaking memories. She could make you feel better, could make it possible for you to keep your sanity in the face of terrible experiences, simply by making you forget. The memories were still there, but the person she helped would not be able to recall them.

Unfortunately for humanity, she had mostly become a hermit the past several hundred years, keeping to this windy bluff in Ireland. Perhaps she had her own memories she wished she could forget.

I was unsurprised to find her sitting, legs crossed, on a large boulder, looking out over the sea. Her long silver hair flowed around her, tossed by the breeze. Her clear eyes, which reminded me of crystals and were disconcerting to look at, even for me, were open, staring out at nothing. I knew she could feel me there.

"Lethe," I said, and she acknowledged me with a slight nod. I went and sat beside her on the boulder. "The view here is lovely."

"It never changes," she said, and her words reminded me of what Brennan had said of Detroit.

"And is that a comfort or an irritant?" I asked her.

"Sometimes it is both. Mostly, it simply is."

I did not respond. "Angelia is missing," I finally said.

She did not react, merely blinked and continued looking out over the water.

"Eros said you were likely the last one to see her and Penthus. Is there anything you can tell me?"

"I like Angelia," she said after a moment.

"As do I," I said, watching her.

"It never changes," she said again, and I glanced out at the water.

"No, I suppose it does not. Did Angelia say anything to you about where she was going next? Or if she was all right? If anyone was bothering her?"

"She asked me to forget," she said.

I blinked, surprised. I had never heard of an immortal asking for that. Though when I thought about it, weren't there many, many things I would rather not remember? "Anything in particular?"

"I cannot remember," Lethe said, and I furrowed my brow.

"You cannot remember what she asked you to forget?"

"Who?"

"Angelia," I said.

"I like Angelia," she said, and I suppressed an irritated sigh. It had been centuries since I'd had to deal with Lethe. I had forgotten how frustrating it could be.

"I like Angelia, too. Do you remember what she asked you to make her forget?"

"She was here."

"Yes."

"It never changes."

I rubbed my hands over my face, longing for something to hit. "No, it doesn't. Did Angelia say anything to you about where she was going?"

"I like Angelia."

I sat in silence for several minutes, trying to figure out a way to get her out of this loop she was in. "I like Angelia," I said.

"She was here," Lethe said. "Asked me to help her forget."

"Forget what?" I asked, hopeful.

"Love. Wants to forget about it. I refused."

"You did not make her forget?"

"No."

"Did she say where she was going?" I pressed.

"She was here," Lethe said, and I tried not to groan.

"Yes, she was."

"It never changes."

I sighed. "I know."

After a few more minutes, I gave up and walked away, down the hill, across a nearby meadow. I hoped walking would help me get rid of the irritation I felt after dealing with Lethe. And then I thought about how Brennan would have been amused by the entire thing, and I shook my head. I really should have brought him with me.

My mind wandered as I walked, and it was several moments before I realized that I felt the energy of more than one soul nearby. I looked around and, to my right, three souls stood, watching me. Women. One wore a long gray dress, much like the one Mary wore, from the same time period. One wore a simple brown skirt that reached to her ankles, a dark blue shawl thrown over her shoulders. The third looked as if she had died maybe in the early twentieth century. Two blonds, one redhead. Their eyes were on me.

And a quick scan told me my Goddess knew nothing about them. They were not on my list.

"It is you," the redhead said. As one, the three of them sank to their knees, and one of the blonds said. "Finally. We are yours."

I shook my head, blew out a breath I didn't realize I'd been holding, and used one of Mollis's favorite words:

"Fuck."

I stood there for several long moments, wishing fruitlessly that they did not exist, yet there they stood. I gestured, somewhat irritably, that they should stand, and the women did.

I studied them. The tallest, the blond in the long gray dress, was named Claire. Dead for nearly two hundred years. Murdered. The redhead who looked like the most newly-dead of the three had died in 1998. Murdered. Her name was Erin. The other blond had died in the early 1900s and her name was Cathleen. Also murdered.

A pattern was beginning to show itself among my mystery souls. All of them, these three plus Quinn, now, had been murdered. No quiet drifting away into an endless goodnight among them. They'd had their lives cut short violently, painfully.

It still did not explain why my Queen did not know about them, why I knew nothing about them upon seeing them, but, given time, their pasts, their lives, their deaths, became clear.

It did not explain why they'd apparently been looking for me.

"How did you know to find me here?" I asked them quietly.

"I dae na know," Claire said, a strong accent coloring her words. "I sensed ye and followed it. Met up wi' these two along the way. They looked for ye as well."

The other two nodded, still watching me.

"And what is it you expect from me?"

"Only that you'll let us help you," Erin said softly. "We… On the way here, we all realized that we were all overlooked by your kind, by the crows that came later. We've seen them, but they do not see us. And each of us, for whatever reason, found that we started holding souls for your kind to claim. And we were never seen."

"And then a few days ago, we each felt the urge to come this way. It was as if you called us," Cathleen said.

"I surely did not call you," I said beneath my breath.

"Something about ye did," Claire argued. "We're here."

"And you can see us," Erin added. "Those others like you couldn't."

I rubbed my temples. One thing at a time. I had to get back to Brennan. Really, what I had to do was get the shifter and the way he drove me insane as far away from me as I could for a while. It was not something I could afford to be distracted by now, at any rate.

How many others would arrive? How many more would seek me out?

"Listen," I said, and they leaned in. "There is a farm field just outside of Kenmare, about two miles west, down the road. You will find two others like you there. They are with me as well," I said, grimacing. "Find them, and wait with them for me. I have something I must take care of."

They nodded, then turned and walked away, the way they'd come.

"I cannot believe this," I muttered to myself. I looked up into the sky. How I longed to be there, soaring, away from whatever this insanity was for a while. Unfortunately, it would have to wait for another day.

I focused, rematerializing at the inn, where I was relieved to find that Brennan had not yet returned. That gave me more time away, without him asking too many of his questions. The way he studied me made me feel as if he could see right into my soul, and I was not ready to be studied quite that closely, considering that I'd decided to keep a pretty major secret from my best friend and Queen and everyone else, at least for the time being.

Was this what it felt like to have a guilty conscience? I wondered.

I grabbed an apple out of the bag of groceries Brennan had left on my dresser and ate it while checking my email. Hephaestus had sent his almost-daily photo of his son, and I laughed at the ridiculously happy expression on the immortal's face as he mugged for the camera with his little boy. It was beautiful. He'd had centuries of misery, married to the Goddess of Love, Aphrodite, who was among the absolute worst beings I have ever known. She had treated him like garbage, rubbed his nose in the fact that he was true to her while she galavanted openly with Ares. How many evenings had Hephaestus and I spent in the mortal realm, sitting overlooking one city or another with him pouring his heart out to me? How many times had I wondered at the insanity of bonds like the one he was trying, and failing, to honor?

I'd listened, and I'd commiserated, and I'd acted the part of a Guardian, a normal Guardian who knew nothing about things like heartbreak and unrequited love. After she'd given birth to Eros, I had tracked her down and beaten the unholy hell out of her.

The memory of it still made me smile.

Needless to say, I was unwelcome in her presence after that, but somehow I managed to go on.

I finished my apple, sent a quick note to Hephaestus about how cute Michael was and that everything in Ireland was fine. I was about to close the laptop when I looked at the photo again. He'd had so much misery, and now, he had this. Happy as I was for him, it still looked, to me, like a form of insanity to give one being that kind of control over your emotions. How could you ever let yourself relax under those circumstances? Madness.

I shook my head, closed the laptop, and focused. I rematerialized again, appearing near the dilapidated barn at the abandoned farm where I'd left Quinn and Mary. I glanced up at the sky longingly. Flying would have to wait a while longer, I thought with some sadness.

I felt them nearby. Quinn, Mary, and my new additions.

I walked across the field toward where they were. The four women sat on the fallen log where we'd sat the day before, and Quinn stood off to the side, arms folded across his chest, watching me walked toward them. The grass crunched beneath my feet. Apparently, there had been a frost. The sound satisfied me, for some reason.

Or perhaps I would just have rather focused on the sound of crunching beneath my feet than what I actually had to deal with just then.

I looked up and met Quinn's gaze. He nodded at me, then glanced at the newcomers.

"Are you going to say 'I told you so'?" I asked him.

He shook his head. "No need. I wonder how many more there will be."

"As do I," I said. "They are like you. My Queen knows nothing of them. They were not on my list." I paused.

"They also died violently. That, so far, all of you have in common."

He nodded.

"They have all been holding souls who tried to escape their capture by my kind or the crows," I continued.

I thought of Mollis again. This was the kind of thing she would get behind, if it was true. If their entire purpose was working to detain souls who tried to escape their judgment, she would welcome them.

"All right," I said. The women all looked up at me expectantly, and Quinn stood where he'd been. "Our situation here is… it is not the type of thing I have dealt with before," I said, meeting each of the women's eyes. "Other than Mary, none of you is known to my Queen, the Goddess of Death. That is unheard of. That is wrong in every way I can think of. I do not know how to explain you." I paused. "You say you felt compelled to find me. I cannot understand that, either. I am merely one of my kind. We were all created the same. Why you should seek me out makes no sense at all."

"And yet you can see us when the others couldn't, lass," Quinn said. "Tells me maybe you're not all as alike as you've believed."

I did not answer. It echoed too much of what Brennan and I had talked about, and that was something I had no interest in pondering just then.

"I am less concerned about why you are coming to me than why it is that my Queen does not know about you," I said. "If she knew about you, I would know. As it is, I am only able to learn your names and the conditions of your deaths after you've made yourselves known to me. The fact that she does not know about you is wrong. And I do not know what to do about it. She will not be happy to find out about you."

"What will happen when she does?" Erin asked, watching me with a worried look on her face. "I mean… she's not evil, right?"

"She is definitely not evil. She is the exact opposite of evil. But she is also brutal and will do whatever she feels is necessary to protect this world. She has done much already that no one ever would have imagined." I paused. "I need to figure out how to tell her about you without her jumping to the conclusion that you are a threat of some kind. Before I can do that, I need to find out for myself how much of a threat you are."

"We're not a threat," Quinn said gruffly. "Other than to those who try to escape their judgment."

"We shall see," I said. "But I cannot afford to be wrong about this." I looked up into the bright blue sky, fluffy white clouds traveling lazily overhead. I had to know they weren't a threat so I could accurately present the situation to Mollis. But if they were a threat, I was hiding them from my Queen and by the time I realized it, it would be too late. Yet if I told her now, she would demand that I bring them in. And I knew how they would be dealt with then, because I have seen it before. The Furies are merciless if they believe they are in the right.

And let's be honest: as far as the Furies are concerned, they always believe they are in the right.

"Know this. I will be watching you. I will be ready to act the instant I believe you have not been forthright with me. So if there is something you fear I may discover about you, this is the time to tell me."

I looked at each of them in turn.

"We don't understand it either," Cathleen said. "One day, I was here. I was alive. I was working in an inn as a serving woman, and one of the customers decided he wanted more than just a meal. He took me, and he did unthinkable things to me, and then he cut my throat," she said, putting her hand to her neck. "I followed him for years. I do not know why. I was obsessed. Full of rage, unable to get any kind of revenge for the things he'd done to me. And I watched him do the same to others." Her eyes had a faraway look to them, caught in her memories.

"And then one day, he got into a fight with someone who could fight back. And he was left bloody and dying in his home. I watched him die and there was some satisfaction in it. And then he tried to run, as if he could sense someone coming for him."

"Of course he did. Souls always know there will be someone there to collect them."

"I didn't," Quinn said, and the women, other than Mary, each nodded.

"Interesting," I muttered. "Go on," I said to Cathleen.

"He knew someone was coming for him. And he did not want them to take him. He decided to run." A cold smile spread over her lips. "I am happy to say that in death, I was much more of a match for him than I was in life. He struggled and fought and tried to run, but it did him no good. He cursed and screamed, and finally begged me to let him go, just as I had once begged him to let me go. I laughed." She said, her eyes bright with angry tears. "I laughed, and I could not stop, and even as I watched the women like you take him away in chains, I still laughed and they never knew I was there."

"And after?"

She shook her head. "After he was gone, it was almost as if I lost all purpose. I drifted. I wandered. I travelled the world and found I only wanted to be here. And in Dublin, I came across another soul trying to escape his fate. And I held him and watched the winged ones take him away, and I knew what I was meant to be doing."

I crossed my arms. "Have you come across others like yourself?"

Claire shook her head. "Jus' these two," she said, nodding toward Erin and Cathleen. "And that was by accident. They were just outside Dublin, and we all ended up chasing the same soul. Jus' decided to stay wi 'em. The solitude was makin' me crazy."

"Solitude never bothered me any," Quinn said. "I still don't understand why I'm even here. I just know I should be."

I stood, thinking. "All right. Here is what we know. Twenty-seven souls escaped while awaiting my Lady's final judgment and their punishments. Mary," I said, gesturing toward her, "was one of them. Her escape was a mistake, and she has personal reasons for wanting to help me track one of those who escaped."

"Indeed," Mary said.

"You four," I said, glancing first at Quinn and then at the three women who had sought me out, "will stay at my side. You can help me hunt the twenty-four who are still out there. And we will see what more we learn about you along the way."

"So, these souls," Quinn said, and I glanced to my left where he was still standing. "Escaped? How is that even possible?"

"It is not. They had help from the outside. Another mystery that needs to be solved," I added. "There are others like me, as you already know."

"Not exactly like you," Quinn pointed out, and after a moment, I nodded in agreement.

"Not exactly, perhaps. But close enough. They look like me. Sound like me. They were created with the same purpose I was, to collect the souls of the dead and bring them for their final punishment." I paused. Did I really want to do this? Did I want to share the failings of my family with these strangers?

"They are traitors," I said softly, hating it. The word was like hot bile in my throat. "They went against everything we are supposed to stand for. They have kidnapped and tortured innocents. I believed them dead. I have reason to suspect that not all of them are. I do not know how many," I added, guessing Quinn's next question. "There were thirteen of us. I do not know how many managed to escape death. Or how they managed it at all."

"So what you're sayin' is that this is fucked up in about a dozen ways," Quinn said.

"It is."

"Perfect," he said, and when I glanced at him, he was studying me. "And if your boss, your queen, finds about about us, that would be bad."

"For the time being, yes," I said, not really wanting to discuss Mollis and her mental state with these souls.

"So you're lying to your boss," Quinn pressed.

"I am," I said, meeting his gaze. "Am I going to get a lecture on honesty now, or shall we move on with more important things?"

He waved as if to say "floor's all yours" and I watched him for a few more moment, until he clearly became uncomfortable under my gaze and looked down. Only then did I look toward the other souls.

"You will all travel with me. We need to take Mary to the United States so she can begin tracking the soul she seeks. Do you want backup?" I asked her.

She shook her head. "I want the satisfaction of finding the bastard to be all mine," she answered, and there was a feral tone to her voice that I could appreciate.

"Very well. We are going to travel now. Take my hand, join hands so all of us are connected. Soon, you will learn how to do this on your own."

"Do what?" Claire asked as she joined hands with Mary and Erin.

"This."

I closed my eyes, focused. He'd died in Florida, so I would take Mary there, to the town in which he'd died. She would track him from there.

When we appeared in a small town in Florida's panhandle, the souls who travelled with me each looked to be in various states of distress. Quinn, Erin, and Cathleen all seemed like the wanted to pass out. Mary looked confused and a little nauseous. Claire and I exchanged a glance, and she shrugged.

"That was quite efficient," she said, and I nodded.

"He died here," I said to Mary. "You undoubtedly know what he feels like after so long."

"Unfortunately," she said wryly.

I walked a bit away from the group and motioned that she should join me. "Do not try to apprehend him by yourself. Find him, and contact me."

"How do I do that?" she asked.

"We… my kind, respond to telepathic calls. It is how we are able to stay in constant contact with those we serve. Practice it with me now. My name is Eunomia. Focus. Think it."

"I am not a telepath."

"It does not matter. All that matters is that you focus and think my name, over and over again if you must. Do it."

"Like a litany," she murmured, and I decided not to bother arguing with her. I watched as she shook her head a little and closed her eyes. She seemed to scrunch her eyes a little after a few moments, and soon I could hear a very, very faint echo, my name.

"Focus harder," I said, and she gave an irritated sound, but within a few moments, her voice calling my name went from a watery-sounding echo to a clear sound.

"Perfect," I said after a few more repetitions.

"You heard me?" she asked in disbelief, opening her eyes to stare at me.

"I told you I would."

"Yes, but… You are spooky."

I felt a wisp of a smile on my lips. "So I have been told."

She laughed then. "I'll find him. And I hope to hell I get to see you hurt him."

"You will," I said. "It is painful when I take them. I can make it even more painful when I have a mind to."

She gaped at me, and I continued. "When you find him, call for me like that. I can be here within seconds. Do not confront him. Do not try to capture him. If you see him meeting up with any other souls, or anyone who looks like me, contact me."

"Yes," she said, nodding. "I will. Thank you for giving me this opportunity, Eunomia. I will not let you down."

"He will be punished," I promised.

"Thank you." With that, she turned and headed toward the last known place Bates Downing had been in this realm. I watched her go, then turned to the remaining four souls.

My souls. The thought came to me unbidden, and I was not happy with it. I had no interest in having them as my own.

"Back to Ireland. I may be away for a day or so, but I will return to collect you as soon as I am ready." I took them back to Ireland, then I returned to my room, preparing myself to tell Brennan that it was time to return home, and pray that he did not realize there was something I was hiding from him.

CHAPTER TEN

When I appeared in my room at the inn, I could hear Brennan in his room. I took a breath and lightly knocked on the door between our rooms.

"Come on in," he said, and I turned the doorknob and pushed the door open. He was wearing his usual suit, having met with another of his contacts that day, and was in the process of loosening his tie. He had his laptop open, and on the screen, I could see Sean's face as he talked to his father. Brennan held up a finger, asking for me to hold on for a moment, and I nodded and sat down on the other end of his bed.

"Have you been good for grandma?" Brennan asked Sean.

"Yes," Sean answered.

"Really?"

"I was mostly good. Gramma yelled at me for pulling Zoe's hair though," Sean said, and I hid a smile at the indignation in his voice.

"Well, did you pull Zoe's hair?" Brennan asked.

"Yeah."

"You know you can't do that, man. She's littler than you. And she's a girl. We talked about that."

"Yeah but you hit Molly."

"Only when we're sparring. That's different. And Molly is fully capable of beating me up. Someday, Zoe's going to be able to beat you up and you're gonna be sorry."

Sean let out a sound of utter disbelief. "Zoe is not gonna be able to beat me up!"

"We'll see. Either way, you can't pull her hair. Or hit her. Be nice, man," Brennan said, and I hid a smile at the stern tone of his voice.

"She's bad, papa," Sean said.

"She is not."

"She bugs me and she messes with my stuff."

Brennan sighed. "She's littler than you, Sean. And I know for a fact that you do the same to her stuff. Remember that doll you destroyed last week?"

"Only a'cause she lost my Iron Man."

"Sean."

"Okay. But she still bugs me."

"I know, buddy. Be good though, okay?"

"Okay. When are you coming home?"

"We should be back in a little while. I love you," Brennan told his son, glancing at me and raising his eyebrows as if seeking affirmation. I nodded.

"Love you too, papa. Bye."

"Bye," Brennan said, and he watched as his son left, and Artemis gave him a wave before disconnecting the call. Brennan shook his head and closed his laptop.

"Hey," he said in greeting. "He does that sometimes, drives Artemis nuts until she lets him FaceTime me."

"So he is irritatingly persistent. I wonder where he gets that from," I said, and he shook his head. "So... how was your day?" I asked him. He stood. His eyes flicked over me, and he pulled his tie off.

"Infuriating."

"Oh?"

"The thing the guy wanted to tell me? Basically there's this one little town where everyone is batshit terrified of shifters. And they're organizing hunts, and the dipshit in charge of supernatural affairs here isn't sure what to do about it."

"Have them arrested and tried for murder, perhaps?" I said, watching him.

"That's what I said. You know what he said?" A muscle in his jaw jumped, and his entire body seemed tense.

"What?"

"They're not human, so it's not murder," he said, meeting my eyes. The look in his eyes, more than anything else, let on how angry he was. "He said shifters are more like animals than people, so it's hunting. Can you freaking believe that?"

I shook my head. "Did he know what you are?"

"He knows now," he growled, and I stared at him. He must have seen something in my face, because he shook his head. "I didn't kill him. Scared him, maybe. Let him know what I thought of his ideas about shifters. They're used to witches here. Witches are their thing. They are terrified of the idea of their neighbors turning into wolves or bears."

"Thank goodness they have not encountered vampires yet," I said, trying to lighten his mood a bit, and was rewarded with a small snort of laughter from him. "Were there threats made?" I asked, studying him.

"Who, me?" he asked innocently, and I laughed. "Yeah. I maybe said something about how I'd be checking back in and that I have his scent. Maybe," he said, and I shook my head.

"I think I am ready to leave this place. Shall we go home?"

"What about Lethe?" he asked.

"I paid her a visit earlier. I meant to wait for you, but you were out and I wanted it over with. She says Angelia was there, and that she asked Lethe to help her forget, but we never got any further than that. Lethe is…" I trailed off and made a wiggling gesture with my fingers, indicating her unstable mental state. "It was mostly a dead end. But at least we know she did actually see them. Eros was not lying about that part." I paused. "So we can go home now."

He nodded. "You're just trying to get out of watching *The Avengers* with me."

"Not at all. I will watch with you whenever you want."

"That's a date, Tink," he said, and I felt the blush rise to my face.

"I am going to gather my things. I will be back in a moment," I said, hurrying out of his room, his low chuckle following me. Damn him.

When I returned to his room with my duffel bag slung over my shoulder, he was standing near the windows, his own bag in his hand.

"I am sorry we did not get to see the store your family owned," I said, remembering.

"I saw it," he said. "On the walk back from talking to the supernatural affairs asshole. I needed to clear my head, so I walked around until I found it."

I smiled. "Good. And?"

He shrugged. "It seemed very normal. Normal feels weird to me now, I think."

"Welcome to immortal life," I said softly, and he nodded. "Ready?"

He came to me, took my hand in his. "Not a word about the Golden Girls. I promise," he said, tiniest of smiles on his lips, mischievous sparkle in his eye.

"I will hold you to that," I said. And then I focused, and moments later, we stood just inside the foyer at the loft. We were surrounded, immediately, by noise. Children laughing and shouting, adult voices. It was jarring, going from the calm and quiet of our rooms. Brennan seemed to sense it as well, and he squeezed my hand, then pulled me with him into the main living area. Sean, Zoe, and Heph's son, Michael, were chasing one another around the dining room table. Hephaestus, Mollis, Nain, and Artemis were in the living room, and they called greetings to Brennan and me as we approached.

"Glad you're back, E," Mollis said, standing up and hugging me. I embraced her, then backed away, looking at her, and focusing, harder than usual, on keeping my mental shields intact.

"Those are new," I said. She wore what looked to be reading glasses, but the emanations of power coming from them led me to suspect they were nothing of the sort.

"Oh, aren't they great?"

"What do they do?" I asked her, then I glanced back at Brennan, holding a finger up to Mollis to forestall her answer. "They are not what they appear to be. Do you feel any power emanating from them?"

"I don't think so," he said, looking unsure.

"Try. Just focus for a moment. You should be able to feel something."

He looked at the glasses, and his brow wrinkled a bit as he focused. "I think, maybe? It's hard to tell, because all of your power signatures are scrambled together."

I nodded. "All right. So what do they do?"

Mollis was grinning, and even the demon seemed happy. "They block what I can see!" she said, her excitement leading her to clap her hands together in delight, and I had to laugh at her obvious happiness. And with relief. I was trying hard not to think about the mystery souls I was still trying to figure out. This would buy me more much-needed time.

"Really?"

"Yes! I think the constant barrage of seeing every damn thing about everyone I know is making this harder. I'm still learning how to handle my dad's powers, right?" I nodded, and she continued. "So these make it so, as long as I'm wearing them, I don't have that barrage of information rolling over me. I can see when I need to, but I can go about my life without being assaulted by everyone's thoughts and sins all the time. Hopefully it will make me feel a little less insane," she said, this last part in a lower, less cheerful voice.

I smiled. "You are not insane. It is a lot to deal with all at once, and I am so happy you found something that works. I assume these are Hephaestus' design?"

She nodded, and I turned to Hephaestus to see him raising his fist. This human habit of giving fist bumps was something he seemed to have adopted, and I raised my own fist and went through the ridiculous ritual. He grinned at me and I rolled my eyes. "Nice work, genius," I said, and he practically beamed.

Mollis sat down beside Nain. "I'm so glad you're back. Fill me in?"

I glanced around, and Molly nodded. "I told Heph and Artemis what was going on. They deserve to know."

I nodded, in complete agreement that the more support Mollis had in what was going on, the better. I sat on the loveseat near the window, and, to my utter confusion, Brennan stayed at my side, sitting right next to me. His son had leapt at him the instant he'd seen him, and he sat contentedly on Brennan's lap, breathlessly telling him about the adventures he'd had in the past couple of days as if they hadn't just spoken to each other less than an hour ago. I began filling Mollis and everyone else in on the soul I'd found, my searches for the others. I did not say that I had found them, and I absolutely said nothing about the souls Mollis knew nothing about. Not yet. And it would be something I would feel more comfortable talking about to Mollis alone, not with the demon sitting there glowering at everyone, as he tended to do. Brennan picked up, telling them about the incident with the shifters. I left out my conversation with Lethe, because I was not sure if Mollis was keeping the issue of our missing immortals quiet or not.

"Where next, E?" Mollis asked me.

"I think Germany, and then Russia. I can probably do both in one trip."

"We can," Brennan said, and I shook my head.

"You do not need to come with me. You have responsibilities here."

"I'm not letting you go alone," he argued.

"Me neither," Mollis said.

"You have a job. You have a son. You can't go with me every time."

"All right. All right," Hephaestus boomed over whatever Brennan had begun arguing. "Ya twisted my arm. I'll go with you."

"I… I do not need anyone to go with me," I argued.

"We've been over this," Mollis said mildly, in a voice that, though I was her closest friend, made it clear she was not in the mood to debate. "You're sure, Heph?" she asked him, and he grinned at me, obviously delighting in my irritation.

"Absolutely. Me and my prickly little pal on a road trip? Sounds like fun. And I think Meaghan would welcome a bit of quiet for a few days as well," he added.

"Great. So that's settled, " Mollis said, and I didn't say anything, because arguing with them was pointless. At least it would be better than being flustered and overheated every time the shifter looked at me. A few days away from him, and I would regain my sense where he was concerned.

I sat and talked to the team for a while. Brennan's phone rang and he carried Sean into the kitchen so he could answer it. I excused myself, grabbed my bag, and headed toward the stairs.

"Hey," Brennan said, and I turned.

"What?"

"That was Ronan. We're going out with them tonight," he said, and I immediately started shaking my head. "Oh, yes we are, Tink. You promised you'd go with me."

"I think 'promise' is overstating it a bit," I said.

"You did," he said, that tiny smile on his lips that made my entire body warm. I glared at him, and his smile widened, well aware of what he was doing. "And," he continued, "you're taking off on me for a few days. I'm not exactly happy about that."

"Somehow, you will survive," I said, turning and starting up the stairs.

"Nine, Tink," he said, and I could hear the smile in his voice.

"I might have to patrol," I said hopefully.

"No, you're good," the demon said, overhearing the conversation. "We didn't put you on the schedule because we weren't sure when you'd be back."

I shook my head a little. "Very well." I continued up the stairs.

"Don't sound so excited," Brennan said with a laugh, and I directed a rude gesture at him I hadn't used very often. It only made him laugh harder.

In my room, I flopped onto my bed and buried my burning face in my pillow, groaning helplessly. Would I never get rid of him?

CHAPTER ELEVEN

Before I knew it, it was eight o'clock, and I forced myself up. I changed into a white button-down blouse that I liked almost as much as my t-shirts, a less-worn pair of jeans, my boots, and my coat. I glanced at myself in the mirror. Maybe I could pull my cowl up over my head and face and fade into the background.

I brushed my hair, applied make-up, which I hadn't done the past couple of days, distracted as I was by the new souls I'd found and how I would work out convincing Mollis not to imprison them immediately. I leaned on my hands on the vanity and looked at myself in the mirror. This was a normal thing, yes? For people of this world, anyway. Going out with friends. I have done this before. I had gone out with Mollis, the demon, Hephaestus, Meaghan. Shanti.

So why were my palms sweating?

"This is so ridiculous," I muttered to myself. I looked longingly at my knife harness on the bed. I felt naked without it.

I picked up my Netherblade and stuck it into the sheath inside my left boot, my regular dagger in the other boot.

"Come on, Tink. We need to go pick the vampires up," Brennan called from the bottom of the stairs.

"This is not a date, or anything like that," I told my reflection. As if saying it aloud would make me less nervous about it.

I stepped out of my room and went down the stairs. Brennan was waiting there, wearing a pair of dark pants that hung in a very nice way from his body, a blue shirt that set off his eyes perfectly. His hair was down (which I really, really liked) and he smelled of the cologne he wore sometimes. The last time I'd smelled it on him had been Ada and Stone's wedding.

"You smell good," I said to him, lacking for anything more complex to say to him.

"You look good," he told me.

"That's just going to make Rayna want to taste you even more," I said, hiding a smile at the way his eyes widened, even as I thought "over my dead body."

What in the Nether was wrong with me?

"Uh. Maybe I'll go wash it off," he said, and I laughed.

"Don't worry. I'll protect you from the gorgeous, rich, sultry vampire," I said in mock sympathy, and he grinned.

"I'm counting on it, Tink."

Mollis laughed from the living room, where she, the demon, and their two kids were sprawled across one of the sofas watching some cartoon. "Go, before you make Rayna mad. She hates waiting."

"We're gone. Call us if you need anything," Brennan said, grabbing my hand and pulling me toward the door.

"Are we rematerializing?" I asked him.

"Nope. Old fashioned travel. I'll drive."

"I would feel safer my way," I said wryly.

"Ha ha," he muttered, keeping my hand in his as we walked on to the elevator.

"I have driven with you before. Do we really need to recount that ill-fated trip for the deep-dish pizza you absolutely *had* to have after Mollis and the rest of us moved back into the loft? And how we got lost and how you drive like one of those fastcar drivers?"

"I think you mean NASCAR, Tink."

"Whatever it is. You are a terrifying driver," I said as he led me to the black sports utility vehicle he drove. He opened the passenger side door for me.

"Want me to teach you to drive?" he asked with a grin.

"I would rather kiss a satyr, Cub," I told him, meeting his eyes, and he laughed. He closed my door and got into the driver's seat.

"I'll try to take it easy. You're already on edge."

"Am not," I said, looking out my window.

"Uh huh. You'd think you were going to an execution instead of out for drinks with friends," he said.

I sighed. He was not wrong. "This is outside the realm of things I am comfortable with. Going out for food, fine. Coffee, even, okay. But going somewhere specifically to just, what? Sit around and drink and be sociable?"

"And dance."

I stared at him, and he laughed. "You are joking."

"I am most definitely not."

"I hate you," I said, and all it earned me was a wink and his hand searching for mine. He enclosed my hand in his, gave it a squeeze.

"Take it back," he said.

"Definitely not."

"We both know you don't hate me, Eunomia."

"But it makes me feel better to say it anyway," I said, and he tangled his fingers with mine. "Do not even think I am setting foot on the dance floor."

He did not answer, and that should have been my first indication that things were not going to go my way.

I held onto his hand with my left hand, the door handle with my right. I could tell he was driving slower than usual, zipping in and out of traffic less than he usually did, but he was still nightmarish to drive with. Mollis tends to drive fast, but there is not this feeling of recklessness. And

Hephaestus usually drives slowly, only because he is looking at everything outside the windows. A thought struck me, and I glanced over at him.

"Let me guess. The demon taught you how to drive."

He grinned. "Yep. I was twelve."

"He is the only other one I know who drives this horrifically," I muttered, and he laughed. Before long, we were pulling into the circle drive at Rayna's mansion in Indian Village, her guards waving us through the large iron gate upon recognizing Brennan.

"They'll meet us out here."

"You just do not want to go in and be surrounded by vampires," I said.

"Damn right."

"Shanti is a vampire," I reminded him.

"I know," he said. "I am fine with vampires. I just…" he shrugged. "It's stupid. I know. It's a prejudice I'm trying to get over. I spent my entire life believing vampires were the bad guys, and now some of them are our allies. I recognize that it's something I need to work on."

I studied him. It was comfortable now that the car was not moving, and the night was dark around us, the lights from Rayna's home casting just enough brightness for me to see his face clearly. "Good. I expect better from you," I said to him.

He met my eyes and nodded. "I'm working on it, Tink."

I glanced toward the house to see Rayna and Ronan walking down the front steps. A guard opened the door behind mine for Rayna, and Ronan climbed into the backseat behind Brennan. Brennan turned around and shook hands with Ronan, greeted Rayna, and I said hello to them both.

"Where are we going?" Brennan asked, pulling toward the gates.

"That new place near Greektown. You know the one I mean?" Ronan asked. I did not, but Brennan nodded.

"You been there before?" Brennan asked.

"I own it," Rayna said, and I smiled.

Brennan laughed. "Of course you do." It was true. Rayna was one of the smartest businesspeople I have ever met. She had a hand in just about every legal business imaginable. Some vampires got involved in drugs, human trafficking, which was why they ran afoul of our team so often. Rayna was completely legitimate, with manufacturing businesses, retail, restaurants, bars, bakeries and undoubtedly other things I did not know about. Aside from being the vampire queen of our region, she was also singlehandedly changing the economy within the city for the better. She employed thousands of people, and every one of them was from the area.

I held onto my handle, as well as Brennan's hand, for the entire ride to the nightclub. Happily, it wasn't a horribly long drive, and when we got there, Rayna told Brennan to park in a spot marked "reserved." A bouncer-type was coming to reprimand him when he saw Ronan and Rayna with us, and immediately apologized.

We went into the large brick building, which had once been a department store, according to Ronan, and I was assaulted by bright flashing lights and music that made me immediately wish for ear plugs. Brennan was walking beside me, still holding my hand, and I glared up at him in irritation. He simply smiled and squeezed my hand.

Rayna led the way to a round table on a slightly raised dais, and slid into the accompanying dark purple leather bench seat. I slid in beside her, Brennan beside me, and Ronan on the other side of his sister, rounding out our group. Drink orders were placed, and I ended up with some concoction I had no intention of drinking. I held the fluted glass between my hands, because at least it gave my hands something to do.

"How's Shanti doing?" Brennan asked Ronan, his voice raised above the music.

Ronan gave a proud nod. "Deadly. She's only grown faster and more effective in the time since she's come to join us. Thank you again for the training you gave her," he said, and Rayna murmured a "here, here" and raised her flute of champagne to Brennan, taking a sip.

"She took to it really easily. It's all her," Brennan said.

"Don't play it down, man," Ronan said. "She's irreplaceable. She goes after thee rogue vamps… she's unstoppable. She finds them every time. There's no hiding form her. She's following in our demon lady's footsteps."

"How so?" I asked him, and he gave me a quick grin, his light gray eyes lighting up a bit.

"Our enemies speak her name with fear. It's beautiful."

I smiled. "Good."

"She's also relentlessly loyal, which I appreciate more than I can ever say," Rayna said. "She, and, by extension, her man. They are as close to me as Ronan is. I am lucky to have them with me."

I studied the vampire queen. She owned every bit of her royal title. Her warm, light brown complexion was set off by those same light gray eyes her brother had, and her dark hair fell in thick waves down over her shoulders. She wore a form-fitting black dress, heels that made my feet hurt just looking at them.

"So Brennan, are we dancing?" Rayna asked, after studying me for a moment. There was no denying she was gorgeous. There were rumors, of course, that like me, she was not only interested in men. That was not something I would be investigating further. Not with one of Mollis's allies.

And not when the man sitting beside me currently had my life twisted in knots.

"I stink at dancing," he warned her as he slid out of the booth.

"Don't worry. They'll all be looking at me anyway," she said with a sultry smile, and he shook his head, glancing back at me before following her out onto the dance floor.

Ronan sat back down beside me with a low grunt. "You don't want to dance, do you?"

"Oh, gods no," I said, and he laughed.

"I'll drink to that," he said, holding his beer bottle up. I clinked it with my glass, and we each took a sip of our drinks.

Ugh, alcohol. I never had gained a taste for it. I set my drink back down.

"So how's life been treating you?" Ronan asked me.

"Not too badly. I am working, so I am happy."

"Yeah? What's so great about working?" he asked me.

"It is all I know. I feel odd when I am not put to work."

He nodded slowly, seeming to be thinking. "Can I ask you something?" he finally said,

"I suppose so."

"You're a god, right?"

I grimaced. "I am a lesser god. Lesser immortal."

"What's the difference between you and any other god? What makes you lesser?"

I thought for a moment. "My kind... we were created to serve the higher gods. We were created with specific jobs and roles in mind. My kind, the spirit daemons—"

"Like that Strife bitch?" he asked, undoubtedly remembering the way Strife had destroyed so much of the city before we were able to take her down.

"Yes. Like her. Gods of the seasons. Earthly gods, beings of that type. We have one role. It was what we were created for, and without that role, we are lost. Adrift," I said. He was listening intently.

"Does that bother you?" he finally asked.

I watched Brennan and Rayna dance for a while. They looked stunning together, and despite Rayna's assurances, there were more than a few women looking at Brennan as he moved with Rayna to the music.

I had the urge to pull my dagger. That would be wrong, I reminded myself. "It does not bother me. I would not trade places with them for anything."

"No? Why not? It seems like they have more options than you do. They got to choose their lives, right?"

I shrugged, continuing to watch Brennan and Rayna. "In some cases they did. Others had their roles assigned to them, but they made the roles in their own images, if that makes sense."

He nodded again.

"Why do you ask?" I asked him, tearing my gaze away from Brennan, aware that my body was heating as I watched him.

"Trying to understand our allies. Can I be honest about something?"

"Of course," I said, meeting this eyes.

"You all freak me the fuck out."

I laughed then, and after a moment, he joined me. "You do realize many of us say the same thing about your family, yes?" I said, and he smiled at me, more relaxed than he'd been when we'd first sat down.

"Oh, sure. But I can't blame them for that."

"Well, I cannot blame you for being uncertain about us. Really, any of us has the power to destroy whatever we want, whenever we want."

He sobered. "And what keeps you from doing so?"

I took a breath. "In my case, I love this world. I do not understand it. I do not feel conformable here necessarily. But I recognize the beauty here and for better or worse it is my home now. As far as the rest of them… Mollis."

He snorted. "She's it, huh?"

"She is the only threat any of my kind need. They will continue to push her. They will look for weaknesses. And they will fail."

"You have a lot of faith," he said.

I gave him a small smile. Remembered my nickname, "the Zealot" among my kind for my devotion to Hades, and, now, his daughter. "I have every reason to," I said.

"Well you don't seem like a fool, so I'm gonna trust you on this," Ronan said. "You sure you don't want to dance?"

I shook my head, watched Brennan and Rayna come back to the table.

"Come on," Rayna said, and it took me a moment to realize she was talking to me.

"Oh. No. I do not dance."

She appraised me. "What a shame," she murmured. "I don't bite, you know. Unless you want me to," she added with a smile.

I smiled and shook my head. "I don't think you need me to dance with. Take a look around."

"Mhmm. I know. But I think I'd really enjoy you," she said, and the flirting tone in her voice was unmistakable, even to me. I am not as clueless as I once was, but I am not precisely experienced, either.

"Maybe another time," I said, and she smiled at me.

"I wonder if you taste as good as you smell?" she asked.

"I have no idea," I said. "Come now, Queen Rayna. Is that all you are interested in? Blood?"

She smiled again. "I never said I was asking about blood."

I could not help it. I laughed, surprised by her forwardness. "You got me that time," I said, and she winked at me. I was well aware of Brennan watching me, his hand on my knee under the table.

"I have the feeling someone else has laid a claim on you already anyway. Poor me. I won't be getting lucky with either one of you," she said with a pout. "Unless both of you want to play?" she asked hopefully. Brennan had been in the process of taking a gulp of his beer, and he choked a little in mid-swallow.

"Guess that's a no," she said, eyes twinkling mischievously.

"You want to dance?" Brennan asked me, and I started shaking my head. He was already standing, pulling my hand, and I shook my head more vigorously. He lowered his face closer to mine, looked into my eyes.

"You wanted to learn to be more human, right? How to live here without feeling like you're lost?"

I gave a small nod.

"Making a fool of yourself on the dance floor is a very human experience. Let's go." He pulled again, and, against my better judgement, I let him guide me toward the dance floor, with its throngs of undulating bodies, the lights flashing overhead, the music thumping loudly.

"I have no idea how to do this," I shouted at him over the music.

"Just move your ass, Tink," he said. He started moving, bobbing a little, and he pulled me toward him, resting a hand at my lower back, at the base of my spine, drawing me close enough to his body that our thighs bumped when we moved.

I must have been glowing, I was blushing so hard.

After a few awkward seconds, I forgot about figuring out how to move my body without feeling like a fool. All that mattered was that hand at my lower back, strong thighs and hips pressing against my own, the scent of him surrounding me. I placed my hands on his biceps, and we moved together. The words in the song were lost to me, and, when I finally chanced looking up into Brennan's face, it was as if everything else around us faded into nothingness. His gaze was hooded, his eyes on me, and that hand at my back drew me closer until all I knew was his firm body pressed to mine, every move he made making one part or another of my body ache in ways I had only ever felt fleetingly before.

"You're good at this, Eunomia," he said, lowering his mouth to my ear.

I let out a breathy laugh. "I am barely doing anything at all."

"See how easy it is when you loosen up a little?"

I did not answer. I could not. The idea of stringing more than two words together felt like an impossible task, and it was enough just to move with him and let myself forget, just for a moment, why whatever it was I was feeling for him was a terrible idea.

The song ended, and I prepared to head back to the table, but the DJ played something slow and dark next, and Brennan held me closer, one hand rubbing up my spine while the other rested at my lower back, holding me close to him. I had no choice but to put my hands on his shoulders, though I could not make myself look up at him.

"Is this so bad?" he asked me in that low voice that did ridiculous things to my pulse.

"I suppose it could be worse," I managed.

"There's that ringing endorsement I was hoping for," he said, and I knew he was smiling by the way his voice sounded. He pulled me even closer, and I rested my head against his chest, and heard him sigh in what might have been contentment. "Is this your first slow dance?"

"Mmhmm," I said, closing my eyes for just a moment, wishing everyone else would just disappear.

"Good," he said. "Nice to know I can be your first something." The song ended, and he let me go, reluctantly. I stepped back, my face burning, and I looked up at him in embarrassment.

"Thanks, Eunomia," he said.

"Thank you," I said back, and then I turned back to our table, hoping my suddenly wobbly legs would get me there.

The rest of the evening passed in a blur of noise and too many bright lights. When the club closed at three, we walked out together.

"I'm starving," Ronan said as we headed toward Brennan's car.

"Don't look at me, man," Brennan said, holding my door open for me.

"No, jackass. For actual food. I need to eat before I go to sleep for the day."

"There is nothing open now," I said.

"Denny's," Ronan and Brennan said together, and Rayna rolled her eyes. Seeing my confusion, she explained.

"It is a chain that serves breakfast twenty-four hours a day. We will likely find many others who were out late there as well."

"Okay with you if we go?" Brennan asked me, and I shrugged.

We piled into the car again and took the freeway to one of the nearer suburbs. I glanced at the clock on the dashboard.

"Are we going to make it back in time for you to get in before sunrise?" I asked Rayna, turning a little in my seat so I could look at her.

"Trust me, Ronan eats fast," she said. "It'll be fine."

I nodded. Soon, we were pulling into a mostly-empty parking lot, then walking into a place that seemed too brightly-lit after the time we'd spent in the club. A tired-looking waitress brought us coffee, and we ordered. Rayna hadn't been wrong. There were two other groups of people there, rowdy and reeking of alcohol.

"We are not inebriated enough to fit in here," I said, and Rayna laughed.

"The fumes coming off them are almost enough to make me feel drunk," she said, and I nodded.

"Last time I was drunk was 1911," Ronan said.

"Oh, here we go," Rayna said with a groan.

"There was this place not too far from our house. Whorehouse, bar, gambling. It was perfect for a dude like me," he said.

"Was this before you turned?" I asked, and he nodded.

"Rayna was pissed because I wouldn't let her come with me. It wasn't the type of place women hung out, and I wanted to have fun and not babysit my big sister."

"As if I have ever needed babysitting, you ass," Rayna said, digging into the pancakes the waitress had just set in front of her. The rest of us started on our meals as well. French toast and strawberries for me. I was hungrier than I'd realized.

"If you say so," Ronan said. "Anyway. I had some fun with a lady upstairs, and then I went downstairs and started gambling. And the drinks were flowing, and I was winning, and my favorite lady from upstairs was sitting on my lap…" He grinned. "It was fun," he said with a shrug.

Rayna seemed to have sobered, and she pushed some of the pancake around on her plate.

"Why do I feel like there is more to the story?" I asked, and Ronan flashed a smile at me.

"It was fun. And then there was a brawl, and even that was fun at first."

"Men," Rayna muttered.

"One of the guys brawling… no matter how hard I hit him, he kept getting up. And he hit hard, man. Fast. Soon it was just me and him. Everyone else cleared out, because he was unstoppable and they were smarter than I was. And less prideful, I guess."

"Maybe less drunk, too," Rayna said, though there was affection in her voice.

"Maybe," he agreed. "He beat me to the edge of death, and then he ended my mortal life. And when I woke up, nothing was the same."

"He was your sire?" I asked, and he nodded.

"He found out about Rayna, and he turned her too. He wanted her for himself," Ronan said, the anger in his voice still hot after all the years that had passed.

Brennan and I sat, listening. He met my eyes for a moment.

"He had us do things. You know how it is with vampires and their sires," Rayna said, and I nodded. Sires have a great amount of influence over the vampires they turn. It is why Ronan was the only choice when it was time for Shanti's mate, Zero, to be turned. "He claimed me as his own. I had no choice at first but to comply."

"Where was this? I asked. "You are not originally from here." There was still an underlying accent in their voices, barely there, but it added a richness to their speech and I had wondered about it the first time I had met Rayna.

"Egypt," she said. "We have been everywhere. We settled here about fifty years ago and it felt like we were home, finally."

"So I'm guessing you took out your sire to be able to get free," Brennan said.

"She did," Ronan said, pointing to his sister beside him. "She started working on herself mentally to be able to resist his influence. It wasn't easy. We were with him for over thirty years by the time she'd finally managed to break his hold on her and end him. We ran, because the rest of his children were after us. Those that caught up with us didn't live very long," Ronan finished with a shrug. "I knew then that my sister was gonna be something. If she was strong enough to do that, to do what everyone thought could not be done, she could do anything."

"We are teaching Zero the same skills I used to free myself so that he is not bound to Ronan as I was bound to our sire. We do not want slaves. We want loyalty," Rayna said, and I looked at her in surprise, my respect for the vampire queen rising with every word she said.

"That's amazing," Brennan said. He raised his coffee cup to Rayna. "I'm glad you're on our side."

"Absolutely," I murmured, and we all clinked our coffee cups. I was just about to dig into the rest of my breakfast when I heard it.

"Eunomia. Eunomia. Eunomia!"

Mary's voice. She'd found the soul she was hunting. Or she was in trouble. Either way, it was time for me to go to her.

"I have to go," I said, standing up.

"Huh?" Brennan asked around a mouthful of food.

"I am sorry," I said, standing up. "I need to take care of this and it cannot wait. I will see you back at the loft."

Before he could argue, I was already somewhere in the Florida panhandle.

CHAPTER TWELVE

I stood outside of what I understood to be a trailer park, rows of single and double-wide trailers arrayed in orderly rows behind the chain link fence before me. Mary was crouched near some shrubs, and she smothered a small cry of surprise when I appeared.

"Sorry to have startled you," I said in a low voice, and she waved it off.

"He's in there," she whispered. "That fifth trailer to the left. The one with the big deck porch," she said, and I nodded, spying the building she was speaking of. "It doesn't look like anyone lives in it. He keeps looking out the window as if he's expecting someone."

Now I really was glad I'd decided to stick my dagger into my boot rather than leave it at home the way a normal person would on a night out.

"All right. Excellent job, Mary," I said. "Wait here for me."

"I want to see him suffer," she said, her eyes hard, and I could only imagine the memories she was reliving, having seen her tormentor again.

"All right. Follow me, quietly. And stay back." I could feel the energy signature of Bates Downing. It would be one more off of Mollis's list.

I pulled my dagger from my boot, and Mary and I crept quietly toward the trailer. Once we were just outside of it, close enough to be sure that he was the only one inside, I took her arm and we rematerialized into the trailer.

"Finally," he muttered upon seeing me, and then his gaze found Mary behind me. "And you brought me a present. How'd you know? I missed you, sweetling," he said to Mary, and she stayed silent.

This… yes. I could not deny it any longer. This was twice now one of them had been expecting someone. Someone who looked like me. It could mean only one thing: I was not the last of the Guardians. At least one of my sisters still lived somehow, and she was involved in these lost souls. Not alone. None of my kind are powerful enough to break into the prisons in the Nether and start removing souls. But involved just the same.

"Sorry it took so long," I said, deciding to play along.

"You were supposed to bring me someone else, though," he said. "Happy as I am that you found my toy, she's not gonna help me live again."

"I wanted to get her to you first," I said, hoping Mary knew I was playing along.

"Very thoughtful. Did you do something to your hair? It was longer before."

"I'm trying to remember how many I've brought you so far," I said. "Do you remember?" Something nagged me. Memory, the ghost of something that felt too familiar about this.

He grinned. "This was to be lucky number three."

My stomach sank. "Right. Come with me, and we'll go get you someone."

I took Downing's hand, and he trustingly put his hand in mine.

And in one swift, smooth movement, I stabbed him in the side with my Netherblade, the thin dagger sliding easily between two of his ribs, and he screamed and thrashed and weakened as my blade sucked the vitality from him.

"How did you get free? Who freed you?" I asked, and he just screamed and tried to break free of my grip. I drew my dagger out, twisted his arm roughly behind his back, and stabbed him again, this time in the side of his neck.

"Who freed you?" I asked again, my voice cold and expressionless.

"I don't know, you dumb bitch," he screamed in agony. "She didn't give me a fucking name. You're the only one I've seen and I thought you knew what you were doing," he ended on a whimper.

I wound the thin black chain, which I'd worn as a necklace that night, around his wrists behind his back and pulled the blade from his neck. I flipped it in my hand so I held it by the tip of the blade and presented it to Mary.

"Did you want a turn? I think he owes you some pain."

She grimly took the knife, and he tried to scurry away when she advanced on him. I held his arm.

She looked into his eyes and stabbed him, hard, in the stomach, and then again in a place no man, ghost or not, ever wants to be stabbed. After one final stab to his shoulder, she handed me the blade, weeping openly.

"Thank you," she said hoarsely.

"I will be right back. Stay here," I told her, and she nodded, settling into a corner of the room, face in her hands.

I focused, and in the next moment, Downing and I were standing inside the soulprison in the Nether. Megaera was on duty, and I handed him over to her.

"Is Mollis around?" I asked, and she shook her head.

"She and her mate are still in their home in Detroit. It has been a quiet night overall, so my sister and I are catching up on punishing some of our souls. Mollis will be glad to have this one back."

"Indeed. I will leave her a message and let her know I have dropped this one off."

"I can tell her when she gets here," Megaera said, pulling Downing back toward the pens.

I watched her go, then pulled my phone out of my pocket. I'd expected to get Mollis's voicemail, but she picked up on the first ring.

"You got one!" she practically shouted into my ear.

I winced, holding the phone away a bit, and laughed. "You can feel it?"

"Yes! Thank you, E!"

"You are very welcome, demon girl. I handed him off to your aunt."

"Great. I'll deal with him when I get there in a bit."

"Mollis—" I began.

"E, I'm sorry. I can't talk now."

"What is it?"

"Nether is fighting me again. I need to focus. I'm sorry. Love ya, E." And with that, she hung up, and I was left staring at my phone.

"Love you too, Mollis," I said quietly.

I had to get this mess under control. It was only getting worse.

I stuffed my phone back into my pocket. Now to get Mary back to Ireland with the rest of them, then make one more jump back to Detroit.

I would be lucky to still be standing when it was finished. But it would be worth it, I thought. Every soul would help, at least a little bit.

When I rematerialized back in the trailer, I called out for Mary. She was not where I'd left her, in the main living area. I walked through the trailer, and there was no sign of her. I stood and sensed, trying to pick up her energy signature. It was faint, like the lingering scent of perfume when someone's left a room. She was gone.

I walked outside, dread curling in my stomach, and walked around the trailer, still trying to pick up on something. There was nothing.

I went back inside, and after another survey of the house, I ended up leaning against the kitchen counter, looking into the empty living room.

It was only when I turned that I saw the small piece of torn paper, as if it was ripped hurriedly out of a notebook, lying near the kitchen sink.

"You took one of mine, so I'm taking one of yours, zealot. Come and get her, if you can find me. I'll take good care of her in the meantime."

I took a deep breath, cursing my stupidity. I should have taken Mary with me. Even if I'd had to turn her over to the Furies, it would be better than what she was likely dealing with now.

I crumpled the paper in my hand, shoved it in my coat pocket.

"Don't come. It's a trap." I heard in my mind. "Don't come don't come don't come."

I had no way to ask where she was. No way to ask how many held her.

Thousands of years old, and I am still capable of making moronic mistakes.

"I will find you," I promised the empty trailer. With a sigh, I rematerialized back into the loft. The multiple jumps had tired me a bit, in addition to the fatigue and stress over losing Mary. And so much worse. One of my sisters, a Guardian, was alive. Alive, and working against Mollis. I did not understand what the point was. Why? And why did I feel like there was something here I was missing?

I was lost in thought and heading for the stairs to my room when Brennan's voice came from the dark living room. "Where'd you go, Tink?"

I closed my eyes. I'd missed him completely. The loft was dark, the sky barely beginning to lighten in the east.

And I was most definitely not in the mood to deal with the turmoil he caused within me.

"Did the vampires get home? It's nearly dawn."

"Yeah. I dropped them off after your little disappearing act." He stood up and came toward me, clicking on the lights in the kitchen as he did, which was where I was standing. He took me in in a quick glance.

"Bloody and pissed off," he murmured. "What happened?"

"I found one of Mollis's lost souls," I said quietly. "I am sorry I left like that. I had to leave before I lost track of it again."

He nodded. "This is which one?"

"Bates Downing. American," I said, and he nodded.

"He bled? Or are you hurt?"

I glanced down. I'd zipped my coat over my white shirt, but the leather of my jacket and my jeans, boots were spattered with blood. "It is not mine."

"How does a soul bleed?" he asked.

"Brennan, I am tired. Can we do this another time?"

I should have known that trying not to talk about it would make him even more intent on doing so. "There's something you're not telling me, Eunomia."

"There are plenty of things I don't tell you," I said.

"How does a soul bleed?" he pressed.

"This is the third one now that has. They are on their way to developing corporeal forms…" I trailed off, remembering why this felt so familiar. We had only seen this once before, during what the humans called the Black Death in the fourteenth century in human time. Too many dead, too quickly. My sisters and I had been overburdened, and it took us longer to get to some of the dead. By the time we had, some of them had been in a similar state as the souls I'd just been collecting. Not alive, just not dead anymore. Not a ghost. We'd dubbed them Undead. The most powerful ones, three of them that were fully capable of dealing with the physical world, had finally been captured and the Furies had finally learned their secret, how they'd managed it: eating the still-beating heart of a human. Three hearts, and they had a fully-capable form. Strong. Endlessly hungry. Violent.

"Tink," Brennan said, stepping closer to me.

We'd never figured out how they'd known to do it. We had never heard of or seen such a thing. That was what both Boyd O'Connor and Bates Downing had been waiting for. They'd expected my sister, who looked almost exactly like me, to bring them a human to help them on their way to full undeath.

"I need to sleep. Good night," I said, shrugging him off.

"Damn it, Eunomia," he said. "You can't do that to me."

"Do what?"

"Shut down and walk away."

I sighed. "I am not. All right?"

"It sure looks like you are," he said, crossing his arms over his chest, those overly-perceptive eyes locked on mine.

"I do not think I could do that if I tried," I said softly. "I do not want to talk about this right now. I need to think."

He did not answer. He was irritated.

"This is reminding me a little too much of why I don't handle relationships like this well," he finally said,

"I am so sorry I will not just simper and do whatever you want me to do, cub," I said, heading up the stairs. "And for the record, this is reminding me that you are much too young and immature for me."

With that, I slipped into my room, closing the door quietly behind me. I went to the tiny bathroom attached to my room, stripped off my clothing, then stood under the almost too-hot shower and scrubbed blood that should not have been there off of me.

And I thought.

If I remembered those undead during the Black Death, it was likely my sister did as well. And if we did… I was convinced there had to be another piece of the puzzle. Something we were not seeing. Something more powerful had broken those souls out of Tartarus. Something had targeted the worst humanity had to offer, and ensured those souls were the ones freed.

Someone was working with my sister to being those souls to undeath.

I had to find these souls before they did. This would be a mess. The death toll just one of the undead could cause with its incessant hunger was terrifying. With over twenty of them still out there, it would be a nightmare.

I needed to tell Mollis about this. She needed to know.

I got out of the shower and pulled on clean jeans, one of my old concert t-shirts, and my boots. I sat on my bed, pulled out my laptop, and started an email to Mollis, laying out what I knew about what was happening, and my suspicions that someone bigger was behind it, because someone had to help the souls escape.

I thought for a moment, then continued typing.

"Demon girl: tell no one, please. If we alert them now to the fact that we are on to them, they may get careful, and it will be that much harder to find them. Or they will get reckless, and people will get hurt. Please trust me to do my job. This is what I was made for. And trust that this needs to stay quiet. I am leaving with Hephaestus for Europe. I need to find these souls, fast. Stay safe, E."

I hit "send," then closed the laptop and picked up my phone, hitting Hephaestus' number.

"You are so lucky I wasn't having sex with my wife just now," he growled into the phone.

"Yes, I will count my blessings. Time to go. We need to move."

"What, now?"

"Now. Right now."

I heard him swear under his breath. "Fine. I'll be there in a couple of minutes." With that, he hung up. I tossed a few things into my bag, thinking. I would need to gather Quinn and the others from Ireland, which meant getting away from Hephaestus for a few minutes. It would not be too difficult. He was easily distracted.

This latest realization about what the souls were doing had me second-guessing my wisdom in keeping Quinn and the others to myself. If they betrayed me…

Well, that was easy. If they betrayed me, I would hurt them, badly. And then Mollis would hurt them, badly.

I zipped my bag, pulled my (cleaned) coat back on over my dagger harness, and zipped up. By the time I was heading down the stairs, Hephaestus was standing in the still-dark kitchen, holding a bag of his own.

"Have I ever told ya I'm not a morning person?" he growled at me.

"Have I ever told you I really do not care?" I answered with a smile, and he released a snort of a laugh.

"Okay, you miniature pain in the ass. Where are we going?"

"Germany," I said, taking his hand in mine.

CHAPTER THIRTEEN

Hephaestus and I appeared in a train station in Beelitz, Germany. Train stations and airports tended to be good places to reappear, because usually no one was focused on anything other than getting to their gate, and, if they were not, nowadays they were usually staring at a phone or other device.

"Okay. Fill me in here. Who're we lookin' for?" Hephaestus asked me.

"Friedrich Munch," I said, leading him out of the train station. "Mass murderer. Killed seventeen teenage boys in an attempt to regain his lost youth."

"Sickening."

"Agreed. But of our two souls here in Germany, he's the less evil of the two. We are also here to hunt the soul of one Peter Stumpfe. In his time, in the late sixteenth century, he was known as the werewolf of Brandenburg. He claimed the devil made him do it, and he was tried with cannibalism and murdering sixteen women and two infants."

"And was he a werewolf?" Hephaestus asked

"He was. There was a werewolf clan here at the time, but he was a loner."

"And what makes him so much worse than the other one?" Hephaestus asked.

"Stumpfe was a sadist who enjoyed playing with his food before he ate it," I answered, and he nodded. "If you need to get an idea of how monstrous he was, those two infants he killed? He ate their hearts. One of them was his own son."

"Those are the ones I most would like to kill," Hephaestus growled, and I nodded in agreement.

"This was where he ran after he was executed. I had to chase him down. This is as good a place to begin as any, considering how long he has been free," I said. "There is a small inn down this road, I think."

"E, when was the last time you were here?" Hephaestus asked with a laugh.

"Not that long. It is still here, I am sure," I told him with a glare, and he laughed.

'If you say so. Are we walking or traveling the sensible way?"

"We will walk. It is the best way for me to sense for energy signatures. Is that all right?"

"It's your party," he said.

I furrowed my brow. "I would not call it a party."

"It's a figure of speech, E."

"I do not like those."

"I noticed," Hephaestus said, and I shook my head. We walked on, and I noted with some amusement that, as I'd predicted, his eye was caught by every distraction presented to us. Car models we did not usually see in Detroit, the man playing some one-man-band contraption on one of the street corners. He was in his element.

"You should take your family on travels more often," I said to him. "You love this."

He shrugged. "I will someday. When things settle down."

"That could be never, my friend," I told him, and he nodded.

"Eventually," he said with a shrug. "So… what's the deal between you and the shifter?"

I stumbled a little and swore under my breath in irritation as he laughed. "Yeah, that's what I thought," he said.

"There is nothing going on. He is my friend, and Mollis has us working together on this mess."

"Sure. Yeah. That's all," he said, and I could tell from his tone of voice that he did not believe a word of it.

"He is too young for me. He has no understanding of our world, and he wants someone who will be a meek, delicate little flower," I said, waving away my irritation, able to be more open with Hephaestus than I allowed myself to be with most beings. "He wants to know every detail of my life, and gets irritated when I will not tell him every single thought in my head."

"We both know he doesn't want someone who's meek," Hephaestus said.

"Well, he thinks he does, except when he thinks he does not," I answered. "I can be honest with you. I like him quite a bit. He is the single most beautiful male I have ever laid eyes on, and I have thought so since the first time I saw him. But he has had a whole mess in terms of relationships before me. And I am not particularly adept at putting in the time long-term with anyone. The relationships I have had the past two years have all been short and I was able to walk away before they became ridiculous."

Hephaestus scratched his chin, thinking. "From experience here, E, things don't really get good until they start getting ridiculous, until you start arguing about shit you'd never imagined yourself arguing over, and then you just look at one another and laugh. Until you've been through late nights and tears and anger and every other emotion, and you know one another inside and out. That's when the relationship shit gets good."

I shook my head. "I will have to take your word for it."

"Why not find out for yourself?"

"It would be stupid," I said. "And I do not want to talk about it anymore."

He sighed, but he let it go and I was grateful.

We quickly found a room at the small inn, a tiny room with two twin beds. Hopefully, this would go quickly and we would not need them for the two nights we'd allotted.

I glanced at Hephaestus, who was clicking through television channels.

"I am going to see if there is anything decent to eat in that shop down the road, and then we can eat and start hunting. I am starving," I told him.

"Me too. Get me something, okay?" he asked, mesmerized.

"Of course." With that I left our room, headed down the stairs, and ducked into the empty sitting room, where I focused and rematerialized. I went a bit farther than I told Hephaestus I would, ending up at the abandoned farm in Ireland where I had left Quinn, Cathleen, Erin, and Claire. They were there, and filled me in on their activities the past could of days. They'd helped the crows find two souls, and spent a lot of time listening for any word on others like them, but had heard nothing.

I nodded. I filled them in on what had happened with Mary, and they were shocked.

"We will find her. I swear it," I told them.

"How?" Claire asked.

"The best way to find Mary is to find those who are working with our lost souls. With that in mind, we have souls to hunt in Germany." I held my hands out, and the four of them linked hands, Quinn and Claire each taking one of my hands. I focused, and within moments, we were standing in an abandoned military hospital in Beelitz, on the outskirts of the town. Thick pine forest surrounded the abandoned facility, and I could smell its clean scent through the broken windows. Weak light filtered through the arched windows, and the tile walls and floors smelled of moss and death. Just as it had been the last time I'd been there.

I waited a few moments to allow Quinn, Cathleen, and Erin to steady themselves, and Claire shared an amused glance with me.

"Who knew the dead could be such delicate things?" she asked wryly, and I gave Quinn an amused glance. He was currently bent double, hands on his knees.

"Stuff it, witch," Quinn groaned, and she laughed out loud. "That is the worst. I'd rather be stabbed again than go through that."

"You will get used to it," I told him. "We will be traveling that way often."

"I don't want to travel that way at all," he grumbled.

"Well, it is a good thing I did not ask what you wanted, then, isn't it?"

He laughed then and shook his head. "You're the kind of woman who would have driven me nuts when I was alive."

"Meaning?"

"Bossy as all hell and too confident for her own good."

"I have every reason to be those things," I said.

"I don't doubt it for a moment, lass," he said, looking at me with amusement. I looked away from him toward the woman.

"Are we all right now?" I asked them, and Erin and Cathleen nodded, though they both still had the pinched look of someone dealing with nausea.

"Good. As I said, we will be doing that rather often, so you will just have to deal with your discomfort. Whether you want to or not." That settled, I focused on the task at hand. "I told you we are missing twenty-four souls. We are now down to twenty-three. The sooner we find them, the better. This means we will not linger. We will not waste time. We will catch who we come for, and we will move on to the next. It's not as if any of us has anything else to do, yes?"

They all nodded. I had their attention now. Their postures were straighter, their attention more focused.

"How do we find him? I don't know about them until I see them," Claire asked.

"I can sense them. I can pick up their trails. But it takes time and focus," I said, and they nodded. I started walking through the dilapidated hospital, focusing, feeling if there was anything there. I kept my focus, walked out of the building and down the crumbling steps, which led to the pine forest. I walked, and focused, and I could sense the four souls following closely behind me.

I stepped into the tangled forest, ducking under tree branches and, after ripping yet another hole in my jeans on a thorny branch, envying the souls their ability to merely walk through anything in their way. This. The footwork, more than anything else, was what I found annoying about my work. I felt like a bloodhound, nose to the ground, endlessly shuffling through my life trying to find what I was after.

And for the most part, it was endless frustration. We walked through the woods, and I stepped into what was left of a small hunting cabin.

Nothing.

I let out a breath of annoyance. If someone had told me of this mess sooner…

I pushed it out of my mind. Complaining about the way things had been done wouldn't make them any better. It was my mess to clean up now, and I would handle it.

I would make it clear that something like this couldn't go unreported so long. Not that I expected it to happen again.

At least, I hoped it would not.

We walked through the woods more, and then back to the hospital. It was a huge complex, and it was the most likely place to find Munch. I sighed in frustration and turned to my team.

"Here is the situation. I am here with another immortal. My Queen worries about me doing this alone. Meanwhile, I am more worried about having those she sends with me getting hurt," I said in irritation. "He does not know about you. As an immortal, he would be able to feel you, at the very least. More likely, he would be able to see you, given enough time and attention."

"How?" Erin asked. "Is he a death god... thing like you are?"

I shook my head. "All immortals, whether they are like me or not, can sense all beings, living or dead. In your case, we can assume that a god or even someone like me would have to know to look for you. I still wish I understood how it all worked," I said in frustration. "But for now, he does not know of you, and I am not ready to have you revealed yet."

They nodded.

"I need to return to him. Please do some searching of the hospital and see if you find any evidence of a soul. I will return as soon as I can, but it may be a while. I am going to take him with me to hunt the other soul."

"We will take care of it," Claire promised.

"Thank you. Be careful. Watch your backs. I am not the only one anymore." I hated leaving them alone, especially in light of what had happened with Mary, but I had to remind myself that for whatever reason, these souls were different. I would have to trust that it would keep them safe, that they would have the sense to watch themselves.

They nodded, and I focused and rematerialized back in town, remembering at the last moment to stop in the shop for food. I threw a bunch of random items quickly into a basket, paid for it, and carried it into our inn.

"You were gone a while," Hephaestus said when I walked into our room.

"I was not sure what to get," I said, setting the white plastic bag on the bed beside him. He started rooting through it and opened a bag of potato chips and a soda.

"When we finish eating, we will go looking for Stumpfe," I said, and he nodded, still watching the screen.

One hour later, we had one more soul for Mollis. He had been nothing more than a spirit, and it took almost no effort at all to bring him in. While Hephaestus exalted in how easy my job was, all I felt was unease. I do not trust it when things go easily. Nothing about Mollis's assignment had been easy so far.

"Why don't we split up for the next one, now that you see how really *not* dangerous this is, hm?" I asked him. "The sooner we get this finished, the sooner you can get home to your family."

"We're on to Russia after this, right?"

I nodded. "And hopefully you can tell Mollis I do not need help. You know I am happier on my own "

"I know. I know," he repeated. "We'll split up for a bit. I'll ask around. What? We're looking for rumors of hauntings, things like that, right?"

I nodded, then gave him a pat on the back. "Thank you."

"Sure thing. Just don't get yer ass kicked or Molly is gonna have mine," he warned.

I smiled. "Do I ever get my ass kicked?"

He rolled his eyes and started toward the other part of town, and I watched him go. After another moment, I rematerialized back at the hospital, hoping to hear that my team of new Guardians had turned up something.

I didn't have much time to wonder more about it.

The second I rematerialized into the large foyer of the hospital, where my team was gathered: there. I could feel the energy signature of Munch.

"One just arrived not ten minutes ago. This the one you're hunting?" Quinn asked in a low voice.

I felt a grim smile on my lips, unaware that I was doing it, and I nodded. I could feel him clearly. This was going to be a good day for Mollis.

I glanced around at my team, motioned for them to stay quiet.

I walked down the long corridor, so many empty rooms off to the sides, the black and white tile of the floor slippery with mildew beneath my feet. The occasional rat ran across our path as we disturbed their home with our presence. We neared a room where I saw a large apparatus, something that may have been used for lighting during surgery, over an old gurney. An operating room, I supposed. I stopped, holding my hand up for my team to be still. I listened, and heard a groan. Not of pain. Pleasure.

I focused harder, and realized he most definitely was not alone.

Faint, as if an effort had been made to hide it somehow, I could feel the trace of one of my own kind.

One of my sisters.

If she were not distracted, she would have felt me there. I turned my head, met the eyes of each of my new Guardians. This would be even more vital to do right than I'd initially planned, and I was glad to have them with me.

I held my fingers up, signaling that there were two. Then I pointed to Quinn and Erin, and pointed to the west wall of the operating room. Pointing at Clair and Cathleen, I gestured to the east wall. "Keep Munch occupied," I whispered, and they nodded, then left, following their orders. I reappeared inside the room. The man and woman on the filthy floor were very immersed in what they were doing. The female, on top, fluttered her bat-like wings in tempo to the way they moved.

"This is utterly disgusting," I said.

The other Guardian stood up with a shriek.

"Don't you know where this thing has been?" I asked Munch, gesturing toward my furious sister as he scrambled on the floor, intent on getting away. It was then that my four souls converged, surrounding him. He started hitting, trying to fight his way out.

I had no more time to focus on him, trusting that my little army had it under control. The Guardian, my sister, Kleio, snarled at me again and lunged, her own Netherblade in hand, and she slashed out at me.

"Sister of mine," she hissed. "So nice of you to drop in." She slashed out at me again and I ducked it, kicked out hard and heard her ribs crack under the assault. She screeched.

She would heal, of course. The point was to weaken her enough to be able to detain her. I am powerful, and so are those like me. None of us should be underestimated.

"Defective bitch," she hissed, lunging at me again. She narrowly missed the side of my neck with the dagger, and I punched, hard, and heard her nose crack. Blood flowed down her face, and she gave a maniacal shout and rushed me. She stabbed toward my stomach, but the blade scraped off, deterred by the metal embedded in my coat there.

"Weakling. Depending on armor like a mortal."

"Better weak than dead," I said coolly. "She is going to kill you," I promised. "And I am going to watch." I kicked out again. This time, the force of it made her crash back into the cabinets behind her. She crumpled for a moment, and then sprang back up at me. "If I could, I would kill you myself. Traitor," I said, and I was all too aware of the coldness in my voice, the menace that only came out at moments like this. "You have failed everything we are. You have fouled your entire reason for being."

"You are the only failure I see here," she snarled, jumping at me again.

It is hard to describe how I feel during times like this. My breathing slows. My muscles are tense, yet fluid. I become cold, steady.

I felt like nothing more than a vengeful spirit. And I embraced it.

There was no blur of rage, no heat of battle. There was cold, mechanical destruction.

A kick to her face.

Her arm wrenched so hard behind her back I could feel her humerus break, and even as she screamed and tried to wrench away from me, I held fast.

The wrist holding her Guardian blade broke as I twisted it, and she screamed in agony.

I did not stop until the blade, a blade she no longer had any right to wield, fell to the floor.

She slumped, raging, screaming in pain, and I felt nothing but cold satisfaction. I knocked her face into the white tiled wall, cracking several of the tiles with the impact, which was perhaps a bit much but it felt good to do it. I bent to pick up her blade, adding it to my sheath.

It was only then that I finally glanced toward my souls. They had Munch's soul surrounded, and Munch looked like he hadn't fared much better than Kleio had.

"Keep him there. I will return as soon as this one is imprisoned."

Quinn nodded, indicating that he'd heard the order.

I took Kleio's arm roughly and focused on the Netherwoods. More specifically, on the cells that held the souls of the dead. I knew I would find one of the Furies there.

Tisiphone was on duty then, and I thanked Nyx for small miracles. I was in no mood to deal with Megaera and her nonsense.

The second she realized I was there, Tisiphone's eyes widened.

"What in the Nether?" she asked as she stared at my sister.

"That is what I would like to know. How is this one not dead?" I gave Kleio a rough shake, and she snarled at me.

"I thought Molly killed all of them," Tisiphone argued.

"Yet here she is, alive and well and aiding those who escaped. We need to know why and how, right now."

"And we will." Tisiphone took Kleio's other arm and the two of us led her to a cell. The black walls echoed with the screams of other souls undergoing their punishment.

"Tisiphone."

"Yes?"

"Trust no one. Do not let this one out of your sight."

"Don't you think you're being overly suspicious—"

"This one has no right even being alive. Someone was able to bring her back. Someone helped those souls escape. Do not make me have to hunt her again."

Her expression became even more serious. "This is wrong. How is this possible?"

"That is what you need to find out. Set Mollis on her as soon as possible. I have no doubt our Queen will enjoy speaking with her."

"Indeed," Tisiphone said.

"I have one of the escapees for you as well. I will be right back."

"How can you be sure it hasn't run off?" Tisiphone asked.

"He was in poor shape," I answered, focusing on returning to where I'd left my souls and the soul of Munch. As I'd left them, my four souls surrounded his, and he sat, shouting, on the floor, battered and desperate.

I took the thin black chain out of my coat pocket and approached him. He tried to run for it and Quinn punched him, hard enough to make his head rock back at a painful-looking angle.

I nodded my appreciation for the help and wrapped Munch's wrists quickly.

"I will return."

"Won't he tell them about us?" Claire asked.

"It is time for me to talk to my Queen anyway," I said. "It matters not."

I took Munch by the arm again, and he trembled in my grip. I exchanged a glance with Claire. She seemed to understand; I would be back as soon as possible. Moments later, I was standing in the cells in the Netherwoods again, and I handed him off to Tisiphone wordlessly.

"Looks like you had fun with this one, too."

"Indeed."

"Remind me not to anger you, Guardian," she said with a smile, and I found myself smiling back.

"You never have yet," I said. "How is my Queen?" I wondered if she had gotten my email, and, more, if she had kept my advice about keeping it quiet. If she had said something, Tisiphone would tell me.

"She is… this will likely help some. She needs to work off some of this rage."

I nodded.

"She and the demon have been talking about moving their family here more permanently. Nether is less of a problem for her here, and Zoe is better able to handle her… issues as well." Mollis's adopted daughter, Zoe, was the child of a demon and a shifter. The opposite types of energy in those two beings usually make it impossible for them to breed. When they do, the results are not good. The demonic side is suppressed by the shifter side, but always bubbles just below the surface. Usually, any offspring that result are put down as soon as possible. Mollis refused to allow that to happen, taking baby Zoe (who was now three years old) into her family instead.

I nodded. The energy of the Nether was soothing to my kind, as well as demons. It was a good plan on her part.

"And what about Detroit?"

"They will leave it in the hands of the vampire queen and the shifter coalition, for the most part. They will continue to work under Nain, but he will be more hands-off. It seems to be the best way to handle things for now. Each soul you find will likely help," she said, pleading to her tone.

"I will not stop until they are all found," I promised. "Is she around? I need to speak with her."

"She is in with your sister. Do you want to go in?"

I shook my head. "I will catch up with her later."

She nodded, and I focused one more time, reappearing in Germany. I went back to my team.

"Amazing work. I need you to move on now. I will meet you at our next location when I can." I held my hands out, and they linked hands with me again.

"Where to now?" Quinn asked.

"Russia," I said, and then we were gone.

CHAPTER FOUREEN

As soon as we arrived in the woods in southern Siberia, I dropped their hands and stepped away, my head spinning.

Too many jumps, too quickly. I did not want them to see me tired. Weak.

And now that the cold calm that came with violence had passed, I was feeling all of the emotions I'd been holding in check upon discovering my sister. In having my theories confirmed, that my kind were not only alive and well in some cases, but also involved in what we were doing.

I did not want them to see that, either.

I stepped away, and breathed, and tried to retain some semblance of calm. Why did I even care? My sisters, those that still lived, as well as those who were dead, were traitors to my kind.

If nothing else, I know what I am. I know who I serve. There is no question about that. Yet Kleio's comment about me being defective struck me, hard.

Why was I the only one who still believed?

I'd heard the whispers from them, of course, in the thousands of years at their sides. They'd gone from gentle taunts of "the good soldier," to derisive commentary.

Zealot.

Servant.

Machine.

They were not wrong. I was all of those things at heart.

My belief in the necessity of my role, in the rightness of what I do, does perhaps make me a zealot. And I am the first to admit that I am more like a machine than anything else.

"You all right?" Quinn's voice said behind me. I had walked further into the woods and hadn't even noticed that he'd followed me.

"I am fine," I answered. "You should be with the others."

"Is that an order?"

I did not answer. We stood in silence for a bit, and I felt my strength coming back.

"So that was the scariest fuckin' thing I've ever seen," he said finally, and I found myself smiling a little.

"Then it was a good demonstration of what happens to those who get on my bad side," I said, looking back at him.

"You could definitely say that. Yeah," he said, meeting my eyes. "I have no intention of getting on your bad side, Eunomia."

"Good to know."

"She was your sister?"

"In a manner of speaking. Though she has no right to call herself that."

"Why not?"

"Because she is so far beneath me, she has lost the right to do so."

He was watching me. "You're a god?"

"I am a servant of gods. I am immortal. But I am not one of them. I am one of the oldest things in this realm."

"That seems overwhelming," he said, looking up at the sky peeking between the tangled branches above us.

"Not really."

He was watching me. "I've never seen anyone give a beating like that before and not show an ounce of anger."

"That is what makes me so efficient. Anger clouds the senses, distracts your focus. So does fear."

"And you don't have that, either," he said.

I shook my head. "My only fear is of failing. And I have no intention of doing that."

He tore his gaze away from mine. "If she demands that you turn us over…"

"It will not come to that. I will not fail in that, either. Trust me."

"I do trust you."

"Good. You should be with the others. And this time it is an order, Quinn."

He nodded, and I watched him walk away.

I turned back toward the woods and pulled my sister's dagger out of my pocket, where I'd quickly stuffed it after picking it up. I inspected the blade, noting that it was immaculately clean, as it should be. I unzipped my coat and reached inside, pulling the steel dagger out of its sheath and putting the black stone dagger in its place. The steel dagger, I sheathed inside my boot.

After a while, I returned to my team. "I need to get back to Germany, but I will return as soon as I can. You can rest here." It was not the most hospitable of places, but I knew souls did not feel cold, or warmth. It was deserted enough that, should anyone else arrive, my new Guardians would be able to detect them quickly and protect themselves.

Claire and Erin nodded gratefully, and they each settled onto a different area of the forest floor. Cathleen went to where Erin was resting, and settled in next to her. Quinn still sat where he was, back against a large log.

"Something is troubling you," I said quietly, settling myself next to him.

"Can't quite get the way you looked earlier out of my head."

"What do you mean?"

"Seeing someone so emotionless when they're causing the kind of damage. It's not natural."

"It would have been better if I'd been hysterical?"

"No. I just—"

"Or maybe if I'd been crying? If I'd needed someone to soothe me? Someone to hold me together before I fell apart?"

"That would be more normal, yes."

"It will take a lot more than that to break me," I said, running my fingers through the thin layer of snow on the ground between his thigh and mine. "And I am not a human. Do not expect me to act like one."

"That other one, though. She was angry. And scared. What makes you so different?"

Good question, I thought to myself. "She is broken. Compromised. I am not."

He did not answer, and I sensed that he was trying to figure it all out somehow.

"She called you defective," he reminded me.

"Yet she was the one riding the soul of a mass murderer as if he was a prized pony. If I am the defective one, I choose to wear the label proudly."

"Zing."

I hid the smile that came to my lips.

"When I said earlier that you're the type of woman who would have driven me nuts?" he said.

"Yes?"

"I meant that in a good way. Just so you know."

"Hmm, compliments. Trying to get on my good sides? Are you scared of me now?" I asked with the hint of a smile on my lips.

"Completely terrified," he said. "But I've always had a thing for dangerous girls."

"Is that a hint, Quinn?"

"A not very subtle one, boss."

"Are you wanting me to ride you like a prized pony?" I asked.

"Without a doubt."

I rolled my eyes. "You must have been a real charmer when you were alive," I said drily.

"Not so much, no."

"That was sarcasm."

"Oh," he said, and I laughed.

We sat in silence for a few moments. "You say you're one of the oldest things in existence," Quinn said, and I nodded, still absentmindedly messing with the snow between us. "Yet this, us being here and your Queen not knowing... you've never seen this?"

I shook my head. "It is wrong. And the fact that I discovered a sister who I've since confirmed did, in fact, die, is wrong. These souls getting helped out of the Nether—"

"Wrong," he said, and I nodded again.

"I wish I knew anything that would help you figure it out. I keep trying to think about when I died and what happened after. The only thing I know for sure is that nobody came for me. Nobody like you, no crows, nothing."

I didn't answer. "We know you all died violently. That you were drawn to the idea of forcing those trying to avoid their judgment to stay put until they could be retrieved. There is something there. And if my Queen knew of you, I'd feel better about all of this. But something like this just doesn't belong. I do not understand it."

"That must not be something you say often," he said, watching my hand as I drew in the snow.

"I say it much more often than I'd like to," I muttered. "Humans are nonsensical."

"He's a human, then? This person who's all under your skin?"

I glanced up, met his gaze. Was I really that obvious? "We are not talking about this."

"Fine," he said, shrugging. "Just seems to me maybe a male perspective might help."

I gave him a disbelieving look. "Males are the most clueless of all humans."

"Hey now," he said, laughing.

"That is not saying much. The females are not that much better."

"Yet one of them has confused you so badly you don't know what to do with yourself. What does that say about you, boss?"

"It says I need to focus on the things I am supposed to be thinking about. Some things are better left alone."

"That wasn't exactly the point I was trying to make."

"The point you were trying to make was idiotic," I said, standing up and dusting my pants off.

"You definitely have a way with people," he said, standing as well.

I did not respond. I cleared my throat. "I will be back when I can," I said. "We have a handful of targets here in Russia. Once we've apprehended them, we will move on to Japan. Hopefully we will get these souls tracked down quickly. Time is rather of the essence."

"Maybe we'll find more like us, who's looking for ye," Claire said from where she was resting.

"Gods, I hope not," I muttered, and focused, and when I next opened my eyes, I was in the room I shared with Hephaestus at the inn in Germany, and he was sound asleep.

We moved through five cities in Russia, and it quickly became clear that my little team of souls were becoming a disciplined, well-organized force. Once I'd found the energy signature of each soul, they'd spread out, almost like hounds tracking their prey. They were relentless, tireless, and they did not let up until the souls were found. It was all much faster than I'd eve been able to track a soul on my own. So much more efficient.

And with each soul we found, they seemed to grow even more dedicated to me, to their role at my side. And I found myself feeling the same about them. To his credit, Hephaestus was very good at staying out of my way and asking no questions. He knew me well enough, and had known me long enough, not to worry when I went out to hunt.

Aside from the bond I was starting to feel with my New Guardians, as I'd begun thinking of them, there was more.

I also felt something changing in their energy signatures. They were stronger. A glance at Quinn showed that he looked more solid, more real.

They were on their way to developing fully corporeal forms. Without the grisly methods that usually brought the change about.

I studied Quinn as we stopped to rest after apprehending our final Russian soul.

"See anything you like, boss?" he asked with a smirk.

"Don't be an idiot," I said. "You're becoming corporeal."

"Huh?"

"You're becoming solid. Soon you'll be easily visible to other immortals. And likely to humans as well, if you aren't already."

"I don't think so," he said, shaking his head.

"What makes you say that?"

"We're becoming more real to you, maybe to the rest of your kind, I suppose. More full. I know I'm stronger the longer we fight by your side. Them, too," he said, nodding toward the women. "We're only real and solid in your eyes. Watch," he said, walking away from me, where a teenage boy was walking past, earbuds in his ears. I was about to shout to stop him, but I reminded myself at the last moment that the humans could actually see me and it would look ridiculous. He drew back and gave the teenage boy a hard shove... And the teenage boy did not move. Quinn went straight through him, despite how solid he looked.

I crossed my arms, and he shrugged. "Just you, boss."

"Did you have to be quite so dramatic about it?"

Quinn grinned. "Was fun watching you trying to decide whether to freak out or not."

I rolled my eyes and turned away.

I checked my phone and there was a text messages from Mollis. I opened it immediately. I'd been almost ceaselessly haranguing the Furies and Mollis for any information they had managed to get from my sister, so far, to no avail. Unfortunately, there still was no news, and her message did nothing to alleviate my stress level.

"I want Brennan to go with you to Japan."

"Shit," I muttered.

I thought for a moment and then typed. "Do not need his help."

A moment later, a response. "I know. Heph told me. You're getting it anyway."

Before I could respond, another text. "Heph is swapping with Brennan right now. No more arguing."

"Why? Send someone else."

"Him. He is driving me fucking nuts because you went without him. If you don't take him, I'm gonna kill him."

I threw my hands up in irritation. "Fine," I texted back.

A moment later, "Love ya, E. Be safe."

I smiled to myself. "Back at you demon girl."

By the time I made it back to where Hephaestus and I had been staying, Brennan was the one waiting in our room for me, his bag tossed onto the bed Hephaestus had claimed as his own. He was sitting on the edge of his bed, arms crossed.

All right. He was not happy with me.

"We will move on to Japan soon. I need to get cleaned up first," I said in greeting.

"You left without saying anything to me," he said.

I stopped, resting my hand on the doorframe between our room and the bathroom. "I did."

"And you said I'm too young for you."

I nodded. "I did. But only after you shared your concern that I am too independent for you. You have reservations about whatever this is. So do I."

"Which is exactly why I'm not pushing you," he said.

"Same. I am not even sure what this is, and I am even less sure that it should develop any further."

"Great. Perfect," he muttered.

"Was that not what you were going to say to me?" I asked him, crossing my arms over my chest.

"I don't know," he said, running his hand through his hair. "I missed you though, Tink," he said and when he looked at me, there was that tiny lift of the corner of his mouth that I liked so much.

"You were worried I was unable to handle myself without you shadowing my every move," I said.

"I was worried. I know damn well you can handle yourself just fine without me. It doesn't mean I have to like you being in danger. There's a difference between not believing in you and wanting to be able to help you. I know you're a badass. I know you've got this. I still want to be here for you. Okay?"

I sighed, shook my head. "You confuse me."

"I know."

"I do not like it."

"I know that, too. I think that's part of what's making this so weird."

"Oh? Enlighten me then, Cub."

He grinned, and stood up, and walked toward me, and my stomach twisted and my body warmed a little more with each step he took toward me. "You are used to being in complete control. To knowing exactly how every aspect of a situation will play out. You have seen everything, you are surprised by almost nothing. But you don't feel in control now, and you hate that."

"I am still surprised by things," I argued, and he stopped in front of me, looking down into my eyes.

"Way to not comment on the rest of what I said," he said.

"The rest of what you said was ridiculous," I said. "Be ready to leave in twenty minutes." With that, I closed the bathroom door behind me with a deep breath of relief.

Once this was over, I was really going to have to figure out how to stop being so affected by him.

CHAPTER FIFTEEN

We had three souls to find in Japan. All three were your typical serial killers, and how sad was it that I was beginning to see serial murderers as run of the mill? One was from the thirteenth century, a woman who'd come to be one of the most powerful concubines at the time. Mostly because she murdered and schemed, along with the man she served, accumulating wealth beyond imagine. The other was a man who'd enjoyed drowning his victims. He hadn't been selective at all; it was bad luck if someone just happened to be around when the mood struck him. The third had been an American soldier who had died in Japan after the second World War. The atrocities he'd committed against a people he'd seen as "the enemy" disgusted me.

War was never pretty. There were always those out there who took that additional step and made it even uglier.

Brennan and I appeared on the shore of the small island of Sarushima, which was where our drowner had worked. He'd been a fisherman, and he'd often mixed business and pleasure. It wasn't until the other people from the area realized that all the murder victims were washing up on the same beach, and always on days when his boat had been seen in the area, that they caught on.

They'd drowned him.

I know that humanity has a distrust of vigilante justice. But I believe that sometimes, it really is the cleanest and most suitable form of justice. I knew for a fact that Hades had not found much fault with those who had partaken in bringing the man to justice. According to Tisiphone, he'd shaken their hands before passing judgment.

We walked along the docks, both of us with a duffel bag slung over our shoulder, ready to drop if we came across our lost soul. We hadn't said a word to one another since leaving the hotel room in Russia.

My New Guardians were here already. I'd moved them quickly after I'd locked myself in the bathroom for my shower. I'd instructed them to stay out of sight, but I could feel them not far ahead.

And there. There was the energy signature I'd been looking for. I tugged the sleeve of Brennan's shirt and gave a slight nod of my head to the west, further down the docks.

He gave a short nod. And then he walked off behind a tiny shack with the Japanese word for "bait" emblazoned on it s sign. Within moments, I saw the dark shadow of his panther slinking in the shadows, and I headed toward my soul.

The soul of Hidemi Sato, the drowner, stood on a pier immediately ahead of me.

With one of my sisters.

She had a human with her, and I knew very well what she was expecting to do with that human.

I rematerialized behind her before she saw me, and my team was there, and immediately subdued the soul of Sato in that moment when my sister Delo turned and snarled at me. Brennan streaked up to us, snarling, and Delo shoved me.

"Not today, zealot. The good soldier will have to return reporting her failure." And before I could grab her, she had disappeared.

I kicked one of the railing supports in irriation.

"Damn it," I said.

Brennan shifted, and I didn't look at him.

"She ran pretty fast," he said, and I nodded.

"I have taken too many of them. They will be careful now."

"How many have you taken?"

"Two. I have no idea how many more of them there are," I said. "Go find your clothing. I will turn this soul in to Mollis and return here." I did look at him then, meeting his eyes. "Be careful," I said, remembering the way I'd lost Mary. "And maybe try to contact someone about this human. I do not know what my sister did to him, but he seems confused."

Brennan nodded. "I will take care of it."

I walked over to where the soul of Sako stood helplessly, my New Guardians just in the shadows behind him.

"Watch over Brennan," I said quietly to them. "If one of my kind goes after him, remember that you can fight her. Do not let anything happen to him."

"This is the one then, eh, boss?" Quinn asked with humor in his voice.

"He is. And if any harm comes to him I am going to be very unhappy."

"We will take care of it," Claire said, and I nodded, finished wrapping Sako's wrists with my chain, and in the next moment, I was in the Netherwoods, just outside of the prison. I sent a demon for Tisiphone, and she was there shortly.

"Another of my sisters was with this one," I said, handing him over to her. "Delo."

Tisiphone stared at me. "How many of you can there still be?"

I shook my head. "She killed them, right?"

"I watched her cut many of them down. I know for a fact I watched Delo turn to dust at my daughter's blade," Tisiphone said. "I don't get it."

"That makes two of us."

"This one is less solid than the others. Still just a soul," Tisophone said. "So that is a good thing, right?"

I nodded. "Delo had a human there for him. He was about to become more corporeal." Seeing her, and the human she'd brought only confirmed what I'd suspected. My sisters were providing the escaped souls with human flesh, helping them become more corporeal. After a third infusion, they would no longer need help. They would be solid enough to take a human down on their own.

Tisiphone looked ill. She remembered the days of that period as well. Dealing with the Undead had not been pleasant. "I will fill my daughter in on your theory."

"You do not think I am wrong," I said quietly.

She shook her head. "This is… I had nearly forgotten about that incident. I wish I could."

"As do I."

We stood in silence for a few moments, both of us wrapped up in our own unpleasant thoughts. "And what about the lesser gods you are searching for? Have you seen any sign of them?" she finally asked.

I shook my head. "Not a thing."

"I like Eiar very much. She's kind." She paused. "She created the black flowers that only grow near that statue of Hades. Did you know that?" she asked quietly.

"I did not. I am still looking. Keep the faith. They are immortals. They are stronger than many of you higher gods give them credit for," I said.

She nodded. "I will see what I can get out of this one. Thank you, Eunomia."

I left her, reappearing back at the docks. Brennan was waiting where we'd stashed our bags, fully dressed now. He handed my bag to me.

"Where next, Tink?"

"Tokyo," I said, taking his hand, surreptitiously taking Clair's hand behind my back, aware that my team was standing there, just inside the shadows. He should have sensed them, that close. I realized the only reason he hadn't was because he was distracted, waiting for me to return. He was definitely not using the senses associated with being an immortal, senses any of us have. And here I had promised him to help him learn more about our world. I would have to do better.

"Here we go," I said, and I focused.

When we rematerialized in Tokyo, the first thing that hit me was the noise. Like any busy city, there was the never-ending cacophony of voices, the rumble of cars and buses, horns honking. And, like any big city, Tokyo had a sound all its own, a rhythm, a tone that no other city had.

Despite my general dislike for the modern era, even I had to admit that Tokyo was a marvel. I felt like a child each time I had reason to come to the city, which really was not often enough. Brennan kept his hand in mine and started pulling me out of the alley, toward the street.

Lights. So many lights. Large screens displayed with advertisements, videos. People swarmed around us, walking much faster than we did. I glanced over at Brennan to see him looking around in wonder, as if he did not know where to look first. I smiled, shaking off, for the moment at least, my worry over my sisters and their association with the lost souls.

"This is your first time here?" I asked, and he nodded, still looking around. I continued watching him as he took it all in, and laughed a bit. I tugged his hand. "Come on, Cub. If you have not yet experienced Tokyo street food, we need to remedy that immediately."

"Your lost soul," he reminded me as he let me tug him along.

"It will take time to get a reading, and the only way I am able to get one of those is to wander around until I pick something up, especially in a place this populous." Here, I would be looking for the soul of the concubine, and this entire city was hers for a time. She was active in many areas, including downtown Tokyo, where she'd died. It was as good a place to begin my search as any. "We may as well have some fun while we work."

He smiled then, and my entire body warmed. He squeezed my hand and let me lead him to the corner, where there was a small street-side restaurant selling takoyaki. I held up a finger, indicating I wanted one order of them, and the vendor nodded. I pulled out a few Yen coins and handed them to the vendor as the doughy balls fried.

"Where did you get the money?" Brennan asked.

"I try to keep a bit of as many different types of currency on hand as possible. It is inconvenient having to rematerialize in a place in not have any cash," I explained.

"Always prepared, huh Tink?" he asked with a grin.

"Like the good soldier I am, apparently," I answered.

The vendor handed over a small cardboard basket lined with waxed paper and piled high with takoyaki, as well as some vegetables and a sauce similar to mayonnaise. I thanked him in Japanese, and the vendor bowed his head a little and we made our way to a small table.

"Can't we just walk and eat?" Brennan asked as he sat down.

"It is considered rude to eat and walk here," I said. "Sit. Enjoy. We have time."

He smiled at me. "That 'good soldier' crack. She said that like she thought it would bother you," he said as I held the basket out, indicating he should take some. He plucked one ball from the top of the pile and dipped it into the sauce. I watched as he bit into it, chewed it. "What is this, anyway?" he asked helping himself to a few more morsels.

"Octopus balls," I said, and watched as he stopped in mid-chew. I laughed.

"Uh…"

"Pieces of octopus meat. In a ball of dough. Not… what it is you were thinking of," I said, still smiling.

"Mean, Tink. I almost felt sorry for the poor guy. Do octopi even have balls?"

"I have never thought about it," I said.

"These are good, though," he said, finishing chewing.

"She knew it would bother me," I answered, continuing our conversation and popping a bite into my mouth.

"Why?"

"It was something they used to tease me with, that I did whatever Hades and the Furies commanded. That I was a slave more than anything else. 'The good soldier,'" I repeated. "It does not bother me anymore. I *am* a good soldier."

"None better," Brennan said. We finished and walked on, and I tossed the empty basket in a trash can. "What's that one selling?" he asked, pointing to another vendor. I smiled. I had the feeling we'd be eating our way down the street.

"The vendors here are going to adore you," I said, and he laughed. "He is selling spiced pork."

"Meat. Yes. I want that then," Brennan said, and I ordered, and we sat as Brennan dug into the fragrant pork.

"Good?" I asked.

"Amazing," he said, swallowing a mouthful. "Want some?" he held the fork out to me, and I shook my head.

The pork having been consumed, we walked on, and I kept myself open for any sign of an energy signature from my lost soul, and Brennan stopped at nearly every food cart and ordered something. He was smiling, happy. Relaxed. I did not often see him this way, almost childlike in his enthusiasm. To my surprise, I found myself smiling and laughing much more than I usually did, caught up in his good mood.

"I think I love this city," he said after finishing off some noodles.

"Surrounded by food, I am sure you do," I said, and he laughed.

"It's not just that. That'a part of it, sure," he said. "It's everything. The lights, the crowds… everything. I feel like I can disappear here."

I watched him, and his gaze met mine. "It feels good, does it not?"

He nodded. "It does. And you knew I needed this. We could have hunted for your soul anywhere in this city. You put us here."

"I knew," I agreed. "And I am hoping you accept it as the peace offering it is. I did not expect it to bother you when I left without saying anything to you. I did not think."

"Apology accepted. I'm sorry for expecting things of you I shouldn't. I know you're different. I need to remember it more often."

"I had a feeling you would love it here," I said.

"How? How do you know me so well, Tink?"

I smiled. "I pay attention."

The comfortable mood between us deepened, shifting to something else as we stood there, neither of us looking away. Warmth spread from my center until every part of my body seemed to be flushed, yet a shiver worked its way up my spine.

It was almost difficult to breathe.

"You pay attention," he said quietly, his eyes still on mine. "That night you made me run. Remember that?"

"Of course," I said, barely able to find my voice under his intense gaze.

"No one's ever done something like that for me."

"You are usually the one taking care of everyone else. Sometimes the caregiver is the one who needs to be taken care of," I said softly. "You are so near breaking, the weight of your life heavy on your shoulders. I see it."

"Is that why you let Molly send me with you? You could have argued with her, and she probably would have given in, eventually."

"That first time, yes. This time… this time I barely argued at all. You are good company." I paused. "I am upset over my sisters… what they represent, what I suspect they are doing, should not be. So perhaps I am selfish. I wanted to be with someone who made me feel a little less morose as well."

"Selfish is not a word I'd use to describe you, Eunomia," he said.

Gods, his eyes. Intense. They reminded me of the last time I'd stood looking out over the Atlantic Ocean, the same blue, the same unbridled turbulence.

"I am glad you think so," I said softly.

I could not take it anymore. I could not stand there with him, with him looking at me the way he was. I could not take the way every system in my body seemed thrown into confusion by him. I shook my head a little, as if that would clear it.

His scent surrounded me, and I forced myself to take a small step away from him. "We should keep walking," I managed, and he nodded, tearing his gaze away from mine.

We walked on, and he took my hand again. I knew this about the shifter, that physical contact was something he craved when he felt close to someone. He'd been that way with Mollis. He was the type who easily hugged his friends. Artemis was the same way. I supposed it was the shifter side of them, that physical aspect of their personalities.

I tried to halt my train of thought before it went exactly where I did not want it to go.

The strangest thing was, I tend to be a very hands-off individual. Usually, if I was touching someone, it was because I was injuring or capturing them. Yet with him, it felt natural to hold hands.

"That newspaper vendor has comic books," Brennan said, looking across the street.

"Let's keep going," I said, an idea forming in my mind. "Come on. There's something you might be interested in seeing."

He choked back a laugh. "Oh, I can think of something I'd like to see," he said with a bit of a growl in his voice, and I gave him a withering glare.

"Not that, shifter."

"I would be interested in seeing it, Tink," he said with a wink, and I felt my face burn.

I pulled my hand out of his, and he laughed and took it back. I could not help myself. I laughed.

"Idiot," I muttered, and he grinned. "Just for that, I should not take you where I was going to take you."

"But you will," he said.

"I will," I grumbled. We walked down the street, and turned a corner. I hoped it was still there. When I looked down the street, I could see the large sign, the floodlights dancing in the sky above the store. I pulled him toward it, and we stood in front of the bright orange storefront, its plate-glass windows plastered with comic book covers. He stood before them in awe, and I smiled and pulled him inside the shop.

It was one of the largest comic shops I had ever seen. I have never read a comic book, but I once chased a soul into this exact shop, and remembered thinking at the time that if this were the type of thing I was interested in, I could happily spend hours there. It was like a playground; comic books everywhere, books, action figures, t-shirts… all the types of things Brennan collected.

"Whoa," he breathed, looking around. He looked like a child faced with an endless offering of sweets, and I laughed.

"Do you like it?"

"Not as much as that other thing I was hoping to see, but it's pretty damn awesome, Tink," he murmured, and I blushed. "I am going to go into so much debt here."

He wandered the aisles, and I followed along, enjoying seeing him so loose, so relaxed. And if I glared at more than a few young women who practically looked like they wanted to lick him, it was not as if he had to know that.

I did not understand it myself.

"Are they in Japanese or English?" I asked, watching him flip through another long cardboard box.

"They have some of both," he answered. He was already carrying a decent sized stack of comics, and I took them from him so he could look more easily. "Thanks," he said, and I nodded.

"What's back there?" I asked, nodding toward an area I'd just seen a young man go through with a black curtain over the door.

"Adult comics," Brennan said.

"There is such a thing?"

"Yeah."

"Have you read any of those?" I teased, surprising myself.

He laughed a little, and I noted with some satisfaction that he was blushing. At least I was not the only one now. "No."

"Are you sure?"

He laughed. "Comic book boobs don't exactly do it for me, you know?"

"How do these women even stand up straight?" I asked, nodding toward a superhero comic. The female on the cover could have used her breasts as effective flotation devices.

Brennan shook his head.

"Can I ask you something?"

"Sure."

"Is that what males actually fantasize about?"

He cleared his throat. "Some do, sure."

I looked at him questioningly.

"I don't."

Then I looked at him in disbelief, and he laughed. "I mean, I'm not saying that's not appreciated or anything. I'm just saying that I tend to be drawn more to scary badasses than huge boobs."

"If the scary badass had big boobs?" I asked, and he laughed.

Then he leaned down toward me, lowering his mouth to my ear so only I could hear him. "I'm more of an ass man, actually. And yours is a work of art, Tink." With that, he stood up straight and walked away, leaving me blushing and stammering behind him. I heard him chuckle, and made myself follow him. "I mean, have you ever looked at your ass?"

"No, I have not," I answer icily, trying to fight that giddiness running through me.

"Well, I have. Round, high…" he held his hands up, curved as if he was cradling something in them.

"Oh for the love of Hades. Stop that," I hissed, and he laughed. I was sure I was approximately the shade of Superman's cape by then.

"In fact, I should be walking behind you…" he said, and I smacked his arm.

"You are enjoying this, aren't you?" I asked.

"Very much, Eunomia. I have never seen you anything other than completely controlled."

"I am still completely controlled," I argued, standing straighter.

He smiled. "Mhmm. But every once in a while, that control cracks a little, and you get all flustered, like that night we went out with Rayna. I wonder how flustered I can make you."

Very. Extremely, I thought to myself. "Cub, I am thousands of years old. Your commentary about my behind is not going to make me lose control."

He grinned. "Well. I'll just have to try harder, huh?" He tuned away, strolling down another row of comics.

I followed him wordlessly through the store, and he finished his shopping by grabbing a few action figures for Sean. He paid for his purchases, then took my hand and we left the store, walking down the street toward our hotel.

"No sign of your lost soul?" he asked me, and I shook my head.

"We will try again in the morning. It is a large city. He could be anywhere."

"And you were entertaining me. I should have let you work more," he said apologetically.

I squeezed his hand a little. "I had fun as well. It was nice."

We walked in silence until we reached our hotel, and he opened the door for me, followed me to the front desk where we checked in, then the elevator. When we got in, I noticed that he was grinning.

"What?" I demanded as I hit the button for our floor.

"I like following you. Really, really nice view."

I shook my head and looked away. Damn it all, I was blushing again.

He laughed, and his laugh was low, a little dangerous-sounding to my oversensitized mind.

"Behave, Cub," I managed, unable to look up at him.

"What fun is that?"

He was a hopeless flirt. I knew this. And I had to remind myself that to him, this was fun. It was not the way I was taking it.

And how I was taking it was a shock to me. The way my body responded to his voice, to his gaze. The way my stomach twisted when he was near.

This was starting to look like a dumb idea, bringing him with me.

I got off the elevator, making my way quickly to our room, and I unlocked the door. He came in behind me, tossed his bag on the bed he'd claimed as his, the bed nearest to the door.

"I'm sorry. I'm not trying to make you mad," he said.

"You are not making me mad," I answered, kicking my boots off.

"You seem on edge."

"This flirting side of you makes me feel awkward. And this entire situation with my sisters and these lost souls…" I shook my head.

His expression sobered. "I'm sorry, Eunomia. It wasn't my intention to make you feel that way, and you have enough on your mind."

"It's not… I enjoy it, Brennan. I am not used to it, is all. Not from you," I added.

"Do you want me to stop?"

I shrugged. "I am confused."

"By me?"

"By everything right now," I said, looking away.

He was silent, and then he came over to me and raised my chin gently with his finger tips. "Hey."

I could not breathe.

"Let's try to alleviate any confusion you have about me right now then," he said. "I am definitely flirting with you, Eunomia. I am doing it because I'm attracted to you. You're a sexy, alluring, terrifying warrior and one of the kindest, most selfless beings I've ever known. I don't flirt a whole lot anymore. I used to do it quite often and I think I was good at it, based on how often it got me what I wanted. I was pretty sure I was done doing that, but here you are, and I am more than happy to make a fool of myself for you. If you want me to stop, if it makes you feel uncomfortable, I will stop. If you enjoy it, I will keep doing it. Okay?"

I stared at him.

"What?"

"You are strange."

"What's so strange about me?"

I breathed out, well aware of how close he still stood to me. "Most people do not understand that I need things like that spelled out for me."

He smiled a little. "You're not the only one who pays attention."

I looked down.

"And as someone who pays attention, I can also tell that you've got the weight of the world on your shoulders right now. You talk about me looking like I'm about to break. I think you're nearly there now."

I gave a small nod.

"So, tell me. What does an immortal badass do to unwind? What makes you feel less crazy, Tink?"

"Flying," I said without hesitation, finally looking up at him.

"Flying?"

I nodded. "It is impossible to feel weighed down when you soar among the clouds."

He smiled and held his hand out to me. "Get us up to the roof. I haven't been a bird in a while."

I shook my head a little and rested my hand in his, and in the next breath, we were on the roof of our hotel skyscraper, moonless night sky dark around us. Brennan started shucking clothing, and I shrugged out of my coat. When I turned around, a huge black hawk was perched on the edge of the roof, black feathers shining by the meager light from below, familiar blue eyes looking out at me over a deadly-looking yellow beak.

I smiled at him. "Let's fly." We rose into the sky. Each flap of my wings, each meter I put between myself and the world below made me feel lighter. Saner. Better. And Brennan flew at my side, and when I pulled up and then dove out toward the coast, he was right with me, and we soared and the world and its worries fell away.

Over the water, I pushed myself, flying fast, diving toward the water only to pull up at the last moment and soar back up into the sky. I flew in lazy loops, upside down, in spirals. My wings stretched, my body became more fluid, and if I flew fast enough, it almost felt as if I could leave everything behind. Brennan twisted, turned, soared with me, and at one point, as we pulled up out of yet another dive toward the water, he let out an exultant shriek, shattering the still night, and I laughed.

We flew. And in that moment, I felt closer to him than I have ever felt to anyone in my entire existence.

And I knew I was lost.

I veered toward the city, and we flew above Tokyo. The lights were no less beautiful from above, though the noise and frenetic activity did not reach us. We circled around several times, racing one another, seeing whose wings were more powerful. For the most part, we stayed side-by-side. My heart pounded, and my body felt languid, more relaxed than I had at any time in recent memory.

We flew until my wings grew tired, and when that happened, I swooped back toward the roof of our hotel, and landed, breathless, turning, looking out over the city to let Brennan dress in some privacy. I could hear him. Hear shuffling, his zipper.

The city was bright beneath us, the roof solid beneath my feet, yet I still felt as if I was soaring. I sighed in contentment, and took it all in. Brennan stepped behind me and related his hands on my shoulders, rubbed them gently.

"I have never seen a hawk quite that size," I said, at a loss for words at the feel of his hands on me.

"Are you saying I'm the biggest you've ever seen, Tink?" he asked, and I could hear the teasing note in his voice.

"Quite impressive," I said, crossing my arms over my body as shiver raced up my spine.

He did not answer, and his hands gently brushed the sides of my neck, and a tremor ran through me.

Oh, gods. I could not breathe. He rested his forehead on the top of my head, and I could hear him breathing me in. He rubbed his face against my hair, and I could feel his breath on the shell of my ear as he lowered his face to the side of my neck.

The sensation of his warm lips kissing the pulse point at the side of my neck thew my entire system into chaos and a small sound escaped me, something between a moan and a strangled cry. At the sound, he groaned and turned me around, swiftly. And then his lips were on mine, soft, warm, giving me a chance to run if I wanted to. And I did not. I pulled him to me, burying my fingers in his hair, kissing him like a woman possessed, and he kissed me back just as hungrily, kissing me, tasting me, our kiss deepening until I was sure I was about to die from the way my heart was pounding. He held my body tightly to his, and ravaged my mouth, and trailed hot kisses across my jaw and down my neck, to that place that had started this whole thing.

"Brennan," I breathed.

He released a low chuckle, and it vibrated against my skin. "Not 'Cub' now, huh?" he teased, and I shook my head.

He pressed another kiss, warm and sweet, to my lips, then gently released me and stepped back.

"Is this awkward?" he asked me, eyes on mine.

"Not at this moment, no," I answered. "Ask me in the morning."

He smiled. "Maybe I won't give you a chance to think about it."

"I do not want to think about it."

He smiled, and took my hand, and I rematerialized us back to our room, and the first thing my gaze took in was the two twin beds. I did not know what he expected now. "I…" I began helplessly.

His gaze followed mine, to the beds. "We're taking this slow, Eunomia. I refuse to mess this up."

I took a breath of relief, and he chuckled. "Not that I am not practically dying for you right now," I said quickly, needing, wanting him to know that he affected me.

How bizarre was that, that I actually wanted him to see how weak he made me?

He smiled. "Glad to hear it. I'm going to need a cold shower before I go to sleep."

"That was a mental picture I did not need right now," I said, and he laughed and lowered his face to mine, claimed my mouth briefly, and I let myself fall into him.

He wandered off to the shower after breaking our kiss, and I sank into my bed, lazily watching the talk show on the television and smiling to myself at the memory of his lips, the way we'd flown together.

.

CHAPTER SIXTEEN

I was awakened by a hand gently shaking my hip, and I opened my eyes to see the sun shining brightly into our room, Brennan sitting on the edge of my bed.

"Hey," he said.

"Hey," I answered. "I slept the sleep of the dead, I think."

He laughed. "You did. I came back in here after my shower and you were in dreamland already. I have a meeting this morning with the guy in charge of the Tokyo bureau for the supernatural affairs office. I just wanted to let you know I was leaving."

I looked him over. He was wearing his suit, and I reached out and ran my fingers over the dark tie.

"Eunomia," he said.

"Hm?"

"I don't suppose you're going to wait for me before you go looking for your soul today?"

"No."

He laughed a little. "Would it make any sense to argue with you and ask you to just wait for me? I hate you going after theses assholes alone."

I shook my head. I knew this was one of those moments, one that would set the pattern and tone for whatever there was between us. I can lie to just about anyone without qualms. I do not like lying to Mollis, keeping things from her, yet I was doing so anyway.

Him, I could not lie to. Not anymore. Not now, when I'd admitted to myself what he meant to me. That he'd made me feel something I had never felt for another being.

"I need to tell you something," I said softly. "Do you have a minute?"

"I have as much time as you need," he said, and it warmed me, knowing he meant it completely.

I sat up and held my hands out to him. "Come with me."

He put his hands in mine, and I rematerialized us to a subway station where I'd told my lost souls to wait for me. My New Guardians.

I spied them though the crowd, sitting on a bench, watching the crowds. I led Brennan toward them.

"I am not alone," I told him quietly as we approached Quinn, Claire, Cathleen, and Erin.

"I don't…" he said, trailing off, then his brow furrowed as he felt something.

"You feel them?" I asked. He gave a small nod. "Focus. Hard. Put everything into it. You are an Aether Immortal. You have been healed by my Lady's blood. Open yourself up. See the things our kind can see."

I watched as he focused. "I feel them more strongly, but…"

"Keep trying. I want you to see. I want you to know," I whispered, and he met my eyes, and nodded. "You are a shifter. Grandson of Artemis. You have senses many can only dream of. Use them."

He looked toward where he sensed my team, and Quinn looked at me questioningly.

"You sure about this?" he asked me.

"I am."

"He won't betray you?"

"I would never betray her," Brennan said, looking toward Quinn's voice. And I saw it. I saw the moment his sight opened up, and he saw the souls before him.

"Holy shit," he muttered the next second. Then he looked at me. "Explain, Tink."

"Tink?" Quinn asked with a laugh.

"Quiet," I told him. And I explained. I explained about them, and how I'd found them, and what they did, and the ways they'd helped me. I explained why I had kept them from Mollis, that I feared she would insist on them being imprisoned with the rest of the souls, and how I was trying to understand how they could possibly exist without her knowledge.

"She would see them as a threat," he said quietly. "She could very well be right."

"She would. And she would have every right to. But they are not. They are mine. Loyal. I cannot explain them. The only theory I have is that Nyx had some foresight, that she saw a situation like this arising, in which there were not enough of my kind to maintain the systems as they are. And maybe she allowed for the creation of New Guardians, those who would have a personal reason for wanting to help those who remained. I have no idea if it is right. It fits with what I know of my Creator, but it is only a guess," I admitted.

He was quiet for several long moments. "She hates being lied to, Eunomia," he finally said.

"I know. I just need time," I said. "I need to know if there are more out there. It would be lovely if I had an explanation for why they are here, other than a guess."

"She'll know the second she looks at me now," he said.

"I know. I will tell her about them when I make it back to Detroit. Do you trust me?"

He looked at me, finally turning away from the New Guardians. "Of course I do. I trust you, Eunomia. And I trust your judgment. And I'm glad you're not doing this shit on your own. I'm glad you have them," he said. "Thank you for telling me."

"I did not want to lie to you," I said quietly.

He took my hand in his. "And I won't lie to you, either. And I won't betray the trust you just put in me. But you need to tell Molly before this becomes a mess."

"I know. I will."

"Okay. I need to get to my meeting, and I'll see you after and we'll figure it out." I nodded, and he lowered his lips, brushed a quick kiss across my lips. "Stay safe, okay?"

"I will. I will see you in a while."

He nodded, then looked at Quinn and the others. "Keep her safe."

"We intend to," Claire said, and the others nodded.

"Not that she needs us, especially," Quinn added.

Brennan smiled then. "True," he said, and Quinn laughed. He looked back at me. "Lunch? One o'clock? Sushi? That place across the street from our hotel?"

I nodded, and he grinned. One final kiss, and he was walking through the throngs of people, heading to the train he needed to catch for his meeting.

I turned to my New Guardians. "All right. Let's look for our American monster. All of his murders took place here in Tokyo and the surrounding areas. He murdered Japanese women, with the twisted notion that he would keep his 'enemies' from the second human World War from procreating if he killed all of their women," I said, rolling my eyes.

"What an asshole," Quinn muttered. "How'd he finally meet his end?'

I smiled. "He happened to run across Lord Hades when Hades was in town enjoying a meal... and some human companionship, if you know what I mean. Hades caught him in the act, killed him, escorted his soul to the Nether personally, then judged and punished him."

"Wow."

"Indeed. Hades really did not get much time off, and I think he was even more enraged to have it interrupted," I said with a shrug.

Quinn shook his head. "This is all completely nuts. So where do we start?"

"We walk. Hades caught him near Lake Tama. We will relocate there, and see if he still haunts the place of his death." I took their hands, and we rematerialized on the winding road near the reservoir. There were trees here, sports fields. There were several so-called "love hotels" in this area, the Japanese equivalent of the cheap motels I'd seen in the States. Hades had been in one of those when he'd been interrupted by the American murderer, who had been there as well, choosing his next target.

"His name was Robert Mordell," I said as I started walking, Quinn and the others arrayed around me. "He murdered thirty-nine Japanese women of all ages in his insane crusade against those he saw as enemies. He did it for forty years. One per year, and he would stalk her for months beforehand in preparation. Grown women. Elderly widows. Young girls. My Queen will be especially glad to have this one returned to her," I finished, thinking of Molly and her ongoing quest to make the world, especially her own city, a better, safer place for women. Men like the one I was tracking now symbolized the entire reason she'd started on the path she was on. I can only imagine that she never envisioned ending up quite where she was now.

We walked, and soon, I felt it. "He has been here," I said quietly. We walked on, toward the end of the lake, where the trail was less-trafficked, weeds and saplings growing up in the cracking concrete, the concrete turning to rubble the further off the main road we went. His energy signature grew stronger, and when I saw where we were heading, I shook my head.

"What?" Quinn asked.

"He returned to the building where Hades killed him," I said, nodding to the dilapidated structure, long abandoned, standing before us.

"What was it?"

"Love hotel. Like a motel or pleasure house, depending on which term you like."

"A whorehouse?"

I shook my head. "No. They had to bring their own partners," I said, and Cathleen crossed herself. She did that whenever she heard something that was apparently not looked upon well by her faith. It amused me, considering that I knew very well who judged her, and Mollis did not care about things like that.

We trudged toward the love hotel, its white exterior stained and sooty, graffiti marking the walls. Trash was strewn all around the building, and a large chest of drawers lay across the porch, partially blocking the entry door. Its blue-tiled roof still gleamed in the weak sunlight. I noted, absentmindedly, the bodies of several large crows nearby as well.

I headed toward the door, ducked inside, and my New Guardians followed me. The entry room, with its long wooden counter where guests would check in, was just as full of trash and debris as the outside. I stepped over it gingerly, pulling both of my Netherblades from my sheath, then re-zipping my coat and pulling the cowl up, covering my head, nose, and mouth, leaving only my eyes visible. I knew, after so much time doing this, that even as small in stature as I am, for whatever reason the cowl adds to the menace beings see when they look at me. And I wanted this one to be afraid.

Perhaps I needed to feel tougher than I did at the moment. It was like stepping into a costume the moment my face was covered, and it centered me.

His energy signature was strong here.

I walked down the corridor, peering into the first room on my left. It was empty, its gaudy orange wallpaper still bright, and an elaborately ugly bed sat in the center of the room. I exchanged a look with Quinn, who just shook his head. The room across the hall, on my left, was wallpapered in red, with a shiny black bed. Mirrors shone from the ceiling. Many of them were cracked, I noted.

The building smelled dank. Almost putrid. It smelled of filth and decay. We walked a few more steps, and I stopped short.

"What?" Quinn whispered on my left.

"There are others here," I said in an almost imperceptible voice.

Lesser gods.

What in the Nether were they doing here? And then it hit me, that they were working with my sisters, with Mollis's lost souls.

I was walking into a situation where I would be facing the soul of a serial-killer and several powerful beings who were likely aiding him. I paused for a moment, considering it. I could go back and get Brennan. I could call Mollis or Tisiphone.

No, I decided. If the lesser gods had chosen to side with monsters, I would show them what a monster truly was. And I knew my New Guardians could handle Mordell.

I took a breath and walked forward. "Go after Mordell," I said quietly. "Leave the others to me."

The door in front of us was closed, and I pulled my foot back and kicked it in and my team flooded into the room around me. Robert Mordell stood there, and he laughed. With him was the other soul from Japan I'd been seeking, Ayame Takahashi.

And he was powerful. Too powerful. Not merely corporeal. Not merely undead. *More.*

I had a moment to glance toward where I felt the other lesser immortals, and what I saw nearly made my heart stop. They were weak. Beaten. Bound. Two of the four, the goddesses of Autumn and Winter, had ragged slices down the center of their chests. Dead, but not truly. Lost to this realm, at the very least, because they would resurrect in the world of the gods, and they would be trapped there.

And it hit me.

"No," I murmured, and in that instant, Mordell charged me as my New Guardians fought with Ayame. I met him, slashing up and out at him, and he knocked my hand away, struck out at me with a knife of his own. Not a Netherblade, luckily. I smacked his arm aside, stabbed up with my left hand while slashing across his throat with my left. I managed to cut him, but he shoved me back, and I hit the wall. Next to where I was, a gaudy bed was tucked into a wall alcove. The wallpaper in this room was black and white, images of nude women.

"You have the world's most horrible taste. Of all the places in the world, you chose this one?" I asked, leaping forward and stabbing at his stomach. I caught him, and he grunted and shoved me back again. I kicked, and it was almost like kicking a brick wall. The things he'd done to gain this power, this strength… I felt coldness settle over me, and my heart slowed, and I could breathe again as I went on automatic, as I let my body do what I was created to do.

As I punished him.

I moved, not thinking, not really feeling it when he slashed across my arm, my hand. I felt my blood dripping down my arm as I stabbed him in the chest and he screamed. He pushed me back, and I had a moment to peek at my team, who were holding their own against Ayame. I was relieved she was not as far along in his process of becoming undead as Mordell was.

And if that was the case, who had taken the heart of the second goddess that had been sliced open?

Because that was how this happened. Still-beating hearts were eaten by those wanting to achieve undeath.

I never stopped to think about what would happen if one could devour the heart of a god.

I launched myself at Mordell again, a flurry of stabs. He shoved me back in rage, grabbed my arm and pulled it back, hard, and I felt my shoulder dislocate.

I refused to scream, even as the agony washed over me. He backed up, laughing.

And that was his mistake.

I just watched him, pulled my dangling arm with my good hand, and popped my shoulder back into place.

"Fuck," he growled, lunging at me again, and this time he did so in earnest, not toying with me, not prolonging things the way he'd always done with his victims. He fought me like a man possessed, desperate, fearful, angry. My body wept blood. Cuts crossed my sides, my arms, my throat. I was weakening, but I was winning.

I glanced to the side to see Quinn victoriously wrapping the chain around Ayame's wrists.

And in that moment, everything changed.

Two of my sisters, Delo and Anthousa, appeared behind my team, and each stabbed one New Guardian, then another.

My team was down, lying beside their prey, in agony as Anthousa stabbed them, over and over and over again. I quickly stabbed my knife into Mordell's throat, wrapped my own chain around his wrists, keeping him in agony and out of the fight.

I had one dagger left, and two deranged sisters coming at me. I was weak, bleeding, and furious for my team, who lay there weak and gasping in pain, taken out of the fight by the agony of having my sisters' Netherblades used so ruthlessly upon them.

"Oh, little sister. Your game ends now," Delo said. "You have lived like a good soldier, but your time is done."

"You can't kill me," I said, my voice stronger than I felt.

221

Anthousa smiled. "No. But we can use you."

"Like them?" I asked, nodding toward the captive lesser gods, and Delo smiled. It was all the confirmation I needed. "You are vile."

"We are survivors. And your pretender Queen will not be allowed to hold what she never should have had."

"You are kidding me, surely? And how are you alive? She killed you. Others watched her do so."

Anthousa laughed. "After seeing her use that damned blade against our other sisters, we smartened up. It is very easy to make it look like you fell to dust. All we did was relocate before she cut through us. It hurt, to let her injure us. But we lived. And here we are."

"But not all of you," I said, feeling a cold smile in on my lips. "I took care of two of you already."

Delo's face became a mask of rage. "And that is where it ends. And believe me, zealot, you will suffer."

And they advanced on me. I was a flurry of movement, taken by the rage I hardly even knew I was feeling, determined to save those they held there. Determined to save myself. Angered I had been so stupid, that I'd walked into what was now clearly a trap.

It was not long before, despite the way they attacked me, Anthousa fell and became dust. Whether it was an act or for real, I could not be sure, but Delo's enraged scream convinced me I had actually succeeded in ending her life in the human realm. She would live, but in the realm of the immortals, the realm we here in this realm only gained access to upon the failure of our bodies in this world.

We fought, Delo and I, and we both bled. I fought her like a woman possessed, keeping a hand on her so she could not rematerialize as I started to feel the tide turn. I was doing well. She fell, breathing hard, and I decided it was my chance to get the injured out. I shed my jacket and grabbed two of the lesser gods, preparing to fly them out and get them out of the room at least, away from Delo.

I had just risen into the air when there was a weight on my back, on my wing, from behind, and I felt the bones in my wing snap as Mordell attacked me. Delos still lay there, but she'd freed Mordell from my chain as she tried to regain her feet. I dropped the lesser gods, and a scream escaped my lips. I saw Mordell grin, and the wicked knife he carried slashed, not at my body, but at my already broken wing, and I watched in agony and horror as the leathery appendage fell to the floor beside me.

I screeched, and lunged, both hands around the handle of my dagger, and I stabbed him through the eye as he struck out with his own blade. I felt the cut across my shoulder, but he fell just the same, gurgling, the handle of my dagger sticking out of his face. I advanced on my sister. I was seeing spots in front of me. Everything felt like slow motion, and I was dizzy. She still lay there, gasping, her breath raspy, and I picked my other dagger, the one Mordell had pulled from his body after she'd freed him, and I brought it down to her stomach and she screamed in agony.

I was almost out. I wrapped my chain around Mordell's wrists one more time.

I fell down onto my sister, and I laughed, madness, pain, fear setting in. My other wing, the one I had left, had been bashed at some point during the struggle, and hung limply.

I could feel the blackness coming to me.

I pulled my phone out of my pocket and hit the number of someone I knew could easily find us, because we were so near water.

"Lake Tama, Tokyo. Help. Love hotel," I managed, and the phone fell from my hand. My sister had stopped moving beneath me, and I followed her into unconsciousness.

CHAPTER SEVENTEEN

Slowly, as if I was moving through quicksand, I eventually pulled myself out of the darkness. Out of the cold, toward warmth. Out of the anger and hurt and fear toward something better.

I dipped in and out of consciousness, every once in a while catching bits and pieces of conversation, cool hands on my forehead. My Queen, murmuring how sorry she was, pushing my hair back off of my face. I wanted to ask her what she was apologizing for, but consciousness floated away from me, overtaken by the pain.

The most constant presence was the warm one that never seemed far away, talking to me in a low voice, talking about nothing, but talking just the same. I knew I would not die. I knew I would live, but I have never been so tired, and so, I let myself be pulled under until I was strong enough to open my eyes.

And when I did, I knew immediately that I was in my room at the loft, lying on my stomach, and that Brennan was stretched out beside me on the narrow bed.

I tried to move, and he jerked awake.

"Hey! Hey. You're awake," he said, and, close as he was to me, I could feel his heart pounding.

"I am," I croaked. My mouth felt like sandpaper, and I felt dizzy from the wave of pain that tore through my body. "Hurts," I said, and Brennan gently got up, trying not to jostle me as the mattress shifted beneath him.

"Gaia and Meaghan put together this tea for the pain. They said you should drink the whole thing once you were conscious," he said.

He was pouring some liquid from a thermos.

"My wings have never hurt this badly," I said, still hoarse. "I think it'll be a while before we fly again, cub."

He was silent, and when I looked up at him, he was still as a statue. His eyes glistened with unshed tears, and I looked at him for a moment in confusion.

And then it came back to me.

Pain.

My wing falling to the floor.

My other wing crushed and useless.

I tried to see my back, to reassure myself that it was a nightmare. And I saw nothing. I closed my eyes, tried to breathe.

"Eunomia," Brennan's voice said, and I lowered my face to my pillow. A feeling came up in me, like my chest was being crushed, like I'd forgotten how to breathe, and a sob escaped me, and I forced my face deeper into my pillow in shame.

I have never cried. Not in my entire existence. Not really. I have felt tears come to my eyes in commiseration with those I care for. For myself? No.

And here I was, sobs wracking my body as Brennan knelt beside the bed and ran his fingers soothingly through my hair. I tried to stop. I tried, and the harder I tried, the harder it became.

"Let it out," he said softly. "It's just you and me here, and I sure the hell am not going to think less of you." The emotion in his voice, the knowledge that he knew how much it had meant to me, that I had lost something I would never get back… it was as if a floodgate opened, and then I did. I cried and it felt as if something inside of me was broken.

By the time I had no more tears to shed, I felt exhausted all over again. Everything hurt. Brennan gently helped me sit up, and I bit my tongue, hard, to keep from crying out from the pain in my back. He wordlessly handed me the cup with the tea from Gaia in it, and held me up, sitting beside me as I drank it.

"This is h-horrid," I said numbly as I downed the tea.

"It smells pretty bad, too," he said.

"What did they do to me? To my wings?"

He was quiet for a moment. "One of them was cut off in Tokyo. Do you remember that?"

"I know. I remember. And the other one was broken. But now…" I glanced back, able to see my back. I was wearing a tank top someone had modified, so it was cut below my shoulder blades, which was where my wings had been. Now, there was a huge bandage there.

"One wing was gone, and the other one was badly crushed. There was a bone left from the one that got cut off, and you just kept bleeding. Asclepias did surgery… he removed what was left of both of them completely and stitched you up, did some pretty massive healing. You were a mess, Tink," he said, and his voice was rough, full of emotion.

I rested my hand on his thigh.

"I owe him my thanks."

"There's plenty of time. You need more rest," he said, taking my hand in his. We were silent for several long moments. "You can grow new ones, right? If you change again, you can make them appear. Right?"

I shook my head. "I cannot change something that is not there. I cannot make something appear out of nothing. The skies are lost to me now," I said, biting my lip from having another ridiculous crying jag.

"I'm sorry. I hoped—"

"I know. Thank you," I said, and he gently squeezed my hand. "I am tired."

"Sleep, Tink. I'll be here when you wake up."

I nodded, and he gently lowered me back into the bed, on my stomach so I would not put any weight on my injuries.

I was about to drift away when my eyes shot open.

"My New Guardians! They were hurt—"

"It's okay. It's okay," Brennan said soothingly. "When Triton brought me with him, your Guardians were still there. They seemed to be recovering — they were messed up pretty badly — but they refused to leave your side. Triton called Molly, and she kicked the shit out of your sister and then took her back to the Netherwoods. Triton and I sat with you, and your Guardians told me what happened."

"Did Triton see them?" I asked.

He shook his head. "He thought I was nuts, I think."

I did not answer for a few moments, turning it all over in my head. "So Mollis knows about them now," I finally said.

"Yeah. Molly went back to find them after we had you back here and Asclepias was sure you weren't going anywhere," he said, his voice becoming rough, as if he was holding back some kind of emotion. "I don't know what she did with them. She hasn't said anything to me about it."

"That probably is not a good sign," I said.

"Probably not," he agreed. "We'll deal with it when you're better. Okay?"

I nodded. And then I slept, letting my pain and exhaustion pull me under once again.

The next time I woke, it was to feel someone changing the bandages across my back. I turned my head slightly to see Brennan there again.

"Shouldn't Asclepias be doing that?"

"I got a little territorial, I guess," he said, gently applying new gauze.

"Territorial?"

"Last time he was here, he pulled one of the bandages off and you jerked like it hurt you… and I went all psycho panther. My grandma got between us."

I shook my head, and he laughed. "So now no one else is allowed in here, except Molly."

"You are insane," I said.

"Sometimes," he agreed.

"How long have I been asleep? How long ago did it all happen?"

He finished applying a new gauze pad, and he taped it down with white tape. "You've been in and out of consciousness for five days."

"Is that all? It felt longer," I said. And I started sitting up. He moved to help me, and I held my hand up, stalling any help from him. I was stiff, and sore, but Asclepias's skill and my own healing abilities had worked.

"You're such a badass," he said, and even though I was looking down, I could hear the smile in his voice.

"Please tell me you were not the one who washed me," I said.

"No. That was Molly. She wouldn't let anyone else do it."

Well. That was all right. We had seen one another through everything else. I could stand my Queen and friend doing that for me, at least.

"I want to dress. It is time to get up."

"I'll help."

"Over my dead body, cub," I said, standing up all the way.

"I don't want to even think about your dead body, Tink," he said, coming up to me and taking my chin not exactly gently in his hand. "You scared the ever-loving fuck out of me, you know that? When Triton came to get me and bring me to you, and I saw you the way you looked… damn."

I raised my hand and put it over his. "And you think it would not have happened had you been with me?"

"Damn right," he said, lowering his hand to my lower back and gently pulling me toward him.

"It would have been so much worse, Brennan," I said. "So much worse. I was not distracted. I was not fearing too much for anyone else. If you had been there, I would not have focused. I would not have been able to finish them off. It would have been a loss. Do you understand what I am saying?"

He let out an irritated breath, and then he nodded. "Okay. You're what? A few thousand years old or something? I know better than to try to change your mind about anything by now."

I smiled up at him. "You've changed my mind about some things," I told him.

"Miracles do exist," he said wryly, and I laughed.

"Now go. I want to get dressed."

"They're all here, waiting for you to wake up."

"I know. I can feel them." He nodded and left, closing the door behind him. I knew he was waiting outside in case I needed him. It took me a while, but I eventually shrugged into a t-shirt, jeans, my jacket, which someone had saved from the love hotel and made thorough repairs to. I pulled my boots on, brushed my hair. I was pale from my healing, and I put on some make up, inspecting the new scars across my throat and the knuckles of my right hand as I did. Marks of honor. I'd nearly fallen, but emerged as the victor once again.

My Queen would know it all now. She'd spent time with me as I slept. I have no doubt that she had seen into my mind, whether she meant to or not. How she would handle the things I'd learned, the things I'd kept from her, I did not know.

I took a moment to steady myself, taking a deep breath, preparing myself for what would come next.

I opened the bedroom door, and Brennan pushed away from the wall he'd been leaning against, took my hand in his. I could see the entire team sitting around the loft. Mollis, her mate, Artemis, Megaera, Tisiphone, Gaia, Hephaestus, Meaghan, Stone, and Ada. The children ran around, as always, and imps stood at the windows, always on guard. Mollis's two Netherhounds lay near the door, and watched me as I walked down the stairs.

When I reached the bottom step, there were careful hugs from just about everyone. Tisiphone whispered how worried she'd been. Megaera congratulated me on my work. Triton was there as well, and he quickly thanked me for saving the lesser gods. Finally, it was Mollis and the demon, and Mollis stood there, arms crossed over her chest, her face like stone.

"My Queen," I said, stopping a few feet in front of where she stood.

"Eunomia," Mollis said, Our eyes met, and I knew. I steeled myself for what was coming. For what had to happen.

My Queen hates being lied to.

"You have done an admirable job of returning nearly half of the lost souls to me," she began. "You have captured three of your own sisters, who were working against me." She paused, and her face was an expressionless mask. "However, I see everything. I know everything. And what I know is this: you kept things from me. Important things. You lied to me. You chose to conceal the existence of beings who aided you, beings I had every right to know about."

"Yes," I answered quietly.

"Molly," Brennan began beside me, and I held my hand up. He was practically trembling in rage.

"Do you have anything to say?" she asked me, and I shook my head.

"I did what I believed I had to. I have never worked for anyone but you."

"And yet you lied. I refuse to have anyone in my home, in my inner circle, in my family, who would dare to lie to me as you have. With that in mind, you are officially exiled. You will not set foot in my home, or in my palace again. And you can go with her," she said, pointing at Brennan. "Of anyone, you should know best how much I fucking hate being lied to. We're done here." And with that, she swept up her children and disappeared with her mate.

The rest of the team looked at me in shock.

"E. You can stay with us, girl. You too, Brennan," Hephaestus said, his shock and confusion clear on his face. "She'll cool down later and this'll all blow over. Come stay with us."

"Please," Meaghan pleaded with me, and I shook my head.

"She's going to stay with me," Brennan said, heading to his room. I knew he kept a house that had belonged to his parents. I had been there once with Mollis back when they were mated.

Artemis went to her own rooms. She went where here grandson and his child went, and I knew her loyalty would not allow her to stay in Mollis's home when her family was not welcome.

I stood, uncomfortable under the scrutiny of my now-former team members. Tisiphone and Megaera stared at me in shock and anger. I gave them a terse nod and headed up to my room.

It took me less than five minutes to pack.

By the time I was finished, Brennan and Hephaestus had begun loading bags from Brennan and Sean's rooms into his car, and were coming back for a second load. Like me, Artemis packed light, and she had a bag slung over her shoulder. She put a supportive hand on my shoulder while Nain's team tried to look anywhere but at me.

Brennan and Hephaestus finished, and Brennan grabbed a last bag, picked up his son. Hephaestus stuck his hand out and Brennan shook it.

"You need anything, you fuckin' come to me and Meaghan," he said to me, then looked at Brennan, including him in that. "She wants to be pissed, fine. She can be pissed. I'm not turnin' my back on someone I knew fucking well did what she believed was right."

I could not speak, in danger of sobbing again. Hephaestus hugged me. "What the hell happened, E?" he asked against my ear. "This is wrong."

I shook my head. "She is right. I lied. I am not going to deny it. I will always be hers, but I am not going to deny that I lied, and I did so knowingly."

Brennan seethed behind me, and once I let go of Hephaestus, he took my hand in his free one, and we left the loft, Artemis trailing behind us. We all climbed into Brennan's SUV, Brennan strapping Sean into his car seat. Artemis sat in the back with Sean, and I sat in the passenger seat.

Brennan started the engine and sat, hands on the steering wheel.

"So? Home?" he asked me. "You can stay with us for as long as you want. And if you don't want to, I'll help you find a place. All right?"

"All right. It will all be fine."

"Yeah? What makes you so sure?" he asked.

"I am thousands of years old. There is very little I do not know," I said, looking forward. "I will continue to do what I do, and my Queen will live her life as she sees fit. I can only control my own actions."

"She speaks truth," Artemis said. "And I am starving, so shall we get moving?"

"Okay, fine," Brennan said, putting the car into drive. "Where should we go first?"

"Pizza!" Sean shouted from beside Artemis, and Brennan shot a look in my direction.

"Pizza," I agreed. Brennan shook his head and pulled out of the parking garage.

"I cannot believe this," he muttered.

"It is what it is. I have no intention of falling apart now. My sisters were not working alone. There are more out there, planning to use these lost souls. I refuse to let that happen."

"Why? What does it matter to you now?" Brennan asked.

I raised my eyebrows at him. "I have a choice to make between being angry and spiteful and being what I know I am meant to be. Maybe it makes me a zealot. I do not care anymore. I am what I am, and I have no intention of changing now."

"Everything you did, returning all those, what? Eleven? Souls back to her, capturing three of your sisters who were behind all this shit, finding the missing lesser gods… you did everything she asked of you, and more, and this is how she goddamn repays you," he growled, smacking the steering wheel in frustration.

"It could have gone better," I said, and he grunted in agreement.

"It could be worse, "Artemis said from the back seat. "If Hades had still been in charge, he would have tortured you in punishment."

"See?" I asked Brennan. "There is always a bright side."

He just shook his head and drove toward downtown. Maybe the world was falling apart. Maybe my life was more chaotic than I ever could have imagined. But if there is one thing I know about being immortal, it is that you always have tomorrow. An endless string of tomorrows, and I had the power to make of them what I chose.

I intended to make them worthwhile.

EPILOGUE

Two weeks later…

I was pacing back and forth across the empty pier. I had agreed to this meeting in one of the suburbs of Detroit, and I tried to appear calm despite my inner turmoil. I looked out over Lake St. Clair, barely even registering the view. It was near dusk, and empty fishing boats bobbed in the boat slips nearby. It was chilly. November had roared into the area with torrents of freezing rain, knocking the remaining colorful leaves from their branches.

I had been in Detroit long enough to know that, even to someone as old as I am, a Michigan winter feels interminable. Ceaseless. And for once, I was grateful I would not be there for much longer.

I stretched my back, still conscious, hyper-sensitive, perhaps, of where my wings had once been. I swore sometimes I could still feel my wings, that I could feel them moving, flapping as they once had. I had told Brennan about it, and he had pulled up information on his laptop about humans who had had body parts amputated. Apparently the phenomenon was known as having a "phantom limb." Somehow, that seemed appropriate, all things considered.

I waited, and paced, and then finally stood still once again and looked out over the water. A few moments later, I felt a presence behind me. I did not bother turning around.

"So… do you think they bought it?" the Queen of the Dead asked behind me, and I felt a smile spread across my lips.

"I would say so. You nearly had me convinced for a minute there," I said wryly, and she laughed.

"You told Brennan, right? He doesn't think I'm a complete asshole, I hope."

I laughed. "I told him. And he was furious. And then he was relieved. And furious," I said, and she nodded, coming beside me and resting her forearms on the railing. "I also told him to stay away from your home. For obvious reasons."

She nodded. "Nain knows too. But he's mentally strong enough to keep anyone from prying into his mind. Bren probably is, too, but I don't want to risk it. Not now."

"I know. I do not want Brennan endangered by this." I leaned forward, let my head hang down, stretching my neck. "I am glad you understood. You had every right to be furious."

Mollis shrugged. "I was, at first. I sat next to you when Triton brought you in, and I stayed there when Asclepias healed you… and I saw into your mind. I wanted to know what happened, and I saw everything. At first, it was Brennan and his shit all over again. The lies. But I don't have the luxury anymore to just go nuts and destroy everyone who pisses me off. And you're the person I trust most in this world. Maybe even more than Nain, at times," she said. "You've always been there, E. And so I made myself sit, and I re-read that email you sent me and I looked at what we knew so far… and I know that a lot of it is out of the bounds of what I know. But I don't believe for a second that you'd betray me."

"Good." I looked out over the water. "The souls, my team, the New Guardians... I still do not know how they are possible. My best guess is that Nyx built it into them somehow, that she knew that someday my kind would not be enough. And so we have the New Guardians."

"It sounds like something Nyx would do," Mollis said. "And you believe, as I do, that your sisters were working for someone else. Someone stronger."

I nodded. "None of us has the power to breach the prison and select the worst of the worst to free. That goes beyond us. Imprisoning other lesser gods... let alone four of them, would take a lot of strength." I sighed, unsure how to word the next part. "Whoever it is who is pulling the strings, they have in intimate working knowledge of death. Of the way the Nether, and you, work. They wanted to weaken you, while building an army against you. That is not something my sisters, even working together, could have done. And they would not have come up with this on their own. They are, at their core, meant to serve others."

Mollis was silent for several long moments. "They also have an intimate knowledge of how to make memories disappear. I've hit your three sisters, hard. I can't find a single fucking sign of who did this. There are blanks there." She was quiet, then her voice low. Not in sadness. In rage. "Do you know who the only beings are who are capable of taking, stealing memories from someone?"

I knew. I did not want to be the one to say it. And I also knew she'd come to the same conclusion, which was why her ploy at the loft had been necessary.

"Furies." Mollis said it for me, and I closed my eyes at the obvious pain in her voice. "My mother or my aunt betrayed me. The smart thing to do would be to take them, torture them. Destroy them before there's even a chance they can hurt anyone else I love."

I put my hand on her arm. "I cannot believe Tisiphone would do that to you. I dislike Megaera, but I do not believe she would do it, either."

"Well. I don't want to either, but everything points to them, doesn't it?"

"There are always others, Mollis. You are at the top. There will always, always be someone trying to take you down."

"They didn't do it to my father," she argued. "Damn I wish he was here," she said, and I heard it in her voice. Not just a queen looking for guidance. A daughter mourning her father.

"They did. Zeus alone tried to destroy him every century or so. This is nothing new." It was my job to put this in perspective for her, to try to not let her fall into despair. "We know whoever it was has to have an intimate knowledge of the way the Nether, and death, work. So there are Guardians. Furies. What about other possible suspects? Demons know some things. There are lesser gods who are associated with the Nether. I have no idea if they are around or if they were lost to us when the gateway was destroyed. But that is worth checking out."

"The memories, though, E," Mollis said, and I shrugged.

"All I am saying is, yes, be careful of your family, no matter how much it hurts. But we need to look everywhere. Unless you want to destroy your mother and aunt now?"

After a moment, she shook her head.

"So we keep looking. And I keep tracking down your souls, and we work out a system in which I turn them directly over to you."

"We're missing more," she said.

I sighed. "I know. They are taking them before the crows can get to them now." I relayed the dead crows I'd seen in Japan. Crows that were hers, and she shook her head in anger.

"So my New Guardians are even more important now," I said. "And if there are more out there, I need to find them. This is being done on purpose, to weaken you, to ultimately try to take you down. We will not let it happen."

She nodded, met my eyes. "I went back and looked for your souls. At first, they hid from me."

"They worried you would insist on putting them in the Nether prison."

She nodded. "Eventually, I found them and convinced them I was not going to take them in, but that they needed to come here to help you. They're in that empty boat club building on Belle Isle."

"Thank you, demon girl," I said, and she bumped my arm gently with hers.

"Thank you, E," she said, meeting my eyes. "I don't know what I'd do without you. You know that, right?"

I smiled. "You'll never have to know. No matter what happens, I have your back, and I know you have mine."

"We'll make them regret the day they were created."

I looked out over the water, at the setting sun, and smiled. "We will. And I am looking forward to it."

The End

Eunomia will return in *Betrayer*,
the second book in the *Hidden: Soulhunter* series.

Never Miss an Update!
Sign Up for Colleen's Newsletter at
http://bit.ly/colleensnewsletter

Visit **http://www.colleenvanderlinden.com** for
news and upcoming releases

LETTER FROM THE AUTHOR

And, here we are, back in the *HIDDEN* world. I hope you're as happy to be here as I am. I knew, the moment Eunomia appeared in *Lost Girl*, that she was a character with a story I wanted to tell. I am so excited to be telling it, and I hope you love her as much as I do.

I am extremely grateful to have so many wonderful people in my life.

First and foremost, I want to think my readers. You guys are completely amazing. Your enthusiasm for these characters, for this world, is what makes it possible for me to keep writing about them. Every time you buy one of my books, or tweet, or post on Facebook, or review, or blog, or email, or recommend my books to someone else, I am touched and humbled. Thank you so much.

Thank you and eternal love to my husband, Roger, who is everything. Partner-in-crime, layout and design, technical help, proofreading/beta reading help, not to mention all of the other ways I depend on him every single day. You are the best.

To my kids, who both drive me nuts and make me delirious with happiness, often at the same time. I would be lying if I didn't admit that Zoe and Sean may have been inspired by their antics.

My incredible beta reading team. They are absolutely wonderful. I love working with these ladies, and they are tough as nails and let me know when I go off track. Their love for these characters makes me happy, and I know this book is even better because of them. Thank you to Susan Cambra, Shawna Cerda, Jo Dawson, Kristen Driscoll, Jennifer G., Amber Hegarty, Brenda Hopkins, Sarah Leenart, Kathie Littlemore, Jayna Longstreet, Katherine Peters, Rachel Scott, and Sarah Wicks.

Finally, thank you to the lovely, talented Elizabeth Hunter for reading *Guardian*, but more so for being a really awesome, funny, supportive friend. You're the best.

Thank you so much for reading! Please tell me what you think! Reviews on Amazon and GoodReads are always appreciated, but if you'd like to tweet me (@C_Vanderlinden), drop me a line on Facebook, or email me at email@colleenvanderlinden.com, I would love to hear from you that way as well!

Colleen Vanderlinden
Detroit
April 25, 2015

ABOUT THE AUTHOR

Colleen Vanderlinden is the author and publisher of the *Hidden* series, which currently includes *Lost Girl*, *Broken*, *Home*, *Strife*, and *Nether*. She lives in the Detroit area with her husband, children, and two lazy cats. She enjoys reading, obsessing over comic book characters, gardening, and playing *World of Warcraft*.

Learn more about Colleen at her website, colleenvanderlinden.com, contact her via email at email@colleenvanderlinden.com, or follow her on Twitter and Facebook.

The Hidden Series
Book One: Lost Girl
Book Two: Broken
Book Three: Home
Book Four: Strife
Book Five: Nether
Hidden Series Novellas
Forever Night
Earth Bound

The Copper Falls Series
Shadow Witch Rising

The Hidden: Soulhunter Series
Guardian

Never Miss an Update!
Sign Up for Colleen's Newsletter
http://bit.ly/colleensnewsletter